# THE WALLFLOWER'S GREAT ESCAPE

## THE WALLFLOWERS' REVOLT
### BOOK ONE

VALERIE BOWMAN

JUNE THIRD ENTERPRISES, LLC

This book was updated and expanded in April 2026.



Digital ISBN: 978-1-960015-52-5

Print ISBN: 978-1-960015-53-2

Book Cover Design © Lyndsey Llewellen at Llewellen Designs.

*She was trying to escape one unwanted marriage. She never expected to end up in a deliciously inconvenient one with her brother's brooding best friend.*

Lady Georgiana Chadwick is done being a pawn in Society's games. She has no intention of marrying the ancient marquess her father has chosen for her, no matter how many debts the match would settle. With a daring escape plan in motion, Georgie is finally ready to take control of her life—until her brother's best friend, Lord Jason Pemberton, Earl of Pembroke, catches her in the act.

Jason has no interest in playing the hero. Haunted by the past and determined to keep his heart safely locked away, he only agreed to watch over Georgiana as a favor. But the stubborn, sharp-tongued wallflower is nothing like he expected. She's infuriating, reckless, far too tempting…and suddenly very much his problem.

When one daring escape leads to a very public scandal, there's only one respectable solution: a marriage of convenience. Now Georgie and Jason are trapped together in delicious forced proximity, matching wits, trading barbs, and trying very hard not to want each other.

But the longer they share a house, a future, and one inconveniently irresistible attraction, the harder it becomes to tell where duty ends and desire begins. What started as a scandalous rescue may become the one thing neither of them expected: a forever kind of love.

# CHAPTER ONE

*London, April 1820, The Willoughbys' Ball*

Lady Georgiana Chadwick flung open the door to the ladies' retiring room, slipped inside, and leaned back against it as though she'd just narrowly escaped the jaws of a lion. In truth, she might have preferred a lion. Lions, she suspected, did not leer quite so openly, nor leave one feeling quite so much like a horse being bid upon at Tattersall's.

Her pulse hammered in her ears as she pressed her back harder against the door. Her hands trembled against the soft violet-papered panel, and she took a deep breath of the cool air. The scent here was mercifully subdued, lavender water and lemon polish, unlike the crush of rosewater and beeswax in the ballroom beyond. No footsteps followed her, no sound of a cane tapping the marble. At least not yet.

Safe. For now. She exhaled a long breath.

One would think that a young lady engaged to be married should be smiling prettily at her betrothed, not crouching in a corner, plotting her escape. But then one would also think an engaged young lady's betrothed might be less than *forty years her senior.*

Georgie pushed herself off the door and let her eyes adjust to the dim light. The retiring room was smaller than she remembered, though perhaps that was because of its other occupant.

A young woman sat primly on the chaise, stiff-backed, her blond hair gleaming in the soft glow of the single candle on the side table. Her chin was tilted at a rather impressive angle of disdain. Georgie eyed her carefully. Her gown cost more than Georgie's entire wardrobe.

"Oh," Georgie blurted before she could stop herself. "I beg your pardon. I didn't realize—"

"It's quite all right," the young, blond lady replied, her voice as dry as last week's toast. "And now that you're here, you may as well take a seat."

Georgie complied at once, moving farther into the room and lowering herself onto the end of the settee. She glanced to her right where a tray of biscuits sat untouched. Mother was forever scolding her for eating too many biscuits. She quickly grabbed three and tossed them into her reticule. She'd eat them later. And Mother would never know.

The other young lady said nothing. She merely turned her gaze back to the pad of paper in her lap, muttering something under her breath as she scribbled furiously with a stub of pencil.

Georgie tilted her head curiously. "Are you…drawing?"

"No," the young woman said without looking up.

Georgie frowned. "Yes. You are."

"I'm not."

Georgie caught a glimpse of the paper—sharp, dark lines forming the unmistakable silhouette of a gentleman with a great many embellishments that did not flatter him in the

least. One eyebrow arched as she dared to inquire, "Is that…
Lord Nicholas Archer?"

The pencil froze. The blond woman's gaze snapped to
hers. "You *know* him?"

"Well," Georgie hedged, "it does resemble him. That brow
is rather…unmistakable."

The young woman sniffed and snapped her small sketchbook shut before tucking it discreetly under her arm with more
force than strictly necessary. "It is none of your concern. I have
every right to…record my observations. If my drawing happens
to resemble a pompous hypocrite, that is hardly my fault."

"I see," Georgie murmured, though she didn't. Not
entirely. "Well, don't worry. I'm not here to judge. I'm here to
hide."

The blond woman lifted her chin, an unmistakable spark
of interest flared in her green eyes. "Hide?"

Georgie blinked, unsure how to reply. Before she could
decide, the door burst open again, banging against the wall
and admitting a third young woman who skidded to a stop,
skirts askew, cheeks flushed.

"For heaven's sake," the newcomer moaned, "she nearly
climbed atop the refreshment table again."

Both Georgie and the blond woman turned to stare at
her. The new young lady slammed the door shut and leaned
heavily against it, her pretty red hair slightly mussed from
her flight.

"Oh. Oh no," the newest woman said, throwing an arm
across her face. "You saw, didn't you? *Everyone* saw her
antics."

Georgie pressed her lips together as though trying not to
laugh, while the blond woman simply raised an imperious
brow.

"I saw nothing," Georgie finally said, sensing the poor

redhead was already at her wits' end. She did not want to upset her further.

The red-haired woman groaned. She moved away from the door to sink deeply into a chair. "It was dreadful, wasn't it? Was it as appalling as I think it was?"

The blond woman set down her pencil. "If you're referring to your mother's impromptu…display earlier, then yes, I saw it. And it was appalling."

The red-haired woman sighed heavily. "Well then. Perhaps if I never leave this room, I can die in obscurity rather than infamy."

"An admirable plan," the blond woman replied, her tone still dry as dust.

Georgie cocked her head and stared intently at the red-haired woman. Mention of her mother? Antics? Embarrassment? Oh, yes, this young woman had to be the offspring of none other than Lady Viva Montfort, the widowed Viscountess Montague. She was infamous for her scandalous foibles. She caused a scene everywhere she went.

"She does seem…quite spirited," Georgie said, her voice tinged with sympathy.

"She's a menace," Miss Montfort said flatly. "And she's determined to drag me down with her." She straightened suddenly, realizing she hadn't introduced herself. "I'm Poppy, by the by. Poppy Montfort. Daughter of the Viscountess of Chaos, I mean Montague. And you are?"

Georgie bit her lip. "Georgiana Chadwick."

"Lady Georgiana, are you not?" the blond woman added.

Georgie tucked a strand of her dark hair behind her ear. "Yes, but at the moment I'd give my eyeteeth to sink into oblivion."

"I'm Beatrix Winslow," the blonde continued after a beat. "Lady Beatrix, if you prefer."

Oh, yes. How did Georgie not recognize her before? Of

course the beautiful blond young lady was Beatrix Winslow, the daughter of the powerful Duke of Winston. The Diamond of the Season. The Diamond of *every* Season. She'd received more marriage offers than one could count, yet she curiously remained unattached. What *was* she doing in here?

Poppy nodded. "Lovely. Now that we're all properly acquainted, at least tell me I'm not the only one in disgrace tonight. You"—she gestured to Georgiana—"look as if you've just escaped a firing squad. And you"—she waved at Beatrix—"are far too wealthy and beautiful to be hiding in here." She gave both of them a narrowed-eyed stare. "What are *you two* hiding from?"

Both Georgie and Beatrix snapped up their heads to look at her. Was it so obvious?

Georgie was on the verge of making something up. Something simple. Something that didn't beg questions. But a *feeling* told her that she could speak the truth in front of these young ladies, both of them. The truth was…she did not dream of grand passion or jewels. She dreamed of a room with a lock, a purse of her own, and a life in which no man announced her future as if she were livestock.

"I'm hiding from my *fiancé*," she admitted in a whisper. "The Marquess of Henderville."

Ooh, saying it aloud felt better than she'd expected.

Beatrix gasped. Then she promptly clapped a gloved hand over her mouth and straightened her shoulders, as if trying to regain her equilibrium after having displayed a less than ladylike reaction to what must have been shocking news. "Pardon me, but did you say…the Marquess of Henderville?"

Georgie nodded. "Yes."

"Oh," Poppy said, frowning. "That's rather…unfortunate."

"It is," Georgie agreed. "Quite unfortunate." She swallowed hard. "He's…old. And not in the distinguished way.

More in the 'has a collection of questionable canes and an unsettling fondness for rubbing my elbow' sort of way."

Beatrix made a sound suspiciously like a strangled laugh but covered it with a cough. "I am sorry," she murmured.

Georgie nodded, once. It was nice to have someone apologize to her for her circumstances. All her parents ever did was tell her how fortunate she was to have received an offer with no dowry.

But it was not merely Henderville she dreaded. It was the look in her father's eye whenever her future was discussed—that calm, practical certainty that she could be handed over like a parcel and expected to smile.

This young lady didn't expect her to smile. Refreshing, that. Why was *she* in the retiring room?

"And you?" Georgie countered, leveling her gaze at Beatrix. "What brings *you* to the retiring room?"

Beatrix's chin lifted another imperious notch. "Lord Nicholas Archer."

This time, Georgie frowned. "You're hiding *from* him?"

"You could say that." Beatrix shrugged one shoulder.

Poppy perked up, her own troubles seemingly forgotten for the moment. "But why? He's quite…handsome."

"And he knows it," Beatrix snapped, rolling her eyes. "He's also a libertine, a scoundrel, and the most infuriating man alive. My father insists on throwing us together at every opportunity, convinced it's a brilliant match. Never mind that our politics are diametrically opposed, and I'd sooner marry a goat. Honestly, a satyr at least."

"Ah," Georgie said delicately. "Well. That does sound… unpleasant. Marrying a goat, I mean. Or a satyr. One might expect they have similar scents." Though she secretly thought she'd expire from glee if her father had matched her with the young, handsome Nicholas Archer, Marquess of Vanover, instead of old, crusty Henderville.

"I'm entirely serious," Beatrix muttered. "Nicholas Archer may not be an old man, but he is an insufferable one, I assure you."

Georgie sighed. "I often wonder. If marriage is supposed to feel like triumph, why does every conversation about a young lady's future sound so alarmingly like horse trading?"

An unmistakable smile popped to Lady Beatrix's lips.

"Well," Poppy interjected with a shaky laugh, "you may both feel like horses, but at least neither of you has a mother who's managed to upstage the orchestra, the refreshments, and Lady Cranberry all in the span of half an hour. I shall die a wallflower, trying to live down my mother's scandalous reputation."

Georgie watched carefully as the redhead spoke. She'd spent years learning to read moods before they turned threatening. Which was why Bea's composure impressed her and Poppy's nervous laughter pricked at something tender inside her almost at once. They were not unalike, the three of them.

They fell silent, the air heavy with their collective grievances. Then, almost simultaneously, they began to laugh. Softly at first, then with growing amusement, their laughter filling the small room.

It was Georgie who finally broke the mirth with a sigh. "We are quite the pathetic lot, aren't we?"

"I prefer to think of us as resourceful," Beatrix countered.

"Resourceful?" Poppy repeated with a faint smile.

"Yes," Beatrix insisted. "We've each found the one quiet place in this entire house where no one dares follow."

Poppy straightened in her chair, her blue eyes bright with mischief. "We have, haven't we?" She sighed. "Perhaps we ought to start our own society. For Resourceful Young Ladies Who've Had Quite Enough."

"Oh, yes." Georgie grinned. "I would join straightaway."

Beatrix regarded them both with a considering expression before finally conceding, "If we're forming a society, I should like to be prime minister."

"Very well," Georgie agreed, "then I shall be your *Lady Chancellor*."

"And I suppose I can be the Chancellor of the Exchequer," said Poppy. "Heaven knows I have plenty of experience managing the deplorable state of Mother's coffers. Or trying to, at least."

They all laughed again, the sound less brittle this time, more genuine.

Georgie felt a warmth in her chest that hadn't been there earlier in the evening. For the first time in what felt like forever, she didn't feel entirely alone.

Then...footsteps coming closer.

The laughter died instantly. All three froze, eyes darting to the door. Georgie's heart leapt into her throat as she listened for the unmistakable sound of a cane tapping against the marble floor outside. She shuddered. *Was it Henderville?*

Beatrix's gaze narrowed, her lips pressing into a thin line. "That better not be Nicholas Archer," she nearly growled under her breath.

Poppy groaned, burying her face in her hands again. "Oh no. What if it's Mama, looking for me to introduce me to the footman she was flirting with earlier? She has no regard for propriety whatsoever."

Georgie swallowed hard, her pulse quickening. Her reprieve was over. Any moment now, the door could open, and she'd have to paste that polite smile back on her face and endure Henderville's clammy hand on her elbow.

But when she glanced at the other two young ladies, she found herself squaring her shoulders instead. Something about their presence, about knowing she wasn't the only one trapped in this glittering prison, made her a little braver.

She adjusted her gloves, lifted her chin, and turned to them with a faint smile. Suddenly, the idea they'd laughed about seconds earlier seemed like quite a fine idea instead. "Are we not the Resourceful Young Ladies Who've Had Quite Enough?" she intoned.

Poppy raised her gloved hand high in the air. "I'm in."

Beatrix nodded as she lifted her hand too. "So am I."

"I am as well," Georgie said, lifting her hand to mimic theirs. And then they all lowered their hands into a circle and touched them one atop the other, palms down.

"We hereby institute the official Society of Resourceful Young Ladies Who've Had Quite Enough," Beatrix said in a firm voice.

"Very well. Ladies?" Georgie asked, swallowing and steeling herself against what lay on the other side of the door. "Shall we?"

Beatrix nodded, her expression one of unshakable determination. Poppy looked a bit nervous but straightened nonetheless, smoothing her yellow skirts.

Together, they marched to the door one after another.

Georgie paused with her hand on the knob, feeling their shared strength like a spark between them. Whatever waited on the other side—lecherous *fiancés*, smug MPs, scandalous mothers—they would face it.

But not alone.

She pushed the door open, and the three of them stepped out into the guest-filled corridor, their heads high, their hearts steeled, and the faintest hint of rebellion glinting in their eyes.

# CHAPTER TWO

Lord Jason Pemberton, the Earl of Pembroke, did not belong here.

The mirrored ballroom of Willoughby House glittered with the light of a thousand candles burning in the chandeliers that hung high above the ballroom. The air smelled of perfume and sweat, and everywhere he looked he saw painted smiles hiding calculating eyes.

He should have been in his club. Or, better yet, at Pembroke Court, a hundred miles from London and all its conniving matrons and simpering innocents.

But here he was, smashed in among the lot of them. Not because he desired to be here. Never that.

He was here because he owed Chadwick.

Jason grimaced and adjusted his cuffs as he leaned against the nearest marble pillar, resolutely ignoring the flirtatious glances a bevy of young ladies sent his way.

He wasn't here for them. He was here because his friend, Henry Chadwick, had broken his bloody leg racing Jason's bay gelding across Richmond Park three weeks ago, and in the haze of guilt that followed, Jason had muttered that if

Chadwick needed anything—*anything at all*—he had only to name it.

And Chadwick had named it, God help him.

*Keep an eye on Georgiana. Don't let her do anything foolish. She keeps threatening to run off before her wedding. You know how she is.*

But Jason *didn't* know how she was.

But he knew this much: no woman threatened flight on the eve of marriage unless something had already gone badly wrong.

He'd formally met Henry's younger sister, Lady Georgiana, exactly once, at her come-out ball four Seasons ago, where she'd danced with him one time, flushed prettily, and then disappeared into the throng. He remembered thinking she looked cleverer than most, with shrewd brown eyes taking everything in.

But she was still just another debutante. And watching debutantes was the last thing Jason wanted to do tonight. Debutantes led to courtships, courtships led to marriages, and Jason had seen enough of marriage to last a lifetime. He cursed Chadwick's luck—and the bloody horse who'd thrown him—for the thousandth time.

Jason scanned the ballroom, narrowing his eyes. No sign of Georgiana Chadwick.

His jaw flexed. Because of course. Of course she wouldn't be easy to find.

Honestly, he had no business feeling responsible for a woman he scarcely knew. Responsibility, in his experience, was merely another name for failure waiting to happen.

With an oath muttered under his breath, he tugged at his gloves, pushed himself off the pillar, and began to move through the crowd.

*You're the last man alive who ought to be watching a young lady,* his mind whispered unhelpfully.

And wasn't that the truth?

If Evelyn were here… If she hadn't—

Jason's chest went tight. He didn't let himself finish the thought. He didn't have to. He'd thought it a thousand times before. Evelyn should have been here tonight, standing among the most sought-after debutantes of the Season, smiling prettily as she searched for a husband.

But she wasn't here.

Because of him.

His younger sister had died on his watch.

He straightened his shoulders, scowling as though the force of his glower could keep the memory at bay.

It couldn't.

And that memory alone was reason enough that he should not—*should not*—be entrusted with *anyone's* sister.

And yet here he stood, scanning the crowd for Chadwick's.

Jason was fairly certain Georgiana wasn't in the ballroom. Which meant he needed to expand his search. He strolled out the double doors into the corridor that led to the foyer.

The moment he stepped onto the polished marble floor, a flash of bright skirts caught his eye as the door to the retiring room opened, and out walked three young ladies. One dressed in pink. One in green. One in yellow.

Jason went still.

There she was. The one in pink.

Lady Georgiana, looking quite unlike the shy girl he remembered from three years ago. Her chin was lifted, her dark-brown eyes bright and alive with some secret mischief. Her cheeks were flushed, not with modesty, but with determination. She moved like a soldier advancing into enemy territory.

Beside her in the green gown was Lady Beatrix Winslow, the Diamond of every Season, her golden hair and swanlike neck catching the candlelight as if she'd been born to command it. Was that a drawing pad tucked under her arm?

On Georgiana's other side, was a red-haired young lady dressed in yellow who Jason didn't recognize. Whoever she was, she carried herself with a sort of weary dignity that told him she didn't want to be here either.

He studied Georgiana more closely.

It was subtle, clever, even, but he'd been in enough drawing rooms and military camps to know what plotting looked like. Her eyes sparkled and her mouth turned up just a hint at both corners.

She was up to something.

Jason rubbed a hand over his face.

Oh, excellent. He was meant to look after *that*. Mischief in a pink gown? She was already halfway across the corridor.

Why couldn't she just sit quietly like other young ladies? Chadwick had made it sound as if his sister simply needed a bit of a watchful eye, not a full military escort.

But it was more than that. He did not merely find her troublesome; he found her unnervingly alive, as if everyone else in the room had gone a little dim beside her.

Jason's gaze followed her as she parted ways with her companions and slipped down a side hall.

And that, he thought grimly, would be his cue.

He fell into step behind her, quickening his pace. He managed to keep a respectable distance without letting her slip out of sight.

*One would think,* he told himself dryly, *that if a young lady were trying to avoid scandal, she wouldn't march down dimly lit corridors alone at a ball.*

Georgiana's skirts swished briskly as she moved, her gloved hands clenched into determined little fists.

She had no idea he was behind her.

He followed her past a line of gilded sconces, down a narrower hall lined with ancestral portraits.

She glanced over her shoulder once, and he ducked smoothly into the shadow of a column, watching her with narrowed eyes.

This whole event was a farce. The marriage mart, he thought sourly, was a ridiculous exercise in futility. A grand, overwrought parade of fan-wielding girls and ambitious mothers, each pretending they weren't scheming. He wanted no part of it. Never had.

He wasn't here looking for a wife. Hell, he didn't even *want* a wife.

If his parents' marriage hadn't already soured him on the notion, then Evelyn's death had driven the lesson home: promises were brittle things. He'd promised to keep Evelyn safe, after all, and she was dead. How could he ever promise the same to someone else?

So no, he didn't dance attendance on innocents. He didn't pay calls to drawing rooms, and he certainly didn't haunt the ballrooms in search of some shy, fluttering bride.

He was here tonight for one reason and one reason only: his debt to Chadwick.

Nothing more.

He watched as Georgiana paused at the end of the hall, glanced around, and slipped through a door.

Jason followed her, stopping just shy of the door. He leaned against the wall and let his lips curve into a grim smile.

Right.

So she thought she could simply disappear, did she?

He sighed, waited half a beat, then followed her.

~

INSIDE WAS a small antechamber lined with shelves of books and a potted palm. The faint scent of lemon wax lingered.

And there she was, Lady Georgiana, kneeling on the floor, fiddling with the latch of a floor-length window that opened to the gardens beyond.

Jason crossed his arms over his chest as he watched her progress.

Grunting a little, she managed to get the window open and step upon the sill.

That's when he made his move. He had to. She was only one step away from escaping into the night. He leaned forward, locked his forearm around her small waist, and pulled her back into the antechamber.

First, a gasp and then…

"Unhand me!" she demanded, trying to yank herself free. She twisted to glance up at him, and her demeanor changed for just a moment. If he hadn't been watching her so closely, he wouldn't have seen it. She clearly recognized him, which had to be the only reason she wasn't screaming bloody murder right now.

"Lord Pembroke." Her eyes narrowed. "This is none of your concern!"

"Oh, I beg to differ," he said dryly, setting her down and spinning her to face him. "Your brother asked me to keep an eye on you. And here you are, halfway out a window."

She glared up at him, cheeks hot. "You're ruining everything!"

"I suspect that's rather the point," he drawled.

She yanked her arm from his grasp and smoothed her skirts with exaggerated dignity. "I am perfectly capable of seeing to myself. You needn't play the knight errant."

Oh, if she only *knew* how far from a knight he was.

"You are insufferable." Her lips tightened. "Besides, my brother has no right—"

Jason blinked at her patiently. "Doesn't he?"

Her arms snapped into place across her chest and she eyed him up and down, a look on her face that clearly said she now regarded him as the enemy. "You've no idea what it's like." Her words came through clenched teeth.

Jason's mouth twisted. On the contrary, he knew all too well what it was like. To watch someone slip through your fingers and be powerless to stop it. But he suspected that was not what Lady Georgiana meant. And for some unknown reason, he actually wanted to hear her out.

He shut the door behind him with a soft click. "Tell me, then," he said quietly, stepping closer to her.

Lady Georgiana allowed her arms to drop. She smoothed her skirts again, then her hair, her chin lifting stubbornly. "I have been auctioned off to the highest bidder," she snapped. "But I will not marry that...*man*." She shuddered. "And if my parents and my brother think they can force me to, then they'll find themselves very much mistaken."

Jason raised an eyebrow. Who was she talking about? He hadn't even thought to ask Henry who his sister was engaged to, and now he regretted it.

"Who's your *fiancé*?" he asked, eyes narrowing as he studied the color rising in her cheeks.

Her brows shot up as if the fact that he didn't already know surprised her. "The Marquess of Henderville," she stated, her voice entirely flat.

Jason frowned, certain he must've misheard. "Henderville?" he echoed, disbelief threading through his voice.

"That's right." Her eyes flashed at him, fierce and defiant.

"But Henderville has to be nearly seventy," Jason said, the furrow between his brows deepening with disbelief.

"He is," she shot back. "Tell me, my lord. Would *you* want to marry him?"

Jason swallowed and dragged a hand through his hair,

trying to make sense of what he'd just heard. Outwardly, he kept silent. Inwardly, he was shaking his head with vehemence. No. Absolutely not. If he were a young, beautiful woman—hell, if he were *any* kind of woman—he wouldn't want to marry Henderville. The man was a cantankerous old bag of bones. What on earth had possessed Henry's father to agree to such a match? Money? How much? There wasn't an amount on earth that would convince Jason to give Evelyn to such a man. Then again, Evelyn would have had a sizable dowry. There were many rumors that the Chadwicks were destitute. Regardless, young, beautiful Georgiana Chadwick marrying old, sour Lord Henderville was utterly unthinkable.

Georgiana continued to eye Jason as if waiting for his answer.

"Is Henderville here tonight?" he asked, steadfastly avoiding her original question.

"Yes, and that's precisely why I'm leaving." Her voice remained defiant.

Jason blew out a deep breath. For the first time that evening, a flicker of something strange, something truly protectively, stirred in his chest.

She reminded him of Evelyn. Fierce and stubborn and unwilling to be told what to do. Evelyn had never listened either. Much to her detriment.

Evelyn hadn't gotten her happy ending. Hell, she hadn't even grown old enough to make her debut.

It was too late to save Evelyn, of course, but Jason could save Lady Georgiana. At least for tonight.

Jason scrubbed his hand over his jaw and winced. *Damn it.* He'd come here this evening to keep her from doing anything foolish. And it seemed she'd made his task impossible.

He was going to help her escape.

# CHAPTER THREE

Georgie had nearly made it.

She'd managed to pry open the window, and cool night air had spilled in, teasing the curls at her nape. One foot had already been on the sill, her fingers gripping the frame. If she had just been able to swing the other leg over, she could have dropped down into the garden and made her way to the street where she could hire a hack. From there, freedom.

Freedom from the lecherous Marquess of Henderville, freedom from her father's imperious edicts, freedom from that suffocating ballroom where everyone smiled at her like a lamb fattened for slaughter.

But just as she'd begun to shift her weight forward, a rather strong arm had wrapped around her waist.

Her breath left her in a startled gasp as she was hauled—*hauled*, like an unruly sack of grain—back inside the room while Lord Jason Pemberton's low, familiar voice rumbled in her ear.

He'd spun her around to face him while anger coursed through her veins. Meanwhile, Lord Pembroke was annoyingly composed, despite having just bodily dragged her back from a very tidy escape.

They'd exchanged some heated words. But when she pulled herself out of his grasp and accused him of behaving like a knight errant, a flash of something vaguely like regret shone in his eyes.

Then his brow arched, green eyes glinting with a faint amusement that only deepened her irritation.

It was then, once she stopped wanting to slap his face and actually *looked* at him, that she realized just how unfair it all was.

Because *he* was…handsome.

Not merely handsome in the way most Society men were handsome, well-groomed and stiff, but truly *fit*. Broad shoulders that actually looked as if he used them, the tailored black coat clinging just slightly too snug over his chest. His dark hair, a shade richer than chestnut, fell across his forehead in a way that looked unintentional but somehow perfect. And those eyes, deep green, sharp and assessing, held hers with an intensity that made her stomach flutter in a most traitorous manner.

Hmm. When was the last time she'd seen him? At least four years ago. The man rarely came to *ton* events. Why, he'd be devastating if he wasn't behaving like a self-righteous ass at the moment.

They'd had a bit of a discussion, the two of them. She'd explained why she was trying to escape out a window and, surprisingly, Lord Pembroke had seemed to understand. Now he was staring at her as if he already regretted his next words.

"Where do you intend to go after you leave here?"

A flicker of hope flared in Georgie's chest. He was speaking of it as if it may still happen. But hope was hazardous. Hope was how young women ended up trusting promises they had no business believing. But standing here with Lord Pembroke, Georgie felt it all the same.

"Home," she told him.

"Is your mother in the ballroom?"

"Yes, along with my father…and Henderville."

Lord Pembroke took a slow step closer. His heat and the faint scent of clean soap and starch washed over her.

"I cannot allow you to run off into the night alone," he said quietly. His tone was calm, but it settled over her like an iron weight. For one hot instant, he sounded too much like every other man who had ever tried to order her life. And yet…there was something different beneath it. Not greed. Not vanity. Concern, perhaps?

Georgie lifted her chin. "I don't see why not." Her heart was hammering now, but she refused to let him see her doubt. She *would* run if she had to.

If she let him stop her, even for a moment, she might begin to imagine that some men could be reasoned with. That some men might care what became of her. And that way lay danger of an entirely different kind.

The small room had gone still around them, the night air cool against her cheeks and the faint murmur of the ballroom in the distance was barely audible through the door.

"I cannot allow you to run off alone," he finally repeated. "But I can escort you home."

A ridiculous flicker of relief moved through her. No man had ever made protection sound so much like an offer rather than a demand, and she did not know what to do with that. Both of her brows shot up. "Pardon?"

"I think you heard me. And we must be quick about it."

Lord Pembroke cracked open the door and glanced out, obviously trying to determine if they had been followed.

Georgie took the opportunity to take another look at him,

at the way his coat pulled across his back when he shifted, the faint shadow of stubble on his strong jaw. Even his hands, large and capable, flexed at his sides as though itching to either throttle her or perhaps drag her back to safety again.

Blast it all.

Why *couldn't* her father have chosen *him*? He was unattached, wasn't he? She didn't have the thought because he was handsome—though he very much was—but because he had listened to her. Because he had looked at her as though what she wanted might matter. Instead, she was supposed to be delivered into the hands of a man old enough to have attended Vauxhall's opening night.

Georgie's lips tightened. She already knew why her father hadn't chosen a man like Pembroke, or indeed, Pembroke himself. Henderville was *paying* for her. Pembroke would expect a dowry. He was hardly a man who needed to *purchase* a bride.

Lord Pembroke shut the door and met her gaze again, his expression resigned but steady. For a long moment, they stared at each other, the quiet between them taut as a bowstring.

"Let's go," he prompted.

"You're truly helping me?" she asked, frowning.

He leveled a finger at her. "I will not let you wander into danger. If you're determined to leave, then yes, I will help you. But you will follow my lead. No arguments."

Her lips curved into a smile that she couldn't quite suppress. "No arguments," she agreed sweetly. Though she fully intended to argue if need be.

He muttered something under his breath again—something that sounded like *What the devil am I doing?*—before striding to the window and shutting it firmly.

"That was my escape route!" she protested.

Lord Pembroke shot her a look over his shoulder. "Not anymore. We'll find a better one."

Then he extended a hand to her, palm open, the faintest glint of humor hiding behind his stern expression.

"Well, Lady Georgiana," he said. "Shall we?"

Georgie placed her hand in his and let him lead her out of the antechamber, her pulse thrumming in her ears and the faintest, most wicked thrill curling low in her belly.

And that flicker of hope? It grew a bit stronger.

# CHAPTER FOUR

What the devil was he doing?

Jason asked himself the question for the fifth—no, sixth—time as he descended the servants' staircase at the back of Lord Willoughby's town house with Georgiana Chadwick in tow.

His hand tightened imperceptibly on hers. He should stop this madness now, march her back to the ballroom, and deliver her into her father's custody.

But no.

Instead, he was here. Smuggling her through a dim stairwell, her skirts whispering behind him, her breath coming faster than he liked.

He risked a glance back at her and his jaw tightened. *Damn.* She really was beautiful. But it wasn't merely her beauty that unsettled him. It was the vivid force of her, as though restless life thrummed just beneath her skin.

She wasn't beautiful in the too-polished, perfect way most Society debutantes were, but in some untamed, indefinable way that was neither helpful nor relevant to the task at hand.

Because he had one job. *One*. To keep her reputation intact.

Jason swallowed a bitter laugh. God help them both, *he* was the worst man alive to be trusted with such a responsibility. And already the task felt alarmingly less like duty and far too much like desire to keep her close. Not to mention, if they were caught together alone like this, she would be ruined immediately.

His own reputation was hardly pristine. He'd spent the better part of a decade perfecting the role of solid MP by day and discreet libertine by night. He'd had a string of mistresses, each more manipulative than the last.

His last mistress in particular had made a habit of contriving fainting fits whenever she wanted a new bauble. She'd stop at nothing, sobs, theatrics, even once deliberately slashing her own hem to prove some ridiculous point about his neglect.

And that, come to think of it, was why she was now his *former* mistress.

Jason's gaze flicked again to the young woman hurrying after him, her chin lifted stubbornly even in flight.

Was Lady Georgiana cut from the same cloth?

She claimed to be betrothed to the Marquess of Henderville, after all. That seemed quite unlikely, now that he considered it.

It couldn't possibly be true. Could it? Jason shuddered at the thought. The Marquess of Henderville?

That decrepit scoundrel was old enough to be her grandfather. Jason had seen him just last week at White's, nodding off into his brandy and muttering about the glories of Bath.

Could she possibly be telling the truth?

He scowled. Perhaps she was simply employing the oldest feminine trick in the book, dramatic falsehoods to gain her way.

Except…she didn't seem the type.

And God help him, that flash in her eyes when she'd looked at him with an expression that clearly said, *Now do you see why I'm trying to flee?* Frankly, it had looked heart-breakingly real.

He had seen practiced tears before, well-rehearsed feminine distress meant to bend a man to a lady's wishes. This was nothing like that. This was dread, bright and bare and impossible to dismiss.

Jason forced the thought away. He'd promised Chadwick he'd watch over her, and he would. Who she may or may not be betrothed to should not be Jason's concern.

He stopped at the bottom of the staircase and glanced around. The servants' corridor was empty, save for the faint scent of coal dust and soap. A row of cloaks and shawls hung on a pegboard along the wall.

"Stay here," he ordered gruffly.

Lady Georgiana raised a brow but kept silent…for once.

Hurrying over, he plucked a plain dark scarf from a peg and, after a moment's search of his inner coat pocket, left a pound note in its place, more than enough to cover the cost of the item.

When he turned back, Lady Georgiana was watching him with those large, clever eyes.

"What are you doing?" she asked finally, suspicion lacing her tone.

He stepped close—closer than he strictly needed to—and lifted the scarf. "Keeping you from being recognized."

Her breath caught as he touched her, and the tiny sound went through him with wholly inappropriate force.

Before she could protest, he draped the scarf over her head, tucking it around her face until only a glimpse of her cheeks and lips remained visible.

"There," he murmured. "Better."

He should have stepped back at once. Instead, for one inexplicable moment, he could only look at her.

She opened her mouth.

"Don't speak," he cut her off. "You've already done quite enough for one evening."

Her eyes narrowed to slits. "Do you always order people about like a field marshal?" she hissed.

"Only people who try to climb out of windows," he said flatly.

He took her arm—not roughly, but firmly—and led her out the side door into the night.

The air outside was crisp, laced with the faint scent of roses from the gardens and a distant tang of woodsmoke.

Lady Georgiana stumbled once on the gravel path, and his hand automatically steadied her at the elbow. The contact lasted no more than a second, yet he felt it far too keenly. She was all restless warmth and stubborn grace beneath his fingers.

She looked up at him then, her lips parting as though she meant to speak again.

Jason didn't give her the chance. "I'm in charge here," he said evenly. "And you'll do as you're told. Silently. Understood?"

She huffed, the faintest puff of breath fogging in the cool night. But she nodded.

He nodded back, satisfied, and led her along the lawn, keeping to the shadows.

They'd nearly reached the far wall of the garden when the unmistakable sound of laughter and footsteps spilled out from a pair of French doors leading from the house. Jason froze, tightening his hold on Lady Georgiana's arm.

A trio of drunken young gentlemen stumbled into the garden, all high spirits and flushed cheeks, their voices carrying across the moonlit grass.

"Damn," Jason muttered under his breath.

Lady Georgiana tilted her head up at him, her expression questioning.

He didn't have time to explain. Instead, he backed her into the nearest shadowed alcove and pressed her shoulders gently but firmly against the cool brick wall.

"Stay still," he murmured, bending his head close to hers.

"What—" she began.

"Quiet."

He shifted his body to block her from view and—because he couldn't think of anything else to do that wouldn't draw more attention—he lowered his head until his mouth hovered just above hers.

To anyone glancing their way, they'd look like a couple lost in a scandalous kiss.

She exhaled softly, and he felt it warm against his cheek.

"Pretend," he whispered against her ear.

She made a sound in her throat—something between a protest and a sharp intake of air—but didn't move.

Jason angled his head, letting his lips just graze the scarf near her temple.

The footsteps drew nearer.

He pressed closer, not touching anything he didn't have to, but close enough to shield her completely.

Her hands, trapped between them, clenched briefly in the lapels of his coat. Her eyes flicked up to his, wide and dark and—

*Bloody hell.*

He became suddenly, uncomfortably aware of how soft she felt against him, how sweetly she fit in the circle of his arms.

And just like that—he realized with a jolt of irritation and disbelief—he had a cockstand.

A wholly inconvenient, thoroughly inappropriate cockstand.

He closed his eyes for half a second, breathing through his nose and willing his body to behave itself. Why did she have to smell so blasted good? Like lilacs and soap and—

The drunken trio paused a few paces away, their laughter low and knowing.

"Ah, leave 'em be," one of them finally muttered. "Plenty of other places to drink."

Their footsteps faded back toward the house.

Jason stayed exactly where he was for another beat—until he was certain they were gone—then stepped back, letting cool air rush between them.

Lady Georgiana blinked up at him from behind the scarf, her lips parted slightly.

He cleared his throat, adjusting his coat to cover himself and desperately hoping the shadows hid more than his pride.

"Come on," he said, his voice hoarse. "We're not entirely safe yet."

She didn't move right away. "What was that?" she asked finally, shaking her head as if coming out of a trance, her voice soft.

Jason forced a tight smile, though his pulse was still hammering inconveniently.

"That," he said, "was improvisation."

Her dark eyes sparkled faintly in the moonlight, and she gave a tiny nod. Then, curiously, she smiled.

"Quite effective," she murmured.

Jason ran a hand down his face and exhaled. What the devil was he doing? Whatever it was, he reminded himself grimly, it was for Chadwick.

Nothing else.

Nothing to do with Lady Georgiana's soft lips or her

clever eyes or the way she'd fit against him in the shadows and smelled like a dream.

No.

He had one job. And he'd damned well see it done.

# CHAPTER FIVE

Georgie had no idea what possessed Pembroke to help her, but he'd shoved her into the hack as if he owned it. And here she was, perched on the worn seat, scarf still covering her head, while he barked an order to the driver and climbed in after her.

The door shut with a decisive *thunk*, and then he was there, long legs folding into the opposite seat, his coat settling around him like a dark cloud.

He looked at her squarely, his green eyes sharp even in the dim carriage light.

"I'll escort you home," he said flatly, as though it were the most obvious thing in the world. "To ensure you actually make it there safely."

She narrowed her eyes at him, arms tightening over her chest. "I see," she said sweetly. "You've appointed yourself my gaoler for the evening. How very…gallant."

His brow arched, but he said nothing.

Georgie studied him from beneath her lashes as the coach jolted forward.

She'd seen him with her brother countless times over the

years before Henry had moved to his own apartments, laughing in the billiard room, leaning lazily against the mantel, all easy charm and dry wit. She'd always thought he was rather nice, if a bit aloof.

But now she knew better.

Pembroke was yet another arrogant man convinced it was his duty to control her life.

Just like her father.

Just like her brother.

Just like Henderville.

Just like all of them.

And yet—even as she had the thought—some part of her knew it was not entirely true. Her father controlled her for profit. Henry for convenience. Henderville presumably for lust. But Pembroke seemed driven by something else altogether. Something she couldn't quite place.

Georgie turned her head to stare out the window, the faint blur of streetlamps streaking past in the night.

Still, she grudgingly admitted to herself, for tonight, Pembroke was useful. He was helping her toward her goal at the moment, and she'd let him.

For now.

She grudgingly had to admit to herself that unlike most men of her acquaintance, he felt steady. Capable. Alarmingly safe.

It really was too bad he was such a pompous ass.

Because, unfortunately, he *was* terribly handsome.

And when he'd pushed her against that wall back in the garden—she pressed her knees together at the memory—well. For just a moment, she'd actually thought he was going to take a liberty.

And worse? She'd wanted him to.

Which was mortifying. And wrong.

It wasn't because she wanted roughness or conquest, as

Henderville no doubt imagined all young women did, but because for one lightheaded instant she had felt chosen. Seen. Desired by a man she might actually have chosen for herself.

Pembroke's voice broke into her unhelpful thoughts. "So," he said slowly, "you say you're betrothed to *the Marquess of Henderville?*"

She met his gaze squarely. She hadn't mistaken the hint of disbelief in his voice. "Yes," she said, leveling him with her gaze.

Let him be shocked. Let him finally understand that this was not feminine dramatics or some bid for attention. This was her life—being bargained over by men who would never have to endure the bargain themselves.

Pembroke leaned forward slightly, his expression still faintly incredulous. "The marquess *himself,*" he pressed, "not…his nephew?"

She narrowed her eyes. Still found it difficult to believe, did he? Just like a man. "No. The old man. Apparently he still intends to try for an heir. His nephew be damned."

She let out a breath. Saying it aloud in front of Pembroke made the whole thing sound even more awful than it already was. No wonder she wanted to claw her way out of her own life.

Pembroke's jaw tightened. He actually *shuddered,* his shoulders rolling like a man trying to shake off a particularly bad dream.

"My sentiments exactly," she murmured.

But Pembroke's continued disbelief was written plainly on his face.

Georgie tilted her chin higher. "You don't believe me, do you?" she asked coolly. "That's why you asked again. You think I'm lying to you."

He hesitated…just enough for her to see it. Then he said, "No."

But it came out far too quickly.

She let out a dry laugh, settling back against the worn, dark cushions. She turned her face toward the window again. "I don't care what you think," she muttered. And she meant it. What did she care what a pompous man who enjoyed far too much privilege and control over his own life thought of her? She knew the truth and that was all that mattered.

She didn't speak to him for the remainder of the ride. Instead, she rummaged in her reticule and pulled out a biscuit. She didn't off him one.

Pembroke didn't try to fill the silence. No doubt he thought that was some kind of victory.

When the coach finally rattled to a halt in the quiet lane behind her father's town house, Georgie had finished her pilfered biscuit. She lifted her skirts, opened the door, and stepped down without waiting for him.

The back servants' door loomed ahead, faintly lit by a single lantern.

She could feel Pembroke's gaze burning into her back as she ascended the short step to the door.

He'd followed her, his boots echoing softly on the stones.

He stopped just behind her. "I must have your word," he said quietly, "that you intend to remain here tonight."

Georgie turned slowly, her hand already on the latch. She pulled the scarf from her head and couldn't help but roll her eyes. "As if you'd believe my word," she shot back.

His eyes narrowed faintly. "I do believe it," he said evenly. "And I am asking for it."

She held his gaze for a long moment, then gave a short, sharp nod. "Fine," she said. "You have my word."

And without another glance at him, she flounced inside, letting the door shut behind her with a satisfying thud.

The house was quiet at this hour, the faint scent of rose-mary, from dinner, no doubt, still clinging to the stairwell.

Georgie slipped off her shoes and gathered her skirts in her hands, ascending the back staircase silently.

Her pulse finally began to slow as she neared her bedchamber on the third floor.

She had to give him credit, she thought with a frown, Lord Pembroke was more difficult to shake than she'd anticipated.

But he didn't know her nearly as well as he thought he did.

She'd told him the truth: she had no intention of leaving the house tonight.

No, indeed.

The real escape was planned for her wedding day.

And no one—least of all Pembroke—would stop her then.

# CHAPTER SIX

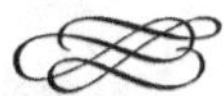

Jason leaned back against the carriage seat, arms crossed, and glowered at the darkened city streets flashing past the window.

St. James's Square wasn't far, but it was far enough for him to stew.

And stew he did.

Lady Georgiana Chadwick.

Fire in her eyes, defiance in her voice, her chin tilted high as though she dared the world to strike her down.

Spoiled. Reckless. A nuisance.

Those were the labels her brother had given her, at any rate. Jason was beginning to suspect those words were merely what some men called a woman they could not easily manage.

"Georgie's a bother," Chadwick would grumble after three pints at the pub. "Too sharp by half, too spirited, too much."

And yet—Jason's jaw worked—he couldn't quite square that image of her with the way she'd looked tonight, swathed in shadows and the scarf, clutching her skirts as she tried to escape the company of a man she had no business being beholden to.

She had not looked spoiled. She had looked cornered. Proud, frightened, and furious at having been cornered—but cornered all the same.

Running from the Marquess of Henderville.

*Henderville.*

Jason muttered a low oath and rubbed a hand over his mouth.

He'd run from Henderville too, given the chance. Hell, any woman with sense would. The thought came too quickly, too instinctively. It felt perilously close to the same hot surge of helplessness he had known once before—and failed to outrun. But the very thought of Georgiana Chadwick being handed over to that lecherous relic made something hard and ugly twist in his chest.

Which was why he was on his way to visit Chadwick and ask him outright if his sister was truly betrothed to that old goat.

BY THE TIME the coach clattered to a halt in front of Chadwick's bachelor flat in St. James, Jason's mood had soured even further.

The driver opened the door and Jason stepped down, straightening his coat before rapping on the door and letting himself in.

Inside, the faint strains of music and female laughter drifted out onto the cobblestones.

Of course.

Chadwick's idea of convalescence apparently involved brandy, women, and no doubt some enterprising footman who'd managed to produce a pianoforte on short notice.

Jason pushed the door open and was greeted by the sight of Henry Chadwick—future earl, notorious rake, and present invalid—lounging on a sofa with his splinted leg propped up on a pillow.

A decanter sat at his elbow, two scantily clad women danced to the lilting music, and the room smelled faintly of smoke and cheap perfume.

"Pembroke!" Chadwick called out cheerfully, raising his glass. "Come to join the revels? Took you long enough."

Jason didn't answer at first. He shut the door behind him, removed his gloves, and surveyed the scene with a dispassionate eye.

One of the women giggled and offered him a come-hither smile.

He ignored her.

The music swelled, and Chadwick gestured at him with his glass. "Don't just stand there looking like you've swallowed a lemon. Sit. Drink. There's plenty to go around."

Jason remained standing another beat before crossing the room and sinking into the chair opposite him, rubbing a hand through his hair.

"I need to ask you something," he said flatly.

This was none of his business. It was precisely the sort of family arrangement a sensible man would avoid. And yet Jason found himself heading straight for it, unable to leave well enough alone when Lady Georgiana's face kept flashing through his memory.

Chadwick took a long swallow of brandy and leaned back, smirking. "By all means. Ask away."

Jason narrowed his eyes on his friend. "Is it true," he said slowly, and perhaps too loudly, "that your sister is betrothed to the Marquess of Henderville?"

The music faltered as he spoke, and Chadwick's smirk

slipped just slightly. He waved a lazy hand at the women. "Darlings, give us a moment, would you?"

They pouted but drifted away to the next room, the footman quietly following them.

Chadwick sighed, refilled his glass, and finally looked back at Jason. "Yes," he said simply. "It's true."

Jason's brows shot up. "You're serious."

Chadwick gave a one-shouldered shrug. "What can I say? My father's always been rubbish at cards. He owes Henderville an ungodly amount of money. And Henderville has agreed to pay even more. That's why I thank the heavens every day I was born a male. Otherwise, I'd be sold off too."

Jason stared at him, incredulous. "But Henderville is—"

"Old?" Chadwick supplied helpfully. "Obnoxious? Pungent? A horse's ass? Yes. Guilty on all counts."

Jason leaned forward, his elbows braced on his knees.

"You don't see why Georgiana might be…loath to marry him?"

Chadwick barked a laugh, throwing his head back. "Of course I do! Didn't I just say I'm damned glad I was born a man?" He grinned, the corner of his mouth tilting upward in an expression that made Jason's teeth clench. "Thank Christ it's not my problem." Chadwick raised his glass in a mocking toast and tossed back the rest of the brandy.

A flare of contempt shot through Jason, so sudden it nearly shocked him. Chadwick spoke of his sister as though she were an inconvenience to be settled, not a woman being bartered into misery.

He studied his friend for a long moment, the heat rising steadily in his chest. He'd known Chadwick for years. They'd gotten foxed together, raced horses together, and, yes, chased women together.

But he'd never—not once—heard him speak so callously about his own sister.

His beautiful, stubborn, spirited sister.

"When is the wedding?" Jason asked, doing his best to keep a grim look of distaste from his lips.

"Three weeks hence," Chadwick replied easily. "And Georgiana has a troubling habit of running away from parties when her *fiancé* is present. Which is why I asked you to keep an eye on her."

Jason's jaw tightened as Chadwick beckoned the women back in and gestured for the music to resume.

Soon, the room filled with lilting notes and laughter once more, but Jason hardly heard it. His gaze remained fixed on Chadwick as a bitter thought settled in his mind like lead…

*No wonder Lady Georgiana doesn't trust men.*

At the moment, he certainly couldn't blame her. For the first time, Jason understood that Georgiana's sharpness was not mere temperament. It was armor. And men like her father, her brother, and Henderville had hammered every piece of it into place.

# CHAPTER SEVEN

*The next morning*

Georgie always took a walk in the mornings—her one sliver of independence in a life that was beginning to feel like a noose tightening with slow, merciless inevitability. The only time she could breathe freely. The only time she could be utterly herself without Mama hovering or her brother complaining about his lack of funds or Society peering over every metaphorical hedge. Her walks were sacred.

But today…something was different.

From the moment she stepped outside, she'd felt it—an odd, irksome certainty in her bones. As though the universe had nudged her in the ribs and whispered, *He'll be there.*

Lord Pembroke.

Which was ludicrous. She ought to have felt only annoyance at the prospect of him appearing where he had no business being. Instead, some traitorous flutter had lodged itself low in her belly from the moment the thought occurred.

Why, she couldn't say. But she simply *knew*. The air itself seemed braced for him.

He'd claimed he was doing her brother a favor by "keeping an eye on her." But that was last night...*at the ball.* If Pembroke arrived today, she would begin to suspect that either he'd misunderstood his assignment...or he had motives entirely his own.

The notion ought to have alarmed her. Instead, it sent a small, forbidden spark through her chest.

Georgie had chosen Hyde Park for her walk today because it was public. Busy. Which meant it should be impossible—for any sensible man—to behave improperly or to meddle in a young lady's affairs.

Unfortunately, Lord Pembroke was neither sensible nor inclined toward minding his own business.

She had just reached the Serpentine, her family's remaining servant, an elderly footman, toddling behind her as chaperone, when she felt it...that unmistakable prickle at the back of her neck. The one that said she was being watched. Possibly by a large, overbearing, broad-shouldered nuisance wearing an entirely unnecessary scowl.

She stopped walking, and slowly...ever so slowly...she turned.

There he was. Pembroke. On horseback. Looking like a brooding angel of judgment sent directly from the heavens to ruin her morning. Or perhaps to improve it in ways she had no intention of examining too closely.

He cut an arresting figure astride his bay gelding—dark coat fitted impeccably over those undeniably wide shoulders, snowy cravat tied with military precision, trousers molded to thighs that were, frankly, indecent. A black riding glove rested on the reins; the other hand pushed dark, wind-tossed hair from his brow. Altogether too dashing for her peace of mind.

Georgie, by contrast, wore a pale lavender walking dress with an old yet neat pelisse buttoned to her throat, her worn bonnet tipped just so, dark hair rebelliously escaping despite her best efforts. She looked perfectly respectable, but she couldn't help but feel slightly self-conscious about the state of her wardrobe compared to Pembroke's finery.

He halted his bay gelding a few paces from her. "Lady Georgiana." He nodded.

She folded her arms across her chest, doing her best to look completely unaffected. But if she was being honest, it was not entirely displeasure making her pulse stumble. "Lord Pembroke."

His attention did something inconvenient to her insides. Most men's notice made her want to flee. Lord Pembroke's made her want to stand her ground and see what he would do next.

"I didn't expect to see you here," he said.

She lifted her brows. "Why do I find that difficult to believe?"

His lips tightened. "I wasn't following you."

She made a small, elegant sound of disbelief. "Mm-hmm."

Pembroke swung down from the horse, boots thudding against the ground. "I wasn't."

"Then why," she asked sweetly, "have you managed to arrive at precisely the spot I chose at precisely the moment I chose it?"

"I was riding," he insisted.

"In *my* direction."

He opened his mouth, closed it, then scrubbed a hand over his jaw. "Coincidence."

"Coincidence," she repeated. "How convenient."

His gaze flicked over her, a brief sweep, respectful but too perceptive. "You shouldn't walk alone."

She pointed to the footman. "Martin is with me."

Lord Pembroke glanced at the elderly man. "He's turned in the wrong direction. I question whether he can even see."

"Be that as it may, I am not alone."

Pembroke's jaw clenched. Hard. Which was gratifying.

She stepped closer, tilting her head. "Tell me, my lord, do you ever tire of glowering at me?"

"No," he said quickly, obviously before he could stop himself.

She froze.

His ears went faintly pink.

"I mean," he corrected sharply, "if I glowered at you last night, it was because you lack self-preservation. As evidenced by your attempt to flee out the window."

She tugged at her glove. "I could argue that fleeing out the window was my attempt at self-preservation."

"It was reckless."

"It was my decision, my lord."

They stood in silence for a moment.

Then Georgie sighed dramatically, turned on her heel, and resumed walking.

Pembroke exhaled a curse and followed on foot leading his horse behind him—because of course he did.

Over her shoulder she said, "If you're going to follow me, at least keep up."

And his answering growl warmed her more than the sun. She smiled to herself. She couldn't help it.

They walked in an uneasy parallel—Georgie with her gloved hands clasped behind her back, chin lifted defiantly; Pembroke half a step behind, leading his gelding and watching her like she might dart into the Serpentine just to spite him.

For several strides, neither spoke. Walking beside him felt strangely intimate, as though they were not adversaries circling one another but something far more alarming: a couple who might have met under entirely different circumstances.

Finally, Georgie broke the silence. "You know," she said lightly, "most gentlemen prefer to *ride* on horseback rather than drag the animal behind them like a poorly matched chaperone."

"I can do two things at once," he replied, dry.

"Glower and lead a horse?" she teased. "Impressive."

A reluctant breath of amusement left him. "I admit the glowering requires some concentration."

She risked a glance over at him—and nearly stumbled.

He was smiling.

Softly. Barely. But undeniably.

It was…disarming.

She turned forward again quickly. "Well," she said, "I should hope you exert yourself so thoroughly on other tasks as well."

"Such as?"

"Oh, I don't know." She waved a careless hand in the air. "Diplomacy. Reading. Polite conversation. Hiding behind shrubbery to lecture young ladies on propriety, perhaps."

"I do not hide behind shrubbery," he insisted.

"I would not put it past you."

There was more glowering from him as they walked another few steps.

Just then, a curricle came too quickly around the bend, forcing walkers to the edge of the path.

"Careful," Pembroke said under his breath.

Before she could object, his fingers closed lightly around her elbow, guiding her aside. The contact lasted no more than a heartbeat—proper enough in a crowded park—but her body noticed all the same, quickening as though he had done something far more intimate.

Georgie drew a breath and straightened at once. "I was not in any danger."

"Of course not," he said, with that maddening calm. "You looked entirely in command of the oncoming horse."

She didn't have long to contemplate a sardonic reply of her own because Pembroke cleared his throat and asked, "What brings you to the park this morning?"

Her pulse hitched. It was such an ordinary question. Yet such a startling one. Because there it was again—that impossible, maddening contrast. The same one she'd sensed last night. In one breath, he spoke as though he meant to manage her, and in the next, he asked her questions as though her answers mattered.

She swallowed. "Fresh air," she said after a moment. "And silence."

His brows shot up. "A young lady of Society has no access to silence?"

"Not the sort that counts." She kept her gaze ahead, watching the glimmer of sunlight on the water. "Everyone wants something. A comment. A promise. A performance. A smile. A bow. Out here, no one asks anything of me."

He considered that. "I can understand the need to escape expectations."

She darted a skeptical look at him. "You? You look as if you *were* expectation carved into human form."

His mouth twitched. "My mother is exceedingly fond of expectations."

"Ah." Georgie nodded. "Mine too."

He hesitated, then added quietly, "She doesn't permit missteps."

"Nor does mine." Her voice gentled. "And yet, here we are. Failing spectacularly to remain where our mothers put us."

His gaze softened, just a shade. Enough that her breath snagged in her chest.

Just then, a boy with a tray suspended from a leather strap ambled past, calling, "Lemonade, my lady? Lemonade, my lord?"

Georgie became abruptly aware of how dry her mouth was. She glanced wistfully at the boy carrying the lemonade tray, then looked away just as quickly. She had the last biscuit from the previous night tucked inside her reticule, but no money for lemonade.

Pembroke, however, had noticed. He stepped forward, pressed a few coins into the boy's hand, and claimed two glasses. He passed one to Georgie with an ease that made the gesture seem entirely natural.

"Thank you," she murmured, lifting her eyes to his before taking a small sip.

He inclined his head and drank as well.

She let the silence stretch for a moment, then said with studied carelessness, "Do your mother's expectations include presenting her with a bride before the Season is out?"

Pembroke promptly choked on his lemonade.

Georgie stopped short. "Good heavens. Was that so appalling a question?"

He coughed once into his fist, then again, shooting her a look of pure irritation as he recovered. "Appalling? No. Alarmingly specific, perhaps."

She bit the inside of her cheek to keep from smiling. "I merely wondered. You have the look of a man frequently pursued by ambitious mamas."

His mouth flattened. "I intend to remain a bachelor as long as is humanly possible," he said. Then, after the briefest pause: "If not forever."

For one incomprehensible instant, her chest tightened.

So that was that. Pembroke was not looking for a wife. It unsettled her more than it should have, which was foolish. Even if he had been, he would hardly have set his sights on a penniless girl from a family with a damaged reputation. Regardless of his friendship with Henry.

She lifted her glass and took another sip as though his answer had not landed anywhere tender. "How very resolute of you," she said lightly.

"I assure you," he muttered, "it is one of my firmer convictions."

The footman wandered past them in the wrong direction entirely.

Georgie sighed. "Martin seems to have embarked on a journey entirely separate from ours."

Pembroke murmured, "We should collect him before he attempts to guide ducks across the bridge."

She stifled a smile. "Lead on, my lord."

They angled toward the footman, but as they walked, Pembroke spoke again, voice surprisingly low and introspective. "You questioned earlier why I was here."

"Yes," she answered lightly. "I am still awaiting a satisfactory explanation. Please note that 'coincidence' remains an unsatisfactory defense."

He inhaled slowly, eyes fixed ahead. "Today was a coincidence. Last night, I was sent by your brother."

"Ah," she said simply.

"Your brother—"

"Please do not attempt to tell me my brother worries about me. He worries about himself," she said.

Pembroke didn't deny it. Instead, he merely added, "He asked me to watch you while he's incapacitated."

Her brows shot up. "Watch me? Or track me?" she asked. "Like a hound."

Pembroke stopped walking. So did she.

"Lady Georgiana," he said quietly, "whatever you think of me, I am not here to do you any harm."

She blinked. That…was not the answer she had expected. And God help her, it sounded sincere.

"Then why are you here?" she whispered.

The wind stirred the budding leaves overhead. Somewhere beyond the trees, a carriage rattled past. Pembroke looked down at her, his jaw tight, his expression shadowed—as though he were grappling with something he would much rather have left unsaid.

At last he said, "Because you concern me."

Her heart gave a heavy thud.

He seemed to realize at once how revealing that sounded. His expression hardened. "You are reckless," he said. "And stubborn. And, at present, being cornered into something you do not want."

Her smile returned, though smaller now, edged with irony. "You make me sound like a trapped fox."

He shrugged. "Trapped creatures are apt to do reckless things."

She lifted her chin. "Reckless things? Like what?"

"I do not know what desperate young ladies consider when they see no tolerable path before them," he said grimly. "Only that I would rather not discover you have done something irrevocable merely because everyone around you has left you with too few choices."

For a moment, she could only stare at him. It was there in his voice—something unvarnished and real. As though he understood, at least a little, that what awaited her was not merely inconvenient but unbearable. "What would you do?" she asked softly.

That stopped him.

He scrubbed a hand through his hair and let out a breath, the sound rough with frustration. "Honestly?" His mouth tightened. "I don't know. But I should not like it any better than you do."

She simply looked at him.

No lecture. No hollow assurances. No sharp reminder that she ought to be grateful for any offer at all, as her parents and Henry so often insisted.

Just the truth. And somehow, that plain honesty moved her more than any polished speech could have.

Then, because the moment had grown too raw and strange, she tipped her head and said, "So instead you intend to follow me about like a chaperone and prevent all possible scandal?"

He shook his head. "I told you. I am *not* following you."

"And I told you...I don't believe you." She smiled at him sweetly.

He exhaled, some of the tension leaving him at last. "You mentioned silence. And fresh air. Both sound delightful to me. May I continue to accompany you on your walk? At least until Martin manages to locate the correct century?"

Her lips parted. He looked almost uncertain. Which was new. And interesting.

"Very well," she said at last, turning back toward the path. "But only if you promise not to scowl the entire time."

"I make no such promise."

"Of course not."

"I do smile."

"When?"

He made a sound of long-suffering. "Occasionally."

"Then I shall keep watch for this rare and possibly mythical event."

And when he fell into step beside her once more, she caught the faintest curve at the corner of his mouth.

A smile.

For her.

It sent the most alarming little flutter of heat through her —somewhere decidedly lower than her heart.

# CHAPTER EIGHT

*Two days later*

Georgie stepped into the Duke of Winston's town house. She'd never been inside a place that looked quite so perfectly proper while harboring quite so much delicious rebellion. The exterior was the picture of aristocratic dignity—white stone, gleaming windows, a perfectly liveried butler who seemed carved from marble.

But once she climbed to the second floor and slipped into Bea's private sitting room, closing the door softly behind her, propriety vanished entirely.

Rebellion simmered inside like a pot left unattended on the hob.

Books lay open on every surface. Cushions were tossed haphazardly about. A tea tray sat perilously close to a stack of parliamentary pamphlets. And in the center of the mess sat Bea, cross-legged on the settee, tapping her pencil thoughtfully against her lip.

Poppy perched on the edge of a chair nearby, her bright

blue eyes wide and earnest, as though she feared her mother might swing in through the window at any moment.

"You're late," Bea declared without turning.

"You're early," Georgie countered, earning a sniff of approval.

"Sit, sit," Poppy said quickly, waving her to the chair beside her. "Before Bea's mother wanders by and wonders why the three of us always look guilty when we gather."

Bea dropped her pencil with a dramatic flourish. "Well. Now that we're all here—"

"We can finally begin the second official meeting of The Society of Resourceful Young Ladies Who've Had Quite Enough," Poppy said proudly.

"Yes," Bea said, "and as the Prime Minister, I have decided that our first order of business shall be renaming the society."

"Renaming it?" Poppy asked, blinking.

"Indeed," Bea continued. "It needs to be more powerful. And, I daresay, a bit more...succinct."

Poppy perked up, her bright-blue eyes going wide. "Oh! Perhaps something that includes wallflowers. I rather like that notion."

Georgie pursed her lips. "But Bea, here, is hardly a wallflower."

"Ooh, you're quite right," Poppy replied, biting her lip and frowning.

"Perhaps," Bea interjected, "but I *aspire* to be a wallflower and that is what matters, if you ask me."

"What do you mean, you aspire to be a wallflower?" Poppy pressed.

Bea shrugged. "I've told my father that as long as he insists upon trying to marry me off to Nicholas Archer, I intend to remain happily unattached. Honestly, I've never seen the point of marriage. It seems a horrible bargain for the lady."

"You told your father you wish to remain unattached and he *listens* to you?" Georgie asked, eyes wide in complete bewilderment. "I wish my father would heed my wishes." She sighed.

Not that she had ever expected such a miracle. In her family, a daughter's wishes were weighed only to determine how inconvenient they might be.

"My father doesn't have much of a choice," Bea replied with a sly grin.

"Why?" Poppy wanted to know, leaning forward.

Georgie was on tenterhooks as well.

"Partially, because my mother doesn't want to see me pressured into marriage," Bea explained. "And partially because I told Father if he forces me to marry, I shall cause the biggest scandal London's ever seen. Why, I'd run away if I had to."

"Really?" came Georgie's breathless reply. Her heart was beating like a rabbit's foot in her chest. She had never met another young lady with the same outrageous plan.

For the first time in her life, she felt as if she truly had someone she could talk to. Someone—two someones!—she could share her deepest secrets with. Not people who would bargain over her future or dismiss her fears, but women who listened as though her life actually belonged to her.

"What about *The Defiant Daisies*?" Poppy offered, refocusing her attention on the society's new name.

Bea made a face.

Georgie pressed her lips together to hide a smile. "It does sound…cheerful."

"Exactly," Bea huffed. "But we are not cheerful. We are plotting. We are strong!"

Poppy sighed. "Fair enough. Defiant, yes. Daisies…no."

Georgie narrowed her eyes. She glanced meaningfully at her friends. *"The Unmanageable Maidens?"*

Poppy flushed scarlet. "Well, it's accurate, at least."

"Better," Bea allowed, biting her lip. "But we need something decisive. Something unyielding." She snapped her fingers. "I've got it. *The Wallflowers' Revolution!*"

"Ooh, that's quite good," Georgie said. "But what about *The Wallflowers' Revolt?*"

"That's it!" Poppy confirmed, beaming. "It's perfect."

"I quite agree," Bea replied.

"It is, isn't it?" Georgie said, warmth blooming in her chest. "It sounds like a small, delightful uprising."

"Small?" Bea sniffed. "My dear Georgie, it will be legendary."

Poppy's smile widened. "I still cannot believe we have a society."

"I can," Bea replied briskly. "A society is the only sensible response to the utter nonsense around us. Now." She sat straighter. "Next order of business: Georgie's crisis."

Poppy clapped her hands once and turned toward Georgie. "Yes! Tell us everything. What are your plans?"

Georgie swallowed. She had told them a little already—briefly, breathlessly—in the retiring room last week, but she had not yet said the actual words slowly, deliberately, aloud in daylight.

"I am going to escape my wedding," she breathed in a rush. "Truly escape it. On the day. Just before the vows."

Neither girl gasped. Neither girl fainted. There was nary a raised voice. In fact, neither so much as blinked.

It was the most encouraging response of Georgie's life.

Bea leaned forward, palms on her knees. "Excellent. Good. How exactly do you intend to escape?"

Georgie hesitated—not from doubt, but from the weight of saying it aloud. Once spoken, it would be real in a way it had not yet been, even in her own mind.

She twisted her fingers in her lap. "I shall hire a hack to

wait for me on the side of the church, then I shall feign illness, act as if I must use the convenience, and slip away right before the wedding."

"The hack will take me to the coaching station north of town where a post chaise will take me away from London," she said carefully, "I shall go to Bath. An old friend of mine is there just now—her family is visiting for the Season. She has agreed to meet me quietly."

Bea's gaze sharpened. "And then?"

Georgie drew a breath. "Then I will travel with the family to Northumbria. My friend's aunt is elderly and in need of a lady's companion. I will live quietly. Under another name, if need be."

The words steadied her as she spoke them. No ballrooms. No bargaining. No being watched and weighed like coin.

"I shall work," she finished softly. "And I shall be safe."

It was not a grand dream, perhaps, but it was hers: a room of her own, honest work, and the blessed relief of not belonging to a man she had not chosen.

Her friends nodded, but Georgie didn't mistake the hint of sadness in their eyes.

Georgie exhaled shakily. "My parents will be furious, of course," she said, a partial smile on her face.

The notion ought to have terrified her more than it did. Instead, she felt only a fierce, determined satisfaction at the thought of disappointing them so thoroughly.

Bea waved this off. "Parents always are. It's their natural condition."

But Poppy shook her head slowly. "My mother wouldn't be furious."

Both girls looked at her, heads tipped to the side.

"She'd be relieved?" Georgie asked hesitantly.

Poppy let out a humorless laugh. "She wouldn't notice."

Poppy folded her hands tightly in her lap, lips pressing

together before she spoke again. "Mama hasn't noticed anything since Papa died. Well, she notices wine. And any man under sixty. And anyone who does anything in the least bit artistic."

Georgie frowned. "Artistic?"

"Oh yes," Poppy said with a miserable nod. "Mama adores artists. All sorts of them. She invites them to the house at all hours. Dancers, poets, musicians who refuse to practice, dramatists who argue with the furniture. You cannot imagine the commotion."

"I quite like the idea of a dramatist arguing with furniture," Bea murmured. "It sounds infinitely more interesting than my father's dull political salons. But go on."

Poppy sighed deeply. "After Papa died, Mama simply… stopped caring about Society. About propriety. About…most things. She drinks far too much. She spends money as if it's her favorite pastime. And she gathers the strangest people to the house whenever she likes. I live in fear that one day she'll invite a contortionist and he'll become lodged in the staircase."

Bea snorted. "Your mother sounds terribly lively."

"Oh, don't get me wrong," Poppy continued with another sigh. "She is quite lovable at times. But it's a great deal of work looking after her. If it weren't for Mr. Ashby—he's Mama's solicitor—I don't know what I'd do. He's the only one who can talk sense into her. Well, he tries at least. She rarely listens. But he does manage to keep her from spending *all* of the money Papa left us. I adore him for that."

Georgie reached for her hand and squeezed it. "I'm sorry, Poppy." It seemed to her that her friend was more of the parent and her mother was the child. It had to have been difficult for the young woman.

Poppy gave her a sweet smile. "I only mean…if scandal results from helping you, Georgie, Mother will be thrilled.

She thrives on it. She'll probably host a musicale in your honor."

Bea groaned. "God save us all from musicales."

Georgie let out a long, deep breath. "I don't want either of you to get into trouble because of me."

"Trouble?" Bea scoffed. "If my father wishes to avoid trouble, he should stop trying to marry me to Nicholas Archer. Frankly, I hope our revolt gives him indigestion."

"And if my mother notices at all," Poppy said, "she will only demand to help."

Georgie frowned. "Your mother? Help me escape?"

Poppy merely nodded.

"That reminds me." Bea's eyes twinkled. "I have news."

Georgie leaned forward. "Do tell."

Bea straightened, looking immensely proud of herself. "I have enlisted the help of the Marchioness of Trentham."

Georgie nearly choked on her own sharp intake of breath. "Scandalton?! I mean…Clare Handleton? You know Lady Trentham?"

Bea grinned. "Of course. She's a friend of Mother's. Well, Mother invited her to one of her gatherings. But unlike the others, Lady Trentham actually stayed and drank tea with me and asked sensible questions and didn't attempt to lecture the me about propriety when I made a few barbed comments about Lord Hargrave's awful politics. She's quite lovely."

Poppy's brow furrowed. "Why is she called Scandalton?"

Georgie leaned back, blowing out a breath this time. "Clare Handleton was the definition of scandal ten years ago. Ruined beyond saving. She couldn't appear anywhere without causing fainting spells. And then," Georgie added, "she shocked everyone by marrying the Marquess of Trentham."

"Not just marrying him," Bea corrected, "but taming him. Lord Trentham used to be the most determined bachelor in

London. My mother says he worships her," Bea continued proudly. "Now Lady Trentham is entirely respectable, of course. And apparently," she dropped her voice conspiratorially, "she has a soft spot for young ladies with…unconventional inclinations."

Georgie pressed a hand to her chest. "But she's—she's a marchioness!"

Bea nodded. "And when I told her about you, she said—and I quote—'If a young lady wishes to avoid a marriage to a lecher who smells like pickled onions, I consider that a cause worth supporting.'"

Poppy slapped her palm to her knee. "Excellent. We have an ally of rank. A powerful ally. And one who is living proof that scandal does not end a woman—it liberates her. I love it."

Georgie felt her throat tighten, emotion swelling unexpectedly. "Why…why would Lady Trentham help *me*?" No one had ever extended a hand to her without expecting something in return. She scarcely knew what to do with generosity freely offered.

"Because she can," Bea said simply. "And I dare say because she remembers what it was like to be trapped. And," Bea added, "I suspect it doesn't hurt that she despises Lord Henderville. She told me he pinched her once when she was eighteen and she still hasn't forgiven him."

"That makes two of us," Georgie muttered. Then she shook her head. "I should be delighted to accept Lady Trentham's help, of course."

The three of them exchanged a look, serious, fierce, united.

Bea straightened. "Well then. The Wallflowers' Revolt has its first official mission."

"The Save Georgie Campaign," Poppy whispered dramatically.

"The Escape Henderville Campaign," Bea countered with a resolute nod.

Georgie laughed, a short, incredulous sound. "I simply cannot believe any of this is real. Last week I was quite alone and now I have two ladies—no, three—helping me."

"Do believe it," Bea replied. "And now that Lady Trentham is involved, our plan is unstoppable. I told her everything. She said she will assist in whatever way we need—alibis, a carriage, an introduction to a sympathetic vicar if necessary."

Georgie's eyes widened. "A vicar?"

"You've only to say the word."

Georgie pressed both hands to her cheeks. "I am truly going to do this, aren't I?"

Bea reached for her hand. "You are. And we are with you."

Poppy reached for her other hand. "Always."

Gratitude bloomed in Georgie's chest. For the first time in her life, she felt as if she wasn't standing alone in the world, waiting for a kind word.

She had friends. She had allies. She had reinforcements.

And she had a plan.

More than that, she had the startling, dizzying sense that another life might actually be possible—one shaped by choice rather than obligation.

Bea stood abruptly. "Right. Before we adjourn, we must assign roles. Lady Trentham, patroness. Poppy, liaison to the bride. I, of course, shall coordinate strategy. And trip the groom should he give chase."

"And what is my role?" Georgie asked with a shaky smile.

To be the one person in her own story who finally chose herself, she thought—but she could not quite bring herself to say it aloud.

"Be brave," Bea said firmly. "And run like the devil himself is behind you if you must."

Georgie nodded once.

She could do that.

The clock on the mantel chimed the hour and Poppy jumped. "Oh no. If I don't leave soon, Mama will start a séance without supervision."

Bea smoothed a hand over her hair. "And if I don't reappear downstairs, Father will send a footman to fetch me."

Georgie rose as well, though a ripple of nerves fluttered beneath her ribs. "And I should go before my mother assumes I've eloped with a stable boy. The last thing I need is to give her more excuses to watch me as a cat watches a birdcage."

Poppy and Bea exchanged knowing looks.

"Until Wednesday," Bea said, giving a solemn nod. "The society's next meeting."

"Until then," Georgie echoed.

The three young ladies paused at the threshold, hands linked just long enough to seal their pact.

Then they parted—three wallflowers with heads high and eyes bright—stepping back into homes that would question, confine, or scold them.

Homes that believed they could still be controlled.

But as Georgie crossed the foyer, a fierce, startling certainty unfurled inside her.

For the first time, she truly believed Society did not stand a chance.

# CHAPTER NINE

*The next afternoon*

Georgie stepped into the little bookshop on Bond Street, the bell above the door chiming pleasantly as she crossed the threshold.

Martin waited outside for her, standing at attention near the shop's door.

Georgie wore a soft sage-green walking dress that complemented her dark hair, the fitted pelisse nipping in at her waist and her bonnet tied with a worn ribbon that insisted on fluttering in the breeze.

Her wardrobe was limited to a few serviceable outfits, the sort that had seen better days, mended here and there with invisible stitches and stubborn pride. She wore them as smartly as she could, back straight, chin lifted, determined to deflect pity with poise. But she never quite grew immune to the whispers behind gloved hands and fluttering fans as she passed—soft, serpent-like sounds that slid between her shoulder blades and curled low in her belly.

It was precisely why she loved bookshops. Books did not care if one's hem had been turned twice or one's ribbon was last year's shade. Inside them, women might be brave, adored, or gloriously free.

Today in the bookstore was no different.

She came to look—nothing more. There was never any money to purchase anything. But it cost nothing to browse. An act that had become a perfectly ordinary part of her perfectly ordinary days. Days that were spent dreading her upcoming wedding and mentally planning her great escape.

But today... Today she did not quite feel so ordinary at all.

Which didn't make sense, because nothing had changed. Henderville still waited at the end of the month. Her plan still had to hold. And yet Lord Pembroke's persistent appearances had begun to make the world feel strangely less certain.

Because she could feel it even before she turned.

That prickle down her spine. That *presence*.

The bell chimed again.

Of course.

"Lady Georgiana."

She closed her eyes for a beat. Composed herself. Then turned with the sort of resigned elegance only a woman persistently shadowed by an aggravatingly handsome man could manage.

He filled the doorway—Lord Pembroke—tall and broad-shouldered, wearing a dark blue riding coat that made him look even more unfairly put together. His cravat was a perfect snowy fold; his boots gleamed; his hair—curse him—refused to stay entirely tamed and curled boyishly over his brow. Altogether, he looked like a man who had just materialized from a particularly fine-looking Greek statue.

"Oh good," she said. "Am I to believe this is *another* coincidence?"

He removed his gloves with infuriating calm. "It is not my fault if I happen to enjoy reading."

She crossed her arms. "You? A lover of literature? In addition to your other qualities? I must sit down before I swoon."

"I do read," he insisted.

"What kind of books?" She blinked at him curiously.

"Ones with pages."

She tilted her head heavenward. "Your wit dazzles."

And there—there it was again. That faint twitch at the corner of his mouth she was not supposed to notice. Except she *did* notice. Far too often.

She noticed everything about him, in fact, which was deeply inconvenient for a woman trying not to imagine him in any role whatsoever in her future.

She shouldn't enjoy sparring with him. She truly shouldn't. But her pulse always quickened, as though some secret part of her delighted in meeting his stare and matching his stubbornness with her own.

It was not merely that he was handsome, though that would have been trouble enough. It was that with him, for a few reckless moments, she could almost pretend she was a woman being courted instead of bartered.

"Well?" she said lightly. "Since you're here, you may as well buy a book."

"I intend to." He promptly looked around the shop. "I saw Martin outside," he added.

"And that fact is entirely unrelated to your appearance here?" she prodded.

"Completely."

She leveled a look at him that suggested he was lying through his teeth, then she turned away from him with deliberate nonchalance and drifted toward the wall of novels, trailing her fingertips along the familiar spines.

She paused now and then, lifting a volume as though she might truly buy it, all while acutely aware of Lord Pembroke standing a few paces off—pretending, with catastrophic ineptitude, to examine a shelf of atlases. Every time she shifted even slightly, he mirrored her with the subtlety of a marble statue trying to be stealthy. At last she sighed, pulled down a favorite Richardson novel simply to have something in her hands, and looked over her shoulder to find him studying the ceiling as though it held all the secrets of the universe.

She turned deliberately to watch him, folding her arms over her chest. "I must know. What literary treasure brought you to Bond Street today?"

He glanced at the nearest shelf, grabbed the first book his hand encountered, and held it up.

She blinked. Then stared. "*A Botanical Study of Ferns of the Upper Hebrides.*"

"Yes," he said, utterly serious.

"Lord Pembroke," she said gently, "you do not look like a man interested in ferns."

He straightened and sniffed. "You don't know my interests."

A warm, unwelcome flutter moved through her chest. She took a tiny step closer, against her better judgment.

"Why can you not simply admit it?"

His brows shot up. "That I like ferns?"

"That you're following me." She gave him a falsely sweet smile.

He went utterly still, his unfairly long lashes touching his cheeks, his breath hitching. It did peculiar things to her heartbeat.

At last, he said quietly, "Because if I say it…it becomes true."

The words struck her unusually hard. As though truth, once spoken between them, might become something living and difficult to contain. Something in her softened in a way she wasn't prepared for.

"And if it's true…" He looked away, jaw rigid. "Then I have no reason for it. And I really should."

This time her brows shot up. "No reason for it? I thought you said my brother asked you to follow me about."

Pembroke shrugged lightly. "Yes…well…I *may* have embellished his words a bit." He cleared his throat. "But I…I cannot help it if I worry for your safety."

Georgie swallowed, unexpectedly moved. She shouldn't be. She absolutely shouldn't be. But she was. No one had worried about her safety before. Her family worried about her compliance…but never her *safety*.

And that, perhaps, was the truest threat he posed. Not his broad shoulders or stubborn mouth or mesmerizing green eyes—but the quiet, devastating novelty of being cared for.

Turning slightly pink, Pembroke shoved the fern book back onto the shelf with unnecessary force. "Buy whatever book you came for," he muttered. "I'll wait outside."

But she surprised them both.

"You may stay," she said softly.

His eyes flicked to hers.

"I mean," she added, gathering up the frayed edges of her composure, "if you are going to haunt Bond Street under the guise of literary devotion, you may as well make yourself useful."

"Useful," he repeated.

"Yes. Stand there and try not to select any more volumes on ferns."

His mouth twitched.

Georgie turned before she could enjoy that too much and drifted deeper into the shop. Near the back, on the highest shelf, she spotted a worn copy of *The Mysteries of Udolpho.* Her heart gave a little leap.

"There you are," she murmured.

A narrow rolling ladder stood nearby. She placed one hand upon it and lifted her foot to the first rung.

"What are you doing?" Pembroke asked at once.

"Retrieving a book."

"Surely the shopkeeper can do that."

"Surely I possess hands."

"That has never been the question."

She shot him a look over her shoulder. "Do stop sounding like a disapproving headmaster."

"Then do stop giving me cause," he said.

Which, naturally, made her climb another rung.

"Lady Georgiana."

"Lord Pembroke."

She rose onto her toes and stretched for the book. Her fingertips brushed the spine. Almost. Just a little farther—

The ladder gave a sudden, traitorous wobble.

She gasped.

The book slipped free at the exact same moment her balance did. For one unsteady instant there was nothing beneath her but air and mortification.

Then Pembroke was there.

His hands caught her firmly at the waist before she could fall. The ladder rattled back against the shelf. The book thumped harmlessly to the carpet. And Georgie found herself half-lowered, half-held against him, one gloved hand fisted in the front of his coat.

Everything went still.

His grip tightened once—just enough to steady her—and the heat of it seemed to burn straight through kid leather, muslin, skin, and sense. She became aware of ridiculous things all at once: the breadth of his chest beneath her palm, the clean starch of his cravat, the faint scent of soap and wool and something unmistakably male.

"Are you hurt?" he asked, but his voice had gone low and rough.

"No," she whispered.

He did not let go.

Nor, she realized with a jolt, did she.

Her gaze lifted to his. His had already dropped—to her mouth.

The look of it sent a small, unsettling wave of heat through her, low and swirling and wholly unsuitable for a respectable bookshop in the middle of the afternoon.

She watched his jaw move.

His eyes came back to hers, darker now.

"This," he said at last, though not with any great steadiness, "is precisely the sort of recklessness I meant."

Georgie swallowed. "I was merely reaching for a novel."

"You were falling off of a ladder."

"Only briefly."

That made him exhale what might almost have been a laugh, though his hands were still at her waist and his expression was anything but easy.

"You are impossible."

"And yet," she said, because someone had to restore order to the universe, "you persist in following me."

His thumbs shifted, almost imperceptibly.

Desire unfurled low inside her.

Very gently now, far more gently than she expected from so stern a man, he set her back upon her feet.

"Perhaps," he said, bending to retrieve the fallen book, "it is because you cannot be trusted alone with literature."

She took the volume from him, though their fingers

brushed and made a fresh mess of her pulse. "A shocking accusation."

"An accurate one."

"You stride into bookshops, pretend to admire ferns, and catch women in compromising positions beside ladders. I do not think you are in any position to accuse anyone of misconduct."

"I did not put you on the ladder."

"No," she said, tucking the book against her chest. "You merely looked very satisfied to find me falling from it."

His eyes flashed. "Lady Georgiana," he said quietly, "you really should take care."

The words ought to have sounded stern. Instead, they sounded very much like something else. Something that made her skin feel too tight.

She cleared her throat. "Well. Since I have now scandalized both you and the architecture, we should go." She tucked the book back onto a shelf. There was no money to buy it.

"An excellent notion."

"You may accompany me," she said, far too brightly. "Provided you refrain from further lectures."

"I make no such promise."

"*Such* a surprise."

"Though," he added, falling into step beside her as they made for the door, "if you insist on climbing things, I shall be obliged to remain near."

Georgie nearly missed her footing again. "How fortunate for you," she said.

They left the shop together, falling into step along the busy pavement. Martin trailed behind, wearing a mismatched coat and an expression of deep philosophical confusion as he paused to investigate a window display of umbrellas.

Georgie sighed. "We should wait for him."

Pembroke looked back. "At this point, I believe Martin survives almost entirely by happenstance."

"Mostly," Georgie agreed. "Once he followed a flower cart for three streets because he thought it was me."

Pembroke's eyes warmed with amusement—a real smile glancing across his face. It made something inside her shift. Pleased. Alarmingly pleased.

She was beginning to understand that what she wanted from him might be as simple—and as foolish—as more. More time. More smiles meant only for her. More of this impossible ease.

They strolled past the milliner's, then a ribbon-and-lace shop. Warm sun filtered between the rooftops, brushing his cheekbones with gold. And she hated that she'd noticed it.

"So," she asked, "if you don't read about ferns, what do you read?"

He hesitated. "History. Philosophy. Occasionally a novel."

"I adore novels," she said.

"I noticed," he answered softly. "Why didn't you buy that one?"

She glanced away quickly and cleared her throat. "I...er... I decided I didn't want it."

In her haste to explain without embarrassing herself, she bumped his shoulder, just barely. The contact was featherlight, almost nothing at all, yet it sent a tiny current through her—as though she had been the one reckless enough to cross some unseen line. "We have something in common, then," she hurried to say. "Novel reading."

His voice lowered, intimate and unguarded. "More than one thing."

Her heart gave a hard little beat, and for the first time, she admitted to herself—she liked this. Their walking. Their arguing. Their impossible, ridiculous...*something*.

She liked feeling chosen by his attention. She liked that he sought her out. And perhaps most troubling of all, she liked the irrational little fantasy that, under different circumstances, he might have sought her out for courtship. Which was madness. First, there was little hope her father would break off her betrothal to Henderville. Not with what was certain to be a small fortune at stake. And second, Pembroke had already made it quite clear that he had no wish to marry. And even if he did wish to marry, she would rather expire on the spot than ask him to *pay* to marry her.

No, whatever this was between them was all it could ever be. Freedom was her future. Not marriage. But that didn't mean they couldn't continue…for the time being.

She looked ahead, heart fluttering wildly. "I'm going to the British Museum on Thursday."

Now, what in the world had made her say that?

Loneliness, perhaps. Curiosity. Or perhaps merely the wish to steal a few more afternoons with him before the rest of her life closed over her like a lid.

"And?" he asked carefully.

"And if you'd like to cut the pretense," she said airily, "you could simply *meet* me there."

His brows rose. "You're inviting me?"

"I'm preventing you from skulking behind sarcophagi."

A slow, beautiful smile spread across his face.

"I'll be there," he said.

"I assumed you would be," she replied, chin lifted. She glanced back at Martin and sighed again. "I am going home now. You needn't worry."

Their steps slowed. He looked at her like she was a puzzle he very much wanted to keep solving.

"Until Thursday," he murmured, bowing slightly.

She dipped a teasing curtsy. "Try not to lose yourself in another book display before then."

And for the rest of the walk home, Georgie could not quite banish the quiver in her chest reminding her…she was beginning to dread her afternoons *less* when Lord Pembroke appeared.

And that was decidedly troubling.

# CHAPTER TEN

*Wednesday*

This time, when Georgie slipped into Bea's private sitting room and shut the door behind her, the first thing she saw was Poppy sitting cross-legged on the carpet, determinedly untangling a string of pearls that almost certainly did not belong to her. The rest of the room was its usual charming storm of organized disarray—half political pamphlets, half sketches, and entirely Bea.

Both girls looked up as Georgie entered.

"Finally," Bea said. "We've been waiting an age. Poppy will have this whole room sorted before long."

"I cannot help it if I'm tidy," Poppy protested cheerfully, wrapping the pearls in a tight circle and setting them atop a nearby table. "If I didn't straighten Mama's house, it would be a bigger mess than it already is. Even with the maids working 'round the clock." Poppy brightened when she saw Georgie. "You look flushed. Did something happen?"

Georgie took a breath. Then another. Then placed her

reticule very carefully on the nearest chair as though if she let go of it too fast, it might explode.

"Lord Pembroke is following me."

Both girls stared.

It was Bea who recovered first. She set down her pencil with a snap. "Tell him to leave you be," she declared, frowning.

Poppy's brows drew together. "What? Why is he following you?"

"It doesn't matter," Bea said firmly. "Tell him to leave you be. Immediately. In fact, say it loudly. Say it at full volume if you must."

Poppy's eyes were shining, far too interested for comfort. "But *why* is he following you? He's so handsome. And rich. And powerful. And did I mention handsome?"

"Several times," Bea said dryly.

Georgie bit her lip and paced. "I don't know why he's following me. Not entirely. That's the vexing part. He just… keeps appearing."

"Appearing?" Poppy echoed, leaning forward, pearls forgotten.

"Yes. Hyde Park a few days ago. And Bond Street yesterday."

Poppy gasped. Bea scowled.

"And last week at the Willoughbys', obviously," Georgie added. She'd already told her friends the entire tale of how Lord Pembroke had escorted her home from the ball.

"Are you certain it's not a coincidence?" Poppy offered.

"I'm certain," Georgie replied. "He admitted it."

Poppy tilted her head. "Because your brother asked him to?"

"No. That's just it," Georgie replied. "He said he's concerned for my safety."

"Oh, what nonsense," Bea nearly growled. "Pure male nonsense."

"Why is it nonsense?" Poppy asked, blinking.

"Because men never do anything unless it's to *their* benefit," Bea insisted.

"I told him I'm going to the museum tomorrow," Georgie admitted, biting her lip.

Bea looked as if a vein in her forehead might pop. "What? Now you're inviting him with you?"

Georgie sank into the chair beside Poppy, tugging at her gloves. "It seemed more prudent than pretending I don't know he's following me. Besides, I must admit…I do find him…intriguing."

"Intriguing!" Bea's face was so red she looked as if she might well have an apoplectic fit.

"He *is* intriguing," Poppy agreed, nodding. "Intriguing and *handsome*."

"What makes him so intriguing?" Bea wanted to know, a full scowl on her face.

"He's *watching* me," Georgie replied. "As though he expects something dreadful to happen at any moment. As though he wants to keep me safe."

"As though you require rescuing," Bea pointed out, frowning.

"He did say I'm reckless," Georgie admitted.

Bea crossed her feet at the ankles, looking every bit the Prime Minister of the Wallflowers' Revolt. The scowl remained. "That is preposterous," she said. "Tell him to leave. With great emphasis. I'll help compose the speech."

Poppy shook her head. "Oh, but Bea, it's not the *worst* thing in the world to have a man like Lord Pembroke keeping an eye on you. He's honorable. And capable. And he has very good shoulders."

Georgie's cheeks warmed. "They are quite nice." She gave Poppy a little smile.

Bea made a disgusted sound. "This is exactly how men lure perfectly sensible women into trouble…by being tall and brooding and developing inconvenient muscles."

"He isn't trying to lure me," Georgie protested. "He's trying to…protect me."

Bea's eyes narrowed. "Worse."

Georgie let her head fall back against the chair. She sighed. "No one—*no one*—has ever cared what I did before. Not my father, not my mother, not Henry. If I vanished entirely, they'd only be bothered that I am no longer available to sell to Lord Henderville."

She swallowed.

"And yet here is this man—this very stubborn man—who seems determined to keep me from falling off a cliff I fully intend to leap from."

Poppy reached over and squeezed her hand. "It's nice to know that someone cares…isn't it?"

"It is unsettling," Georgie said, though her chest did feel… strangely warm. "He watches me as though I'm…worth watching."

Which was strangely affecting, when she had spent most of her life being assessed only for what use she might be to someone else.

"Well, I don't like it," Bea muttered. "You don't need a nursemaid!"

"Oh, how terrible," Poppy said dramatically, throwing herself onto the settee and pressing the back of her hand to her forehead. "A man of excellent breeding and impeccable looks finds Georgie captivating. Yes, we should send him away at once."

"It's not that!" Bea insisted. "You're forgetting. We're planning an escape. If he keeps interfering, he'll ruin everything."

Or worse, Georgie thought, he would make her want things her careful little plan had never accounted for—comfort, companionship, a man who looked at her as though her opinions mattered.

Georgie took a deep breath. "You're right, Bea. Of course."

"Then tell him," Bea said again. "Tell him to *go away*."

Poppy's eyes went wide and her mouth formed an O. "What if he wants to offer for you, Georgie?" Her voice was filled with excitement.

Georgie sucked in her breath. It was too near a thought she'd had. Had and quickly discarded. "Oh, no, no, no. Nothing like that," she hurried to say. "He's made it quite clear that he's a confirmed bachelor."

Poppy's face fell. "Well, that's not very romantic."

"More like a confirmed nuisance," Bea added. "Tell him to leave you alone."

Poppy gave Georgie a catlike smile and fluttered her eyelashes. "Or perhaps just ask him how long he intends to follow you."

Bea groaned. "Never ask a man why he's being absurd. He doesn't know."

Georgie bit her lip, looking between them. "That's a good idea, Poppy. That's precisely what I'll ask him when I see him at the museum."

Bea shook her head. "Are you mad? Don't encourage him. If you told him you're going to the museum, go someplace else."

Poppy waggled her eyebrows. "But what if she *wants* to see him?"

Georgie looked down at her gloves, smoothing a wrinkle that did not exist. "I don't *think* I want to see him," she insisted—too quickly, too obviously—and when she glanced back up, both of her friends' brows were raised.

The lie was so transparent even she winced at it. Of

course she wanted to see him. She wanted to know if he would come. Wanted to know if she had mattered to him after all. Was he just being noble? Gentlemanly? Or—

She hesitated.

Oh, dear. That was the problem, wasn't it? She *did* want to see him. And not merely because he was pleasant to look at, though heaven knew that would have been trouble enough. But because with him, she felt less like a burden to be disposed of and more like a woman who might, under different circumstances, be earnestly sought.

At the same time, she agreed with both of her friends. She simultaneously wanted to tell Lord Pembroke to leave her be and secretly hoped he wouldn't. She wanted to pretend she was entirely unaffected and yet couldn't stop wondering if he'd show up again, if he'd look at her with that furrow between his brows and that maddening, unreadable expression she hadn't yet decided was concern or judgment or...something else altogether. She wanted, at the very least, one more impossible afternoon before the rest of her life was settled for her.

She didn't want to care.

But part of her—some long-neglected, wistful part—was beginning to like being seen.

# CHAPTER ELEVEN

*Thursday afternoon*

Georgie had always considered the museum one of the few places in London where a person could disappear entirely and still be utterly herself. The echoing halls, the smell of dust and ink, the hush of reverence that clung to the marble statues like a prayer—it was all deliciously calming. And today, she needed calm.

Martin was wandering about behind her, squinting at things with such intensity that she had to wonder if he knew what he was looking at.

Georgie paused before a case of Roman artifacts, her gloves tucked into her reticule and her fingers trailing along the cool wooden edge of the display. Inside, a bronze fibula gleamed dully under glass, its pin curved. She read the description three times and still didn't comprehend it. Her mind was elsewhere, repeating a question she couldn't stop asking herself: *Where is he?*

Lord Pembroke had not appeared yet.

That was good.

And also disappointing.

Which was quite telling. A sensible young lady awaiting an afternoon at the museum ought not to feel disappointment over the absence of one particular gentleman. Especially a gentleman who, given the opportunity, could ruin all of her plans. And yet the disappointment was there—like a small, warm ache just beneath her ribs.

She took a step, forcing herself to study the information placard beside the next display. Her brother would scoff. Henry found her obsession with history unbecoming. He once accused her of trying to make herself more interesting than she was by memorizing facts about dead Romans. But Georgie knew it wasn't the facts that intrigued her. It was the stories.

The hidden parts. The private motives. The lives that unfolded beneath the grand public version everyone else was expected to admire. Perhaps that was why Lord Pembroke unsettled her so much. He made her wonder what story might have been hers under different circumstances.

"You're reading that plaque with more intensity than I've seen in a fencing match," said a voice behind her.

Georgie jumped and whirled around. Lord Pembroke stood a respectful distance back, all dark tousled hair and ironic mouth, as though he'd materialized out of the shadowy corners of her own mind.

"Good heavens," she said, pressing a hand to her chest. "Do you make a habit of sneaking up on women in museums?"

"Only the ones who give me false itineraries."

"It wasn't false." She drew her shoulders back, fingers tightening briefly on her reticule. "I said I would be here today and so I am."

"Yes, but *I've* been here for nearly two hours."

Georgie bit her lip. She hadn't meant to arrive late. But

the British Museum charged admission before noon, and she hadn't the coin to spare for luxuries—not even educational ones. So she'd waited, loitering a full hour on the benches along Great Russell Street, pretending to admire a chimney pot while willing time to pass faster. She stepped inside the moment the doors opened for free entry, trying to ignore the way her cheeks burned with a familiar sort of self-consciousness—her threadbare gowns, her thin gloves, her utter lack of coin.

"Are you well?" Pembroke asked after a moment, watching her face too closely.

Georgie blinked, startled. "Yes. Perfectly."

"You're a poor liar," he said gently.

She hesitated. Then she bit her lip and admitted, "I arrived late because I had to wait for the free hour."

A flicker of something crossed his face. Guilt perhaps. Understanding. He shifted, uncomfortable. "I didn't think—"

"No, most people don't," she said. "But money is tight in my household. At least until my marriage."

His brow furrowed. "I… That's why you didn't buy a book at the shop." He bit his lip and shook his head.

She smiled, too bright. "Don't look so grave. It's not your life after all."

Pembroke bowed his head, his fingers tightening briefly around the brim of the hat he carried. "I'm sorry," he said quietly.

She tilted her head, voice featherlight. "Sorry enough to stop following me?"

That made him still. His jaw flexed, the muscle there ticking once. "I told you, I—"

But Georgie didn't let him finish. It was time to ask the question on the tip of her tongue. "Are following me to ensure I don't run off before the nuptials?" She turned back to the display with forced casualness.

But the silence behind her felt weighted. And she didn't need to see him to know her words had hit him precisely how she'd hoped they would.

"Are you *planning* to run off before the nuptials?" His voice was quiet, sincere.

She turned halfway and arched a brow. "Now, why would I ever tell you that?"

The hint of a smile touched his lips. "I suppose that's fair."

She turned fully toward him, took a deep breath, and forced herself to meet his gaze. "Why are you here, Lord Pembroke? It cannot merely be out of concern for my welfare." There. That was direct. Bea would be proud.

Georgie held his gaze, waiting.

He did not answer at once. His eyes flicked away, then back, as if he were bracing himself for a truth he had not yet decided to speak.

"I don't know," he said at last. "I only know that ever since that night—Willoughby's ball—I haven't been able to stop thinking about—"

He broke off, his lips pressing together.

Georgie's heart gave an inconvenient little thud. "About...?" she prompted, before she could stop herself.

For a moment, she thought he might say it. Might say *you*.

Instead, he cleared his throat and gestured toward the case between them. "Why am I here?" A corner of his mouth twitched. "Why, to look at Roman brooches. Obviously."

She forced a smile past the twinge of disappointment in her chest. She recognized the maneuver for what it was...a retreat. A change of subject wrapped in wit. And she ought, perhaps, to have pressed him. Bea certainly would have. But Georgie found she did not want to. Whatever had brought him here—concern, curiosity, impulse, or something he was not yet ready to name—she was enjoying his company far too much to risk chasing him away.

Instead, she kept up the pretense. "You're fond of brooches, my lord?"

"Indeed." His previous jovial tone had returned. "I've a deep personal connection to fourth-century fastenings." He leaned slightly toward the case. "Though this particular piece is third-century, if I'm not mistaken."

She narrowed her eyes. "You knew that?"

"I read the placard."

"Liar."

He gave her a sidelong glance. "Fine. I fear I must admit I'm a student of history."

Georgie turned to fully face him now, folding her arms. "*You* like history?"

"Very much. My tutor called it an unhealthy preoccupation. Apparently, a future earl ought to focus on estate management and bloodlines, not the political system in Mesopotamia."

Her arms dropped. "*You* are fond of Mesopotamia?"

"Who isn't? It's got floods, gods with wings, and cuneiform. What's not to love?"

A laugh escaped her before she could stop it. But then just as quickly, she eyed him with suspicion. "You're serious, aren't you?"

He held her gaze, the humor fading from his expression. "Why is it so difficult to believe that ancient worlds fascinate me?"

She arched a brow. "Perhaps because none of my brother's friends have been anything I might call erudite."

A smile lit his entire face. "Oh, well, I never claimed to be *erudite.*"

She moved to the next display case and when she looked up to inquire after his thoughts on the latest set of brooches, she found his gaze intent upon *her* instead. The look unsettled her far more than it ought to have. It did not feel casual.

It felt chosen. As though, in a room full of relics and marvels, he had decided *she* was the object most worth studying.

She narrowed her eyes at him. "You're terribly different from my expectations. But…"

He arched a brow. "But what?"

Georgie blew out a short breath. She might as well tell him the truth. "Honestly? I'm not entirely certain I can trust you."

To her surprise, instead of looking offended, he merely nodded once. Then his mouth curved in another smile, a more subtle one this time. "And yet you keep speaking to me."

She tilted her head, considering him. He'd mirrored her words from the bookshop. Clever. Charming, perhaps. But he'd also made a good point. She *did* keep speaking to him. That was the risk. Because if she were wrong about him, if he really was watching her on behalf of her brother, it would not be merely embarrassing. It would be ruinous.

Yet somehow she found herself walking beside him into the next gallery, her thoughts stubbornly circling his words.

"Ah, Assyrian reliefs," Pembroke announced as they entered the new space. "I always think these look like they were carved in a rush. As if the artist had a carriage waiting."

"That one's actually meant to show motion," Georgie replied. "See how the legs overlap? They wanted the king to appear fast and strong."

"Like a particularly muscular gazelle," Pembroke murmured.

Georgie smothered another laugh. "I suppose you'll tell me next that you have an opinion on Neolithic pottery," she said, trying for a smirk.

"A firm one. Most of it looks like it was made by drunken sheep."

Georgie shook her head, her curls bouncing against her cheeks. "You can't say that."

"I just did."

They stepped to the next display and Georgie leaned closer to the glass, squinting at the faded inscription. At the same moment, Pembroke shifted nearer, one gloved hand bracing lightly on the wooden edge beside hers as he bent to read it too.

When his arm skimmed hers, heat flickered through her so quickly and unexpectedly that she nearly missed her next breath. She cleared her throat and shook her head.

"This one may have been carved with a bit more leisure." He spoke quietly, the words meant only for her in the hushed gallery, and the intimacy of that private tone did far more damage than any compliment might have.

She swallowed, nodded, and stepped back into the path. They strolled slowly now, their steps in rhythm, the click of her half-boots muffled by the marble floor. It felt oddly normal, almost comfortable. And *that* was dangerous too.

But the true danger of Lord Pembroke. Not simply that he was handsome, or attentive, or irritatingly determined. It was that being with him felt easy in a way nothing else in her life ever had.

She had told herself she wanted only distraction. A few companionable hours before the ugly machinery of her life resumed. But that was no longer quite true, was it? She wanted more of him than was sensible, and the realization left her equal parts warmed and afraid.

"You're quite good at this," she said.

His brows shot up. "At museums?"

"At disarming me."

Pembroke sobered, his voice quieting. "That's not my intention."

She didn't answer. She ought not to have found it so

thrilling that he understood her points at once. But she did. Most men listened merely long enough to contradict. Lord Pembroke listened as though her thoughts were worth following to their end.

"I meant what I said the other day," he added after a moment. "Your brother did ask me to look after you…at the ball. But I'm not here now because of Henry."

Georgie stopped walking. She turned and met his gaze once more. Level. Steady. Unyielding. "Then why are you here? No jests about brooches this time."

He looked down at her, rubbing his tongue over his bottom lip. "I'm here because I want to be. Because I think you're clever and complicated and…in trouble."

Well. Her eyes narrowed on him. That was quite a speech. Quite an *unexpected* speech. "Anything else?"

"Yes. You were honest enough to tell me you don't entirely trust me, so I'll return the favor and admit I think you're planning something."

Georgie didn't immediately respond. Instead, she turned and walked ahead to the next display—a collection of medieval rings, delicate and gleaming.

A cluster of visitors pressed past them, forcing Georgie nearer the display case. Pembroke's hand came briefly to the small of her back—light, careful, gone almost at once as he guided her clear of an elbow and a lady's trailing shawl. The touch lasted no more than a heartbeat. It was still enough to send a hot, startled awareness skittering down her spine.

She briefly closed her eyes. Why? Why was it like this with him? This constant rush of heat at his slightest touch? This attraction both physical and mental that she couldn't deny? Spending more time with him was foolhardy. She'd already begun wishing for things that could not be.

She took a deep breath and forced herself to stare at the rings until she trusted her voice again.

"You think I'm hiding something," she echoed.

He stepped closer and nodded. "Yes."

"You're right," she allowed.

His brows lifted. "You are?"

She nodded. "But you won't find out what it is."

He squinted a little. "Oh, I think I may be able to guess."

She stepped away then, moving into the next room, leaving him standing before the rings. His words had rattled her. She didn't glance up when he stepped beside her once more.

"What is your guess?" she asked, already half-afraid of the answer.

She heard his breath before his voice, a slow exhale, measured, as though he were choosing his words carefully.

"You have a history of escaping from places you do not wish to be, my lady. And being a student of history, I well know...history has a way of repeating itself."

# CHAPTER TWELVE

***Later that afternoon***

Jason scrubbed both hands through his hair, then did it again for good measure…because the first pass had not come close to exorcising the utter madness plaguing him.

His study was quiet, too quiet. Only the crackle of the fire broke the silence. Piles of correspondence sat untouched. A stack of parliamentary briefs leaned precariously near his elbow. His half-finished glass of brandy was sitting uselessly beside him.

And all he could think about was *her*.

Lady Georgiana Chadwick.

He let his head fall back against the leather chair and stared at the ceiling.

"Good God," he muttered. "What on earth is wrong with me?"

Nothing answered, naturally. Not the ceiling. Not his conscience. Not even the brandy, which at least had the decency to remain silent.

He dragged a hand down his face.

He had followed her today.

Again.

Not by accident…by any stretch of the imagination. Not like the other day when he had seen her walking toward Bond Street and had found himself, without conscious decision, striding after her like a man bewitched.

No, today, he'd actually intended to meet her. And he'd stood in front of a display of ancient brooches like a complete fool, pretending to know more than he did, while she stared at him with those sharp brown eyes that saw far too much.

"Brilliant," he muttered. "Absolutely brilliant, Pembroke. You're becoming obsessed."

He stood abruptly, chair scraping across the floor, and began pacing the length of the study. Back and forth. Back and forth. Like a prisoner in his own home.

Why was he doing this?

He knew why he'd started, of course—Chadwick had asked him to. The memory rankled now. He'd agreed in a moment of misplaced guilt over that damned horse race and Henry Chadwick's broken leg.

But that justification had evaporated days ago. Chadwick hadn't spared a second thought for his sister since giving the order. And Jason suspected, with a twist of his gut, that Chadwick hadn't meant it even then.

No, Jason thought grimly. He was definitely no longer doing this for Chadwick.

He paused by the fireplace, bracing an arm on the mantel.

So if not for Chadwick…why?

Because he wanted to see her. Wanted to hear what outrageous thing she might say next. Wanted, with a hunger that was becoming impossible to dismiss, to be the man she looked for in a room.

Damn it. He was doing it because Georgiana had somehow lodged herself beneath his skin, and every encounter with her only drove the barb deeper.

At first, he'd told himself—sternly, repeatedly—that he simply wanted to keep her safe. She had a propensity for disappearing from ballrooms, climbing out windows, wandering alone, and attracting trouble as though she'd been born under a star dedicated entirely to pandemonium.

But safety was no longer the whole of it, was it? He did want her safe—God, yes—but he also wanted her laughing at his side, looking at him with those bright, challenging eyes, choosing to stay when every instinct told her to run.

But he had seen it now—too clearly to pretend otherwise.

Georgiana was not reckless. *She was cornered.* And some dark, possessive part of him had begun to resent every person and circumstance that had put her there.

Like her father who treated her future like a ledger to be balanced. Her brother who was quietly calculating how much Henderville's fortune might secure his own future. And a world that called obedience virtue and left women no honorable path except submission. She was expected to smile, to endure, to accept a bargain struck over her head as though her life were a negotiable instrument.

Georgiana was trapped like a fox, just as she'd said. The realization settled heavily in Jason's chest. How alone she must feel…standing in crowded ballrooms with no one truly on her side, her value measured in pounds and promises, her refusal treated as inconvenience rather than courage. If she ran, she would be ruined. If she stayed, she would be ruined in a completely different way.

He had always known their world was unjust. Every thinking man did. But knowing it in theory was quite different from watching it bear down on one particular woman—one sharp-tongued, bright-eyed, stubbornly brave woman—and realizing there was absolutely nothing fair about the choice being forced upon her.

The thought made his hands curl into fists at his sides. But he already knew…his empathy for her plight was not the only reason he'd been following her.

*Other* young ladies were left to similar fates.

He did not follow them.

He did not trail after them through parks and bookshops like a bloodhound following a strong scent. He did not stand in a crowded aisle pretending to read books about ferns simply to remain near them.

He groaned. Loudly. He did not merely want to pity her circumstances. He wanted—far too badly—to alter them.

Jason closed his eyes. "I am a lunatic."

That at least felt true.

God help him, somehow marriage—the institution he had long distrusted, the bargain he had sworn never to make— suddenly seemed less offensive than the notion of Georgiana being handed to Henderville.

He crossed to the sideboard and poured another measure of brandy. He stared into the amber depths, willing them to supply an answer.

They didn't.

So he drank it.

How, in the span of just a few short days, had he come to care where Georgiana Chadwick walked? Or what she read? Or that her brow scrunched adorably when she grew frustrated with him? Or that she smelled faintly of lilacs and mischief and impending disaster?

He set the glass down harder than he meant to.

He wasn't her guardian. He wasn't her brother—thank God. He had no business keeping track of her whereabouts. And yet every time he vowed to stop…something in him would snap taut like a bowstring.

There she is.

There she goes.

Follow.

He'd tried to blame it on obligation. On guilt. On his failure with Evelyn. On his ingrained compulsion to stop spirited young women from hurling themselves into calamity.

But if that were the reason, logic crept in quietly to remind him, he would not have stared at Georgiana's mouth in the shadows of Willoughby's garden. He would not have felt something warm settle in his chest when she laughed at his jests. He would not have remembered—days later—the way she'd looked at him in the bookstore, soft and disbelieving, when she caught him there.

His pacing slowed. He sank into the chair again, elbows on knees, head dropping forward. Bloody hell.

He wasn't following her to keep her safe. He wasn't following her to appease Chadwick. He wasn't following her out of guilt or duty or any noble intention whatsoever. He was following her because—

He swallowed hard.

Because when she wasn't there, the world felt strangely dull. Because her annoyance was somehow invigorating. Because her wit sharpened his and her defiance sparked something he hadn't felt in years. Possibly ever.

Because—

He exhaled a shaky breath.

Because he missed her when she wasn't near.

The realization hit him in the stomach like a precisely aimed rapier.

"Oh," he whispered grimly. "That's...not ideal."

Not ideal at all.

He leaned back, staring blankly into the fire as the truth settled into his bones with alarming certainty.

He wasn't watching Georgiana Chadwick.

He was seeking her. Wanting her company. Craving it, in fact.

And for a man who had sworn never to entangle himself —emotionally, romantically, or otherwise—it was perhaps the most terrifying revelation of his life.

He scrubbed a hand through his hair once more. He could call it concern if he liked. Obligation. Guilt. Protection. But none of those words explained the heat that rose in him whenever she looked at him as if daring him to understand her. None of them explained why, when he pictured her future, he wanted himself in it.

"What am I going to do now?" he murmured.

The fire crackled.

Jason stared into the glowing embers.

He already knew the answer.

Tomorrow—despite his best intentions—he would seek her out again.

# CHAPTER THIRTEEN

*The next morning*

Jason had just begun to regret his own existence in peace when the butler announced his mother.

He looked up from the dispatches spread across his desk and felt his shoulders go taut at once.

"The Countess of Pembroke, my lord."

Of course.

There were few phrases in the English language less likely to herald tranquility.

"Show her in," Jason said, setting down his pen with more care than it deserved.

A moment later his mother swept into the study as though she owned not only the room but the air in it. Which, in fairness, she often behaved as if she did.

She wore emerald silk despite the hour, the rich color setting off the silver threaded through her chestnut hair. Her gloves were dove gray, her cane ebony and ornamental rather than necessary, and her expression was the same cool, cutting one Jason had known since boyhood. She was still a handsome woman. Striking, certainly. Men noticed her when she entered a room. They also tended, after five minutes in her company, to wish fervently that she had entered some other one.

"Mother," he said, rising.

"Jason."

She did not offer her cheek, nor her hand. She merely took the chair opposite his desk without invitation and looked about the study with quick, faintly censorious eyes.

"You might open the curtains more often," she said. "This room feels like a mausoleum."

"*Normally* it keeps out callers," he drawled.

Her mouth twitched, though not with amusement. "Ah, so I'm fortunate to have gained admittance."

He let that go.

She removed her gloves finger by finger, laying them in front of her on the desk blotter as though staking a claim. "I have not come to trade insults with you."

"A pity. We are both so good at it."

"Indeed." Her gaze sharpened. "I came because there have been rumors."

Jason leaned back slightly. There it was. "Have there?"

"Yes." She settled her cane across her lap. "In Hyde Park. On Bond Street. At the museum, if Lady Penrose is to be believed, though I rather think she invents half what she reports and guesses the rest. Nevertheless, the pattern is sufficiently plain."

He said nothing.

His mother's eyes narrowed. "Do not tell me you are going to attempt surprise. It does not become you. You have been seen in repeated proximity to Lord Chadwick's daughter."

"Lady Georgiana," Jason said evenly, "has a name."

"Of course she does. Most girls do."

His jaw flexed.

The countess leaned back, elegant and composed and entirely intolerable. "I am less interested in her Christian name than in what precisely you imagine yourself to be doing."

Jason reached for the glass of brandy at his elbow, thought better of it, and set his hand flat on the desk instead. "Nothing that requires your oversight."

"That," she said dryly, "has never yet been true where you are concerned."

He gave her a long look. "If you have come to scold me for being seen in public, I should warn you that I am unlikely to repent."

"No." Her voice cooled further. "I have come because I know that look in a man's eye, and I dislike it."

Something in his chest tightened, small and immediate.

His mother continued, "You are not hunting pleasure. You are not amusing yourself. You are circling some species of disaster and attempting to call it chivalry."

Jason let out a short breath. "How poetic of you."

"How accurate of me."

He stood then and moved to the mantel, more to put space between them than because the fire required inspection. The coals glowed low and red. He stared into them.

"If this is about marriage," he said, "you may save yourself the effort. I have no intention of marrying."

"Good."

That made him look back at her.

She held his gaze without blinking. "Because if you have decided to throw yourself away, Jason, I would rather you at least did so with deliberation."

His laugh was short and unkind. "How comforting."

His mother ignored that. "Your father married for desire," she said. "For infatuation. He mistook appetite for compatibility and spent the next twenty years paying for it in misery."

"And you?" Jason asked. "Did you not pay as well?"

Her expression altered by the smallest degree. "I endured," she said. "Which is more than can be said for many wives."

He turned fully now, one shoulder against the mantel. "How inspiring."

"You may sneer, but I am giving you the only useful advice anyone ever gave me. Marriage is not solace. It is not rescue. It is not some fevered answer to loneliness. It is an arrangement. The more sensible the arrangement, the more tolerable the marriage."

"And if one wishes not to marry at all?"

"Then one should take great care not to behave like a man publicly interested in a penniless girl from a disordered family."

There it was.

The room seemed to still around the words.

Jason's voice lowered. "You know nothing of Georgiana Chadwick."

"No?" Her brows rose. "I know she has no fortune. I know her father is notoriously irresponsible. I know her brother is your friend, which is recommendation enough to make any prudent mother uneasy. And I know, most importantly, that she is precisely the sort of creature to rouse all your worst instincts."

He went very still.

His mother watched him with bright, merciless intelligence. "There. That touched a nerve."

"Do not speak of her as if she were an object."

"And do not speak to me as if I do not recognize the pattern."

He pushed off the mantel. "Pattern?"

"Yes." Her tone sharpened. "You see a frightened thing, a vulnerable lamb, and immediately you are compelled to put yourself between it and harm. A laudable quality in a soldier, perhaps. A tiresome one in a son."

Jason's mouth flattened.

She went on, more softly now, which was always worse. "You have spent half your life trying to atone by installments."

The words landed like a blow. They were too near the truth.

He said nothing, but he narrowed his eyes.

His mother's fingertips tapped once against the cane. "You cannot undo what happened to Evelyn by collecting causes, Jason. Nor by choosing some frightened girl and mistaking intervention for redemption."

At his sister's name, the entire room seemed to narrow.

"Do not," he said through clenched teeth.

But his mother had never once obeyed a boundary merely because it was decent.

"You insisted you could watch her," she said, each word neat and cold. "Your father trusted you, and she died for it."

A muscle in Jason's jaw ticked.

"Do you know what your father said afterward?" she continued, mercilessly calm. "That a boy who begged for responsibility ought to understand the cost of failing in it. He would not speak your name for three weeks, as if grief itself had made you unfit for the sound of it."

Jason went utterly still.

"And when he did speak it again," she said, "it was only to ask whether you had at last learned what comes of careless-ness." Her gaze did not soften. "So yes, Jason. If you have carried Evelyn all these years, do not pretend the burden fell upon you out of thin air."

His hand tightened against the carved wood of the mantel until his knuckles turned white.

For one unbearable moment, he was young again. Scared and breathless and soaked to the knees, screaming her name into the trees while servants ran in every direction and his mother stood white-faced on the lawn and looked at him as though something irreparable had already been decided.

When he spoke, his voice was almost calm.

"You will leave."

But she was not finished. Of course not.

"That girl," the countess said, "whatever her name, whatever her charms, is not your duty. If you are sensible, you will leave her to her family and keep your distance."

Jason lifted his eyes to hers. "Georgiana," he said, with deliberate emphasis, "is not a cause."

His mother's gaze sharpened at once.

"No?" she said quietly. "Then that is worse."

He did not move.

She rose, gathering her gloves. "Because if she is not a cause, then she is a temptation. And you, my dear son, are not built for tender domesticity. You would make yourself wretched, and any wife foolish enough to love you would fare no better."

The words might have slid off him had he not spent years fearing some version of the same thing.

He thought of the Hyde Park path. Of Georgie's chin lifted in defiance. Of her asking if he ever tired of glowering at her. Of her teasing him at the bookshop. Defying him by stepping higher on the ladder.

"No," he said at last, his voice low. "I think any wife of mine would fare considerably better than you did."

His mother froze with one glove half drawn on.

A silence fell between them—thin, taut, brittle.

When she finished pulling on the glove, her face was composed again, though colder than before.

"You have your father's talent," she said. "Not for love. For self-deception."

Then she took up her cane and moved toward the door.

At the threshold, she paused only long enough to say, without turning, "Do stay away from the Chadwick girl. There is enough ruin in that family to sully your name."

The door shut behind her with quiet finality.

Jason did not move for several seconds.

Then several more.

At last, he crossed back to his desk, planted both hands on the polished wood, and lowered his head.

The study felt close. Airless.

He had spent years telling himself that marriage was a trap, that desire was unreliable, that domestic affection curdled into bitterness if left long enough in close quarters. His parents had given him proof enough of all that.

But standing here now, with his mother's voice still in the room like the aftertaste of poison, he found that none of it helped.

Because the one thing he could not make himself do—not with reason, not with discipline, not with every bitter lesson of his childhood arrayed behind him—was stay away from Georgiana Chadwick.

If his mother was right, then Georgiana was precisely the sort of woman he ought to avoid.

Which was perhaps why, by the time afternoon came, he was already reaching for his coat.

# CHAPTER FOURTEEN

*Several days later, The Cranberrys' Ball*

Georgie stood with her back to the gilded wall of yet another suffocating London ballroom, holding her half-empty glass of lemonade in front of her chest like a weapon.

Around her, the air was thick with chatter and perfume, and couples whirled across the floor under the glittering chandeliers.

Her violet gown was perfectly respectable, but decidedly out of fashion, the silk softened by wear, its color deepened to the shade of dusk. It did nothing to hide her from notice— only to remind her that she did not quite belong among the brighter hues spinning past her.

Of course she hadn't been asked to dance. Young ladies whose fathers had gambled away their dowries rarely were.

No, they were auctioned off to old men instead.

As expected, her parents had been angry with her for leaving the Willoughbys' ball a fortnight ago. Mother and Father were always angry when she disappeared from ballrooms. Mother had given Georgie the same long-winded lecture she always did. Something about duty and obligation and, most importantly, money.

As usual, Georgie pretended to listen. She'd nodded and blinked and said all the things Mother wanted to hear before finally being left alone in blissful solitude.

But tonight, if Lord Henderville arrived, Georgie had every intention of escaping again. She would not allow that old man to paw at her. No matter what her parents said.

She'd slip away from Mother and Father just like she always did. Honestly, they made it far too easy. All she had to do was tell them she had an urgency to use the convenience and then she simply failed to return. Her parents were too busy talking nonstop to anyone who would listen to notice. It had been Henry's job to watch her.

No doubt Henry would be here himself tonight if he weren't nursing that broken leg. After all, her brother had a vested interest in seeing her married off to Henderville.

The old goat's money would restore the family's coffers, *if* her mother and brother managed to hide the funds from her father long enough to keep him from gambling them away again.

She knew as much because she'd overheard them once, whispering about it outside the breakfast room, unaware she was standing just beyond the door.

She'd learned two things that day.

One: she didn't have an ally in her brother.

Two: she certainly didn't have an ally in her mother.

They both wanted Henderville's money just as badly as her father did…only they wanted to keep it for themselves.

She didn't owe her allegiance to any of them. Which was precisely why she wouldn't hesitate to slip away tonight if she had to.

And when she did the same on her wedding day, it would

be right under her parents' noses as well. The resulting scandal would ruin them. But it would be no more than they deserved.

Georgie had known for quite some that she had no one to rely on but herself. A faint smile touched her lips. Well, herself and Bea and Poppy now. And perhaps…Jason. The thought made her suck in her breath. Yes, Jason had proven to be someone who had helped her.

Her fingers tightened on her glass as she scanned the ballroom looking for her friends.

They'd had another meeting of their new society this afternoon. Bea had informed them that Lady Trentham had agreed to provide the getaway coach and ensure it was sitting on the correct side of the church near the door that led out to the convenience.

Georgie had the thought for the dozenth time that if she ever had a chance to meet Lady Trentham, she would thank her profusely for her generous assistance.

Ah, there was Bea.

Her friend stood near the center of the room, next to her glamorous mother, the Duchess of Winston. Georgie had already come to recognize Bea's imperious poise and biting wit. Both were on full display this evening as she seemed quite in her element, jesting with a group of London's finest. Though, Georgie noted with a bit of amusement, the infamous Lord Nicholas Archer was not among them.

And there, just beyond Bea's group, standing with another set of unwanted young ladies along the opposite wall, was Poppy. Her red curls were pinned too tightly and her cornflower-blue eyes were darting nervously, as though she expected her mother to come galloping through the ballroom atop a steed at any moment.

A faint smile tugged at Georgie's lips. They hadn't spent much time together, but she had already come to value her friendships with Bea and Poppy more than she would have expected.

*The Wallflowers' Revolt.*

A society of their own. A quiet rebellion.

And the first act of rebellion would be hers.

Georgie had been worried when she'd first told them she intended to run away on her wedding day. She'd held her breath after admitting it, half-expecting Bea and Poppy to gape in horror.

But they hadn't.

Instead, they'd immediately offered to help. Today, Poppy had even clasped her hands together near her ear and vowed she'd keep the secret even if they tried to torture it out of her.

Georgie wasn't at all certain who "they" were, but that was when she had known. She might not have her parents or brother on her side, but she had Bea and Poppy.

And that was enough.

Still, standing here now, pressed into the shadows of the room while Society danced on without her, she felt the old familiar chill of apprehension creep back in.

Her gaze wandered again, this time catching on Lord Pembroke...for the third time that evening.

He stood across the room, tall and watchful as ever, his green eyes fixed squarely on her like glittering emeralds.

This time, it wasn't a mystery why he was here. He'd told her. He knew she had a secret. And he'd come perilously close to guessing it. But now she suspected his concern was even more than that.

After their outing at the museum last week, she'd tried to convince herself that Pembroke's talk of enjoying her company might be nothing more than a tactic—a calculated charm designed to lower her guard so she would not question his constant surveillance.

But then he'd continued to show up. Continued to be

charming. In the last sennight, he'd taken her to Gunter's for an ice, bought her a novel from the same bookstore where he'd claimed to be interested in ferns, taken her riding in the park, and paid for her admission to the British Museum where they'd spent a pleasant afternoon discussing the Elgin Marbles and exploring the surprising ease of one another's company.

All in the proper presence of Martin, the footman, of course. Questionable though his chaperonage might be.

Georgie expelled her breath. No. She could no longer lie to herself and pretend that she and Pembroke were spending time together for any other reason than…enjoyment.

She told herself that enjoying Pembroke's company meant nothing. That it was merely novelty, the rare pleasure of being seen as something other than a burden to be managed or a problem to be solved. And yet…she had laughed with him. More than once. He had opinions about history that mirrored her own, a dry humor that surprised her, and a way of listening that made her forget to guard every word. Most unsettling of all, he had claimed—without flourish or excuse—that he followed her not because her brother asked it of him, but because he wanted to.

The thought both warmed and unnerved her.

Wanting was foolish enough. Wanting something—someone—you knew you could not have? More foolish still. Pembroke had been quite clear about his lack of marital intentions. And that had been without knowing of her lack of a dowry.

Still, she could not quite bring herself to regret the afternoons stolen at museums and bookshops, nor the easy companionship she had not known she missed. Pembroke was…more than likable. He was charming. Inconveniently so. He was admirable, even. And she'd come to learn they had a great deal in common. Which was only more of an inconvenience, because she had no dowry and he had no desire to marry. There could be no more than friendship between them. And that would be short-lived given the fact that she planned to leave London quite soon.

She took a careful sip of lemonade, as if that might dispel her unruly thoughts before they grew more insistent.

But she was still turning them over in her mind when the butler's voice rang out above the music.

"The Marquess of Henderville."

The name struck like a clap of thunder.

Georgie's breath hitched. Her shoulders went rigid.

So much for borrowed time.

She did not look for him. She did not allow herself even a single glimpse of the man who believed he already owned her future. Instead, she lifted her chin and caught Bea's eye across the room.

Bea's expression sharpened. One nod.

Then Poppy. Wide-eyed, anxious—another nod.

Georgie returned the nods, her decision sudden and absolute.

She set down her glass, murmured an excuse to the young ladies beside her—something about needing the convenience —and slipped away before anyone could respond, moving fast now, skirts whispering as she vanished into the shadows of the hall.

Her heart thundered. Her palms dampened. But she did not hesitate.

She would not stop...not for fear, not for doubt...

Not even for the inconvenient fact that a part of her wished Lord Pembroke might follow.

# CHAPTER FIFTEEN

Another ball, another marble pillar. Jason surveyed the room with a grim expression, a glass of untouched brandy in his hand.

Tonight, he didn't even bother to try to tell himself he was here for any noble reason.

He was here simply because he wanted to see Georgiana. That was all. He wanted to spend a few moments in her company. He intended to ask her to dance.

Which frightened him. Honestly. He'd never wanted to ask anyone to dance.

Of course he'd had to consider whether he cared only because Georgiana didn't seem to have anyone who gave a toss whether she was ruined or even physically harmed. Her family certainly didn't.

Evelyn had been his best friend, his closest ally, and yet she'd died on his watch. Georgiana didn't even have anyone watching.

He knew it wasn't his duty, wasn't even his right…

And yet. Here he stood.

His gaze slid automatically across the room.

And there she was.

Georgiana.

He couldn't take his eyes off her. Which was ridiculous. Insane, even.

The woman was *betrothed* for Chrissake.

Albeit to a man she loathed. But she wasn't the first young woman to find herself betrothed to a man not of her choosing, and she wouldn't be the last.

His mother might be a snake, but she was right. He had no business thinking about marriage. No hope that he would make a good husband. No right to even assume Georgiana might want him.

No. She would marry Henderville, just as countless others had married for duty instead of love, and the world would keep spinning.

He knew that.

Hell, he'd seen it happen dozens of times.

So why—why—did the thought of her in Henderville's gnarled hands make Jason's stomach twist with something uncomfortably akin to rage?

Because she was vulnerable, he told himself.

Because she reminded him of Evelyn.

Perhaps his mother was right about that too. Perhaps this *was* merely guilt—misplaced, unearned guilt—finding a new target.

He'd failed his sister. And now his mind had decided that failing Georgiana would be just as unforgivable.

Which was wrong, completely wrong.

He took a slow sip of brandy, letting the heat slide down his throat.

And still his eyes stayed fixed on her.

Hmm. She looked as if she was up to something again. He saw it in the set of her shoulders, the spark in her eyes, the way her fingers curled tightly around that glass she was holding as though restraining herself from bolting at any moment.

Jason rubbed the back of his neck, thinking of how she'd grabbed his lapels in Willoughby's garden, her breath hitching softly when he'd leaned close, her eyes dark and wide.

He scowled into his glass.

And not for the first time, wondered what would happen if he offered her father more for her than whatever Henderville had offered. Scandalous, perhaps. Slightly unethical, no doubt.

But probably effective.

Damn it. Every time he had that thought, a far less optimistic one promptly replaced it. His parents' marriage. His mother's outrageous behavior. They hadn't had a moment's peace in all their years together. And his father had assured him that he'd been quite madly in love when he'd been courting his mother.

Courting? God help him, that was exactly what being with Georgiana felt like. As though, for a few reckless hours at a time, he had been allowed to forget what marriage became in the end. Allowed to forget who Georgiana was promised to. Allowed to imagine that wanting her might lead somewhere other than disaster.

Specifically, a messy confrontation with her family and Henderville. Awful, though they may be.

And they truly were awful.

It had taken every ounce of Jason's self-control not to strike her blasted brother in the jaw before leaving his apartment that night.

The way Chadwick had laughed about her—shrugged her off, spoken of her as though she were nothing but an inconvenience to be bartered away—it had made something hot and ugly rise in Jason's chest.

And it was worse now...tonight. After so many stolen afternoons with her.

It hadn't been a hardship, those afternoons. Gunter's, where she'd debated the merits of candied lemon rinds with solemn intensity. The museum, where she'd grown animated in front of the Elgin Marbles and laughed—actually laughed—when he teased her about reading every placard twice. And their ride in the park, where she'd admitted to him that she'd never actually been asked to dance at a ball by a gentleman. She'd laughed again as she spoke, but Jason had felt the pain beneath her smile. She was a debutante without a dowry—a wallflower. He'd never before considered how disappointing it might be to never be asked to dance. It seemed Georgiana made him look at everything with a new pair of eyes. And somewhere along the way, without his noticing, he'd begun to look forward to her company. To the ease of it. To the way conversation with her felt less like performance and more like respite.

Now he realized that in addition to her beauty and her courage, she was funny, and clever, and quietly perceptive.

Georgiana Chadwick, he'd come to realize, deserved far better than the future her despicable family had laid out for her.

And try as he might—as he watched her across the ballroom, her cheeks flushed and her dark hair glinting under the chandeliers, her chin lifted in that defiant way of hers, trying to seem as if she wasn't affected by the rumors and the whispers—he could no longer convince himself that he didn't want her...in his bed. In his life.

The realization made him suck in a breath—only to be cut short as the butler's voice rang out above the hum of conversation. *"The Marquess of Henderville."*

The name cut through the air like a blade.

Jason straightened instinctively, his shoulders tensing as his gaze snapped toward Georgiana.

And right on cue…

Her smile slipped, her spine stiffened, and she murmured something to the ladies near her before turning sharply on her heel and disappearing into the crowd.

Jason swore under his breath.

God help him, he was already moving after her.

# CHAPTER SIXTEEN

Georgie quickened her pace down the quiet corridor, skirts swishing furiously, the faint strains of music from the ballroom fading away.

But she'd barely rounded the corner before his voice came from just behind her. "Lady Georgiana."

*Pembroke.* A wave of awareness shot through her.

She froze. And closed her eyes briefly.

Then she squared her shoulders, lifted her chin, and turned to face him.

He stood there—emerald eyes steady and broad shoulders filling the narrow corridor, the very picture of maddening, unshakable calm. "I did not follow you to stop you."

She blinked and nodded. "I know."

"I followed you to help you."

The words struck her silent for half a beat.

"Again," he added softly, opening his hands in quiet appeal. "For the life of me, I cannot seem to stop wanting to help you."

A small shiver moved through her and for a moment, she could only stare at him. *Wanting.* There was that troubling word again. And worse, the shameful flutter in her chest at hearing it spoken aloud by a man she had no business wanting in return. "I—"

Georgiana stopped. The sound of footsteps echoed from the far end of the corridor. Male voices. Approaching.

Pembroke's gaze snapped past her, alert. In the same instant, he reached for her wrist—not rough, not hesitant—and pulled her toward the nearest door.

"This way."

The door opened soundlessly. He ushered her inside and closed it softly behind them just as the footsteps passed.

They were plunged into darkness.

A library, she realized a second later. Tall shelves loomed on every side, the scent of leather and old paper thick in the air. Heavy drapes muted the moonlight, leaving only a faint silver glow.

Pembroke lifted a finger to his lips.

"Shh."

She nodded, breath shallow.

They stood far too close. Close enough that she could feel the warmth of him, the solid line of his chest. Close enough to catch his scent—clean linen, faint soap, and something purely him beneath it that made her pulse skip.

Too close for sense. Too close for safety. Too close, certainly, for a woman who already knew this man had no intention of marrying anyone if he could possibly help it.

Her gaze drifted upward, unbidden. The strong line of his jaw. The rough shadow of evening stubble. The way his throat worked as he swallowed.

Wanting him had been foolish from the start. Wanting him now—standing here in the dark with his breath in the same air as hers and his body so close—felt like the sort of folly that ruined women completely.

The footsteps faded and silence settled between them.

Georgie cleared her throat, painfully aware of how little space separated them. Her voice came out a whisper. "I was about to say…you needn't involve yourself."

He didn't move away.

Instead, he looked down at her, eyes dark and intent, his expression softer than she'd ever seen it.

"I'm already *far* too involved," he murmured.

And there it was at last—no pretense of duty, no mention of Henderville, no careful gentlemanly excuse. Just him. Just this.

The words lingered between them—quiet, certain.

She ought to have stepped back then. Ought to have made some brisk, sensible reply and fled while she still could. Instead she stood there, rooted by the heady thrill of hearing him sound exactly as involved as she felt.

Before she could draw another breath, his hand came up —firm at her waist—and he hauled her sharply against him as if he couldn't stand the space between them for one more second. The impact stole the rest of her protest. It stole her balance, too, because suddenly she was pressed to the hard line of him, the heat of his body a blunt, undeniable answer.

His mouth took hers with unmistakable intent—no question, no permission asked, only the kind of certainty that made her knees go weak. He kissed her like he'd been holding himself back for far too long and had finally run out of restraint. The first sweep of his lips was possessive, a claiming, and then it deepened—slowly at first, as if he meant to make certain she understood exactly what he wanted.

She made a sound she didn't mean to make. It slipped out of her, a traitorous little breath that turned into something more when his thumb flexed at her waist and he shifted her closer, closer, until she felt the full breadth of him through their clothes. The kiss sharpened, then softened, then sharpened again—his mouth moving with controlled insistence, as if he were testing her, tasting her, learning what made her tremble.

His other hand found her—skimming up, not hurried, not gentle either—until his fingers curved at the back of her neck. He angled her head, taking the kiss deeper, and she had the dizzying sense that he was dictating the rhythm…when she could breathe, when she had to surrender, when he would give her the smallest mercy of space only to steal it again.

And she let him.

Because this was what she had been denying to herself for days now, that part of her had wanted precisely this. Not merely his help. Not merely his attention. Him.

Her hands, which had been useless a moment ago, came alive. She gripped the front of his coat, then fisted the fabric as if it were the only solid thing in the world. She tried to pull him nearer—which made no sense, considering he was already everywhere—and he answered with a low sound that went straight through her, the vibration of it against her mouth making her shiver.

He broke the kiss just enough to drag his breath along the corner of her lips, his forehead hovering near hers, their bodies still locked tight. For a heartbeat she thought he might stop. That he might remember whatever rules he'd been so determined to obey.

Instead he kissed her again—deeper, slower, crueler in its patience—until her thoughts scattered, until all she could feel was his hand at her waist and the steady, unrelenting pressure of his mouth telling her, over and over, that he was done denying this moment.

Georgie gasped, the sound lost to him as he kissed her harder, his grip tightening just enough to make her tremble. The world tilted—dark shelves, silence, the press of him everywhere—and for one wild second she forgot corridors and scandals and escape plans entirely.

Forgot, too, that he was impossible. That he had as good as declared himself a lifelong bachelor. That whatever this was, however fiercely she wanted it, it could not safely belong to her.

When he finally pulled back again, just a fraction, his forehead resting against hers, his breath warm and uneven, he murmured, "Tell me again that I needn't involve myself."

Oh. No. She couldn't.

Because the dreadful truth was that she wanted him involved. Wanted him near. Wanted, with a desperation she hardly dared name, something from him he had already made plain that he did not mean to give.

# CHAPTER SEVENTEEN

"Well," she whispered at last, because the silence felt untenable. "That was…inadvisable."

She stepped back. Just one pace, deciding it best for her state of mind.

Jason's mouth curved. She could hear the smile in his voice. "Is that your formal assessment?"

Her mind raced. She needed to pretend this was nothing. Nothing at all. Nothing of consequence at least. Surely, that's what he wanted too.

"You accidentally kissed me." Her pulse fluttered traitorously at her throat. Her eyes focused on his cravat. "No matter. It's fine. Everything is fine." She nodded and blew out a deep breath.

"It wasn't accidental at all," he murmured. "In fact, I'd say it was rather deliberate."

Her pulse skidded. "It was?"

"Entirely."

She shot him a look, though she knew he could barely see it in the dim light. "You're unrepentant?"

"Yes."

"That's alarming."

"Also yes."

She inhaled, steadying herself, then folded her arms—an entirely useless gesture given the lack of space between them. "We should not be discussing this. We should—"

Heat flickered low in her belly. Her gaze lifted to his, catching the faint outline of his jaw, the gleam of his eyes in the dark. Curse him for being infuriatingly composed. And so very handsome.

"Do you want to do it again?" she asked, her voice betraying her despite her best efforts.

"Very much," he said without hesitation. "Do you?"

She gulped…and nodded.

That was all the encouragement he needed.

He moved suddenly, decisively—pulling her toward him, backing her up until her shoulders met the cool wall. One hand braced beside her head, the other settled firmly at her waist, holding her there as his mouth came down on hers.

The kiss was nothing like the first.

This one was hungry, urgent.

She gasped, the sound swallowed by him as he deepened the kiss, his body pressing close enough that there was no mistaking how affected he was. Heat flared low in her belly, sharp and overwhelming, and before she could think better of it—before she could stop herself—her fingers slid into his hair.

Oh, God. She had wanted to do that for days.

The thought flashed through her mind as her hands tightened, reveling in the silk and thickness of it, in the way he groaned softly against her mouth at the contact. His grip at her waist tightened in answer, anchoring her, claiming space he had no business claiming.

For one reckless moment, there was nothing but this—heat and breath and the way he kissed her as though he had decided, fully and irrevocably, to stop pretending restraint mattered.

Then she broke it, breathless, her forehead resting against his chest.

It was several moments before she was able to speak.

"This need not…" she whispered, trying—and failing—to sound composed. "This need change anything. *Not!* Need *not* change anything," she quickly corrected, feeling her face go up in flames.

He shifted, the humor fading just enough to reveal something more serious beneath it. He cleared his throat. "But I have…compromised you."

She cut him off at once. "No," she whispered firmly. "No one will know. Nothing has changed." A beat. "It was just a kiss…or two."

His gaze held hers in the dark, unreadable. "Just."

She nodded, even as her pulse betrayed her. "Please don't trouble yourself any further on my account." It sounded oddly formal and quite insane given what they'd just done.

"Too late," he replied, his lips twisting sardonically.

Georgie lifted her skirts and made to step around him. "I should go."

"Wait." He gently held her wrist. "I have an offer for you."

She frowned. "An offer?"

For a brief moment—just a flash—she wondered if he might actually mean—

"I'll help you leave unseen. Again."

Of course not.

Disappointment swept through her, hot and immediate. How ridiculous of her to have imagined anything else. He was not offering for her. He was merely offering, once more, to help her run.

"And what is the cost of this generosity?" she asked coolly.

He tipped his head to the side and grinned at her. "One small favor."

Her frown deepened. "I beg your pardon?"

"Don't scowl," he said softly. "Aren't you the least bit curious what I intend to ask of you?"

She narrowed her eyes on him. "I am listening. Begrudgingly."

He paused, as though choosing his words with care. "Tonight, before Henderville arrived, I meant to ask you to dance."

She blinked. Once. *That* was certainly unexpected. "You… what?"

"I still intend to."

"I am not returning to that ballroom," she said firmly.

"I wouldn't dream of asking you to."

She narrowed her eyes. "I don't understand. Where precisely do you imagine this dance will occur?"

Instead of answering, he let his hand slide down to thread his fingers through hers.

She sucked in a breath as his hand enclosed hers—warm, certain, utterly unhesitating. He stepped back just enough to give her space, but did not release her.

"It's time for you to decide, my lady." His voice was low. Steady. "Do you trust me?"

# CHAPTER EIGHTEEN

Georgie ought to say no. She knew it.

She had planned her entire escape on the assumption that trust was a liability. Her future depended on her making the right choice.

And yet—her fingers tightened around Pembroke's.

Against her better judgment, she whispered, "I suppose I'm about to find out."

His thumb brushed once over her knuckles, a quiet acknowledgment, and then he was already moving, opening the door to the library and leading her down the darkened corridor with practiced ease.

They slipped through the house like conspirators, pausing when voices echoed too near, ducking into alcoves when footmen passed, Georgie's heart hammering harder with each step.

She was acutely aware of Pembroke at her back, of the way he seemed to anticipate her movements, steering her gently but firmly, as though this too was something he'd always intended to do.

At last, he stopped before an unassuming door tucked beside the ballroom, half-hidden, easily overlooked.

"Here," he murmured.

Inside was a large storage room—once a cloakroom, perhaps—with tall cabinets lining the walls. The door closed behind them, darkening the room and muting the world, though the orchestra's music carried through the walls, softened but unmistakable.

Pembroke paused. She heard the faint scrape of metal, then the sharp *click* of flint striking steel. A spark flared, brief and bright, and a moment later a single candle bloomed to life on a nearby shelf.

The small flame cast a warm, wavering glow—enough to soften the shadows, enough for her to see him. His face. The intent in his eyes.

As if summoned, the tune shifted.

A waltz.

Slow. Elegant. Intimate.

Georgie's breath caught.

Jason stepped back, releasing her hand only long enough to bow—formal, precise, entirely sincere.

"Lady Georgiana," he said quietly, "may I please have this dance?"

Something tightened in her chest. She opened her mouth, then closed it again, blinking rapidly.

No one had ever asked her that before. Not truly. Not like this.

Henderville couldn't dance—he could barely walk with a stiff, shuffling gait—and no one else had ever bothered. She'd watched from walls and corners while other girls spun beneath chandeliers, telling herself she didn't care.

But she'd told Pembroke... Oh, God. She couldn't breathe.

Standing here now, in the candlelight, with music thrumming through the floor and his gaze fixed only on her...she actually believed he *wanted* to dance with her.

First, she swallowed the lump that had formed in her throat. Then she nodded.

"Yes," she said, her voice barely more than a breath. "And now that we've kissed, I believe you may call me Georgiana."

He smiled—not triumphant, not teasing—but something softer. Reverent. "I'm Jason."

The sound of his name sent a small, startling thrill through her. *Jason.* It was deeper than she had imagined it would be, warmer too, and hearing it in that low voice felt far too intimate for so simple an exchange.

She sucked in her breath as his hand settled at her waist, warm and certain. She felt the contact all the way down to her toes. Her other hand slid into his, fitting there with alarming ease. He drew her closer, just enough that the warm, familiar scent of him stirred the memory of those kisses they had not spoken of again, yet had not forgotten.

They began to move.

The space was small, forcing them close, their steps careful but sure. She was keenly aware of every point of contact...the steady pressure of his hand guiding her, the brush of his coat against her gown, the way his fingers flexed almost imperceptibly when she stumbled and recovered.

This was dangerous. She knew that.

Dangerous because it felt right. Because her body remembered his mouth on hers, because her pulse raced not with fear but with anticipation. Because for the first time in her life, she was not watching from the edges.

*She was dancing.*

And a young lady could get used to attention like this.

Her gaze drifted up, catching the sharp line of his jaw, the focus in his eyes as he watched her—not the room, not the risks. Just her.

"You're very quiet," he murmured.

She swallowed. "I'm trying not to think."

"Probably a wise choice," he said softly.

The music swelled, and he turned her smoothly, the hem of her gown whispering against his boots. She laughed under her breath, surprised by it, and his smile deepened.

For these few stolen minutes, there was no Henderville. No parents. No escape plan waiting in the shadows.

Only the waltz. Only Jason's hands. Only the knowledge—thrilling and terrifying—that once this ended, nothing would ever feel quite the same again.

# CHAPTER NINETEEN

The dance ended without either of them quite acknowledging it.

The final notes of the waltz faded through the wall, the orchestra drifting on to something brighter, louder—music meant for rooms full of witnesses.

"Thank you for the dance," Jason whispered. He lowered his hand from her waist slowly, as though he were reluctant to break the spell, and Georgie forced herself to step back.

"Come," he said quietly. "We must hurry."

She nodded, still a little breathless, and followed him out into the corridor. They retraced their steps through the house with the same care as before—pausing when voices approached, slipping through service passages, moving with the practiced ease of people who had done this before.

The night air struck her cheeks as they slipped out a side door, cool and sharp. Tugging her hand, he quickly led her to the corner where he summoned a hack, unremarkable and anonymous. He helped her inside without ceremony and climbed in after her.

The ride was mercifully short.

London slid past in shadows and lamplight, the wheels rattling over cobblestones, the silence between them heavy with everything they did not say. Georgie kept her hands folded in her lap, staring resolutely out the window, as though she might still convince herself that this evening had not altered anything at all.

But when the hack pulled to a stop behind her father's house and Jason stepped down to help her out, the illusion shattered.

The hack soon rolled away but, conspicuously, he stayed, slowly walking her to the back door. The stoop was dim and quiet, the city hushed around them. For a moment, they simply stood there, facing one another.

"You made it home unseen," he said lightly. "Just as promised."

"Yes," she replied. "Thank you."

She should have gone inside then. She knew she should.

Instead, she was the one who conspicuously stayed this time.

His hand lifted to her cheek, gentle but sure, his thumb tracing the line of her jaw as if committing it to memory. For a breathless instant, he hesitated…just long enough for her heart to slam against her ribs.

Then he leaned down and kissed her once more.

Softly.

Carefully.

His mouth claimed hers with quiet urgency. Georgie gasped, the sound swallowed by him as his hand slid to her waist, pulling her closer until there was no mistaking the press of his body against hers.

She felt it everywhere—the strength in his grip, the heat of him through layers of fabric, the way his mouth moved against hers with slow, devastating intent. Her fingers fisted in the lapels of his coat, dragging him nearer, tilting her head to deepen the kiss without quite meaning to—and then meaning to very much.

He made a low sound in his throat—approval and hunger tangled together—and his hand tightened at her waist as though anchoring himself. The kiss slowed, deepened, became something unavoidably consuming, less a choice than a surrender to how good it felt...to how impossible it was to stop.

She tasted brandy on his lips. Felt the scrape of stubble along her jaw, the steady thrum of his pulse beneath her palm, the unmistakable awareness thrumming low in her belly.

This was folly. For a dozen reasons.

She knew it.

And still, she kissed him.

Not because she mistook risk for romance, as fools in novels often did, but because for one shattering moment she wanted something for herself more than she feared the cost of wanting it.

When he finally broke away, it was only by degrees—his mouth lingering at the corner of hers, his forehead resting against hers as though he needed the contact as much as she did. They stood there, breathing the same air, her heart racing, his breath warm against her cheek.

For a moment, neither of them moved.

Then she pressed her forehead briefly to his chest, steadying herself.

"Jason," she said softly.

"Yes?"

She drew back just enough to look at him. Really look at him. The man who had danced with her in secret. Who had seen her when no one else had bothered to look.

Her voice trembled despite her best efforts. "Will you do a favor for me?"

"Anything," he breathed, squeezing her waist.

"My wedding is next week."

He exhaled through his nose and gave a grim nod. "I know." The words were solemn.

She drew in a breath and closed her eyes for a moment. This would be difficult. Necessary, but difficult. "Will you… stay away until then? I do not think I can—" She broke off, unable to finish.

"Yes," he said, squeezing his eyes shut as if the word pained him. "I will."

"And…" she continued, her throat aching so much she could barely get the words out, "*please*, don't come to the wedding."

He stilled, his jaw tightly clenched. He sucked in a deep breath before finally uttering one word. "Why?"

Georgie swallowed. Why, indeed?

Because if he came, he would look at her again, and she would begin to wonder what might have been. What might have happened if she had met him sooner, or been free, or brave enough to ask for the impossible. She could flee Henderville. She could defy her parents. But she could not endure losing this too—this last stolen moment after their final kiss. She wanted to keep it exactly as it was, before reality had the chance to spoil it.

And then there was the little matter of her escape. If Jason were there, if he saw her run, there was still a chance that he might do something foolhardy. And she could not take that risk. Not along with all the other risks she was already taking.

She swallowed, the words pressing hard against her throat. She wanted to explain. To tell him the truth. But she couldn't. The less he knew, the better…for him.

So, she met his gaze and said only, "Trust me."

It was the cruelest answer she could give him, and still the safest. Better he think her mysterious than desperate. Better he stay away entirely than attempt some noble intervention on her behalf. And she would sooner disappear into Bath under another name than stand still while he did something reckless because he felt obliged to save her once more.

The silence stretched between them.

Then, slowly, he nodded, a wistful smile touching his mouth.

"About this," she said, gesturing faintly between them, "don't worry. No one ever has to know. You don't owe me anything." She swallowed. "Only…thank you. For the dance. For the kiss. For everything."

She stepped away then, opened the door, slipped inside, and closed it behind her—her heart aching with the knowledge that she had just left her most treasured memory on the other side.

# CHAPTER TWENTY

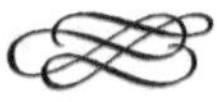

Moments later, Jason was still standing there and still breathing hard.

Damn. He was completely undone.

For one deranged instant, he nearly went in after her. Nearly ignored her request, found Chadwick—or, better yet, her father—and demanded the Henderville arrangement be broken.

But what then? Jason knew enough of her pride by now to understand that any offer he made in the wake of that kiss might look less like devotion and more like rescue.

Georgiana Chadwick would never ask for that. Worse— she would despise it if he offered from mere obligation.

Still, that last kiss had been—

Hell.

He couldn't remember the last time he'd kissed a woman like that.

Couldn't remember the last time a woman had kissed *him* like that.

No mistress, no passing flirtation, no tidy arrangement

had ever left him half mad with the urge to overturn the world for her. Georgiana had.

And yet the very idea sat badly in his gut, because overturning the world for her might look suspiciously like trying to save her. He knew too well where that instinct in him came from. Knew, too, that she would not thank him for swooping in like some dramatic hero if what he truly offered was duty dressed up as desire.

She'd tasted faintly of lemonade and rebellion, her fingers curling into his hair, her body soft and hot against his.

And worse…

*Don't worry,* she'd said, breathless but composed. *No one ever has to know. You don't owe me anything.*

The memory tightened something low and raw in his chest.

What if he wanted to worry?

What if he wanted for someone to know?

What if he—God, help him—wanted to owe her something?

The thoughts startled him, sharp as blades. He had spent his entire adult life avoiding feelings, avoiding emotional entanglements, avoiding precisely this sort of uncontrollable longing. And yet the idea of their kisses existing only in shadow, unclaimed and unseen, stirred an unfamiliar resentment.

It took every ounce of restraint he possessed to straighten and clear his throat. He should leave. That was the *right* thing to do. *Fuck.* A walk home in the chilly night air would do him good.

As he turned and stepped off the stoop, more of Georgiana's words pressed in on him, heavier than the night air.

*Please, don't come to the wedding.*

The request had been earnest. Not coy. Not manipulative.

Spoken like a plea, not a challenge. And that—damn it—was what unsettled him most.

Why would she ask that of him?

Jason dragged a hand through his hair and stared toward the empty mews. If he stayed away, he abandoned her to whatever catastrophe she was quietly marching toward. If he didn't—if he showed his face at that church—he might become the very scandal she was trying to avoid. Or worse, the temptation she could not afford.

*Trust me.*

Two words. Bare. Unexplained. And entirely unfair of her to offer without reason. Though he suspected he knew why.

He closed his eyes briefly, jaw tightening.

He had sworn he would let her go. Sworn he would not interfere. And yet the thought of her standing at that altar—alone, resigned, untouched by joy—set something savage twisting in his chest.

Or worse—her doing something reckless that would ruin her.

Jason turned toward the street at last, his steps slow, his thoughts anything but settled.

Whether he would honor her wish—or defy it—he did not yet know.

Only that either choice would cost him something.

And God help him, he suspected he would pay it gladly.

It had been nearly a sennight since the Cranberrys' ball, and Georgie still couldn't stop thinking about her kisses with Jason.

Not that she had time to dwell on them.

She didn't. She had more important matters to attend to. Like planning her escape from her own wedding.

At present, she was seated in Bea's sitting room yet again, her gloved fingers fidgeting with the edge of her worn shawl.

Across from her, Bea sat perfectly straight in a carved chair that looked more like a throne than a piece of furniture, her cool sea-green eyes scanning some unseen list in her mind.

And beside Georgie on the settee, Poppy, with her fiery red hair and sweet, slightly anxious smile, sipped tea and cast a few nervous glances toward the door.

It was comforting, in its way. Their little trio—the Wallflowers' Revolt—had convened here twice more since the Cranberrys' ball to finalize their plans.

Truthfully, the Cranberrys' ball had been in Georgie's thoughts all week and not only because of the kissing. With

Jason's help, she'd successfully escaped the party. Then she'd dutifully endured her mother's resulting lecture the next day.

But neither of those things were what kept rolling about in her mind far too often.

Ever since that final kiss on the back stoop, Jason had done exactly as she asked—kept his distance, stayed away entirely. Sensible, her mind told her. Necessary.

And yet some traitorous part of her chest ached at the absence, as though it had been quietly waiting for him to appear and could not quite forgive him for not doing so.

Which was ridiculous, of course. She had asked him to stay away because seeing him again would only make everything worse. Might make her hope for things she could not decently ask of him. Might make her imagine him breaking with all sense, going to her father, offering for her himself.

But Georgie could not bear that sort of rescue. Not if it sprang from pity, or honor, or the memory of a few stolen kisses. If Jason ever chose her, she wanted it freely. And since she had no right to ask such a thing, yes, distance was safer.

Bea's crisp voice cut through her thoughts.

"Right," she said, setting her teacup down with finality. "Let's go over this one last time, shall we?" she said in something of a loud whisper.

Georgie straightened. "Of course."

Poppy let out a nervous giggle.

"First, the wedding is at St. George's," Bea began, ticking off each point on her fingers and keeping her voice low. "You'll be in the small room in the back of church where all brides prepare. You tell your mother you're not feeling well and need to use the convenience. You walk out the side door —slowly, of course—and then, when you reach the halfway mark and clear the church wall, feel free to run."

Georgie nodded solemnly. Her stomach roiled, but she

closed her eyes and tamped down the nausea. She had no choice. This was her only chance for a happy life.

"On the other side of the wall," Bea continued, "Lady Trentham's secondary carriage—a plain black one—will be waiting at the corner. Her driver knows the plan. And he's been *well* compensated. He will take you as far as the coaching inn on the London Road, where you'll switch to the post chaise waiting there."

"And that chaise will take me directly to…" Georgie prompted.

"Your friend's home in Bath," Bea finished.

Poppy clapped her hands lightly. "It's perfect," she said. "No one will suspect a thing."

Georgie turned to her. "And you're certain you'll be ready with your part?"

Poppy nodded vigorously, her red curls bouncing. "Yes. As soon as you slip away, I'll distract your mother by telling her how faint you were looking. I'll insist you've only stepped out to collect yourself. That should afford you at least a few minutes before she grows suspicious."

Georgie sighed and shook her head. "My mother will believe that excuse for approximately thirty seconds," she warned.

Bea arched a brow. "Then you'd best move quickly."

"I intend to," Georgie replied firmly. She took a deep breath, still pressing a hand to her stomach. "I cannot thank either of you or Lady Trentham enough—"

Because this—this plan, this friendship, this chance to vanish on her own terms—felt bearable in a way begging any man to save her never could.

"Tut, tut," said Bea. "You will do the same for us when it's our turn."

"I will," Georgie agreed. "You only need write to me.

Only…" She glanced away sadly. "I am sorry I won't be able to see either of you again… Perhaps for a very long time."

The thought made her teary-eyed. She did not add that it was not only her friends she would be leaving behind. She could not bear to name that thought aloud.

"We shall write," Poppy said, forcing a smile to her face.

They all sat back then, a brief silence falling as they imagined the scene to come.

Again, Poppy was the first to speak. "I still can't believe I've been invited to the wedding," she murmured. "With Mama's reputation, I am rarely invited to anything. I'm entirely certain I'm only included in the events of the Season because the hostesses are hoping Mama will do something to gossip about. It's nearly as if *she's* the entertainment." Poppy grimaced faintly. "Honestly, I can't help but worry what Mama will do at your wedding, Georgie. She's bound to cause some sort of gossip."

Georgie gave her a wicked grin. "Are you jesting? I'm *counting* upon it. The more distracted everyone is by Lady Viva's antics, the easier it will be for me to disappear."

That earned a soft laugh from all three of them, though Poppy blushed furiously.

Bea leaned back in her chair, glancing toward the window. "Well," she said at last, "I suppose that covers everything. Now all we need is for the wedding date to arrive."

"Two more days," Georgie said, pressing a hand to her middle once more. She was no longer entirely certain if she dreaded the moment or couldn't wait for it to be over.

Perhaps because escape no longer felt as simple as it once had. Once, she had only wanted to flee. Now she had the far more inconvenient burden of wanting something—or someone—she could not take with her.

Of course she'd *considered* running off in the middle of the night. It held certain advantages. But after her recent stints of running away from parties, Mama had taken to posting Martin outside her door at night. Georgie didn't want to get poor Martin in trouble, and the drop from her bedchamber window appeared to be fatal.

The sound of the Winslows' front door opening down in the foyer carried into the sitting room, interrupting Georgie's thoughts. A deep male voice drifted faintly up to them, followed by the familiar murmur of the butler.

Bea rolled her eyes. "Undoubtedly, that is Lord Vanover," she muttered, rising to peer toward the salon door. "As my father's favorite sycophant, he's forever stopping by to discuss parliamentary business…which means I must take my leave soon."

"Oh, yes, Nicholas Archer, the man you were hiding from in the retiring room." Poppy raised an eyebrow. "But why do you need to take your leave? I thought you didn't like him."

Bea waved a dismissive hand. "Of course I don't like him. But helpfully, my bedchamber is directly above my father's study, and if I press my ear to the floor, I can hear *everything* they say."

Georgie shook her head. But she couldn't help her smile. "And you *enjoy* eavesdropping on their dry, tedious political discussions?"

Bea's eyes sparkled. "How else," she said sweetly, "can I endeavor to ruin their plans?"

Georgie and Poppy both laughed—though Georgie could tell from the set of Bea's mouth that she wasn't exactly jesting.

Not for the first time, Georgie had the thought that she was truly glad to be Bea's friend. It was obviously preferable to being her enemy. In fact, Georgie felt a bit sorry for Nicholas Archer.

As the sound of male voices drifted away, Georgie leaned back into the settee cushions with a sigh.

"Our plan is going to work," Poppy whispered, a little too hopeful. "Isn't it?"

Georgie gave her a half-smile. "It has to."

It had to work because it was the only future Georgie could accept with any dignity. The alternative—staying, pleading, allowing men to negotiate over her life yet again—was unbearable.

Her gaze drifted to the gold-draped window, where sunlight angled in and caught the shimmer of Bea's flaxen hair. Georgie reached up to her own head and patted it, trying to shake loose the thought that had been lurking for days now.

Should she tell her friends she'd kissed Jason? Bea wouldn't like it. Poppy would want details.

Georgie squeezed her eyes shut. "I kissed him," she blurted. Then, because honesty seemed suddenly impossible to contain, she added, "More than once."

Silence.

Then—

"You *what?*" Bea demanded, half-rising from her chair, eyes flashing. "Absolutely not. No. That man has caused you nothing but trouble."

"Ooh!" Poppy breathed, leaning forward, eyes bright. "How was it?"

Georgie groaned and dropped her face into her hands. "I don't know," she said miserably. "It just…happened. I don't know why it happened."

Which was not quite true. She knew why. It had happened because Jason looked at her as though she mattered, because he kept helping when every sensible man would have stepped aside, and because some reckless part of her had wanted him for longer than she cared to admit.

Bea planted her hands on her hips. "This is precisely why

we do not kiss handsome, meddlesome gentlemen in dark corners."

"He wasn't meddling," Georgie muttered. "He was… helping."

Helping in that infuriating, disarming way of his that made it terribly easy to forget he was not hers to want. "And how did you know it was in a dark corner?" she added.

Poppy tilted her head toward Bea. "Why are you so against Lord Pembroke?"

Bea gave a cool little shrug. "Because I hold most men in contempt, if you must know. My father has supplied the example all my life. He is an overbearing brute, and I do not know how Mother has borne him these many years."

Poppy blinked. "That seems rather severe."

"Does it?" Bea asked dryly. "As for Lord Pembroke in particular, if he were honorable, he would have done the proper thing and offered for Georgie by now. Instead, he has merely inserted himself into her affairs—hovering, interfering, assuming she needs his help when she is quite capable of rescuing herself."

Georgie looked down at her hands.

Bea was severe, but not incorrect. Whatever had passed between her and Jason—however real, however difficult to forget—none of it altered the plain truth. He had not offered. Escape remained her only course.

Completely ignoring Bea's diatribe, Poppy turned her smiling face back to Georgie. "Were they *good* kisses at least? Passionate ones?"

"Poppy!" Bea nearly shouted.

"What?" she said innocently, lifting her chin. "I think it's relevant."

Georgie scrunched up her nose. "Yes," she admitted. "Quite good. Amazing, if I'm being honest."

Poppy's smile widened. Bea looked as though she might combust.

"Well," Bea said sharply, drawing herself up, "the good news is that in two days' time, you will be escaping London entirely. You'll be off to Bath, free and unencumbered, and you won't have to see *either* Lord Henderville or Lord Pembroke again. Ever."

The word echoed a little too loudly in Georgie's head.

*Ever.*

Henderville's loss felt like salvation. Pembroke's felt like something else entirely—something perilously close to grief.

The room settled into quiet again, the clink of teacups and the distant sounds of the house drifting in. Georgie leaned back into the cushions, staring at the ceiling, her pulse oddly unsteady.

She had wanted freedom. She still did. She had planned everything around leaving, around never looking back.

But freedom had become more complicated now that it required walking away not only from the future she dreaded, but from the one man who had made her wonder whether a different sort of life might have been possible.

Her thoughts betrayed her, drifting not to Henderville or her parents or even Bath, but to a darkened library, a stolen waltz, and kisses that had felt far too intentional to dismiss.

Did she truly want to *never* see him again?

The thought made her throat ache.

No. That was the terrible truth of it. She wanted to see him again. Wanted him to stop her and yet not stop her, to choose her and yet not from duty, to offer something she could accept without shame.

But such wishes belonged in novels, not in the life of a woman already promised elsewhere. There was no room now for longing, only resolve. In two days' time, she would escape. And if it broke her heart a little to leave Jason behind, she would simply have to bear it.

# CHAPTER TWENTY-TWO

The bells of St. George's tolled brightly in the morning air, mocking her with every joyous peal.

Georgie stood in the tiny back room of the church, the faint scent of lilies clinging to her like a shroud.

The sun streamed through the high windows, catching on the gauzy white veil draped over her head…a veil she had every intention of abandoning before the hour was out.

Her mother sat primly in a chair near the door, her gloved hands folded in her lap, her mouth drawn into the thin line it always became when she was suspicious, which was often.

And she was certainly suspicious now.

"Stand up straighter," Mama growled under her breath. "You'll make the family look ridiculous if you slouch."

Georgie stiffened automatically, even as a sharp reply sat on the tip of her tongue. She swallowed it down. It wouldn't do to start a row now, not when the plan was already in motion.

Her gaze flicked toward her father, who leaned casually against the far wall, his arms crossed, a faint smirk playing at his lips as if he thought this entire spectacle was amusing.

It probably was to him. Why wouldn't it be? He thought he was about to collect the money, his earnings for selling off his only daughter like a prize cow.

Henry was sitting near the door to the vestibule. He'd hobbled in early and sat down with his broken, braced leg jutting out awkwardly in front of him. He, too, had a smug smile on his face, no doubt already counting the money this marriage stood to make him.

The man Georgie was to marry wasn't with them, however. She peeked out the door. The Marquess of Henderville stood waiting at the far end of the aisle near the altar, frail and stooped, his cane planted firmly before him, his face flushed and gleaming with anticipation.

Georgie shivered despite herself. His expression was... unsettling. Too happy. Too eager. Too...*hungry*. She forced her eyes away before her stomach could turn completely.

And then she saw her.

Bea.

Seated in a front pew, flanked by her impeccably dressed parents, her blond head held high and her eyes as sharp and knowing as ever.

Bea turned ever so slightly, and when Georgie's gaze met hers, Bea gave the barest of nods. Georgie winked and fell away from the door.

The plan was set.

And thank heavens for that. A plan was something solid. A plan asked nothing of her except nerve. It did not look at her with tenderness. It did not tempt her into weakness.

In the room with her, Poppy fluttered about nervously, pretending to fuss with the hem of Georgie's gown but really stealing glances toward the door every few seconds.

"Stop fidgeting," Georgie whispered.

"I'm not fidgeting," Poppy muttered, though her hands were twisting the fabric of her own peach-colored skirts.

Earlier, when Georgie had insisted to her mother that her new friend stay with her in the back, Mama had merely sneered. "I didn't realize you *had* any friends."

But Mama hadn't objected. And that's what mattered.

Shockingly, Lady Viva, who was seated in the third pew on the groom's side for some unknown reason, had yet to do anything to cause a scene. She was dressed in an ostentatious confection of pink and feathers, her expression surprisingly serene for once. Poppy claimed she'd begged her mother to act propitiously, but she *also* claimed that that never worked.

Georgie had almost smiled at the sight. Of course Lady Viva would choose this moment—the one time Georgie was counting on a distraction—to sit quietly.

No matter. The plan did not depend on her.

Georgie exhaled and adjusted her white kid gloves, her pulse beginning to climb.

And it had reason to.

She was about to cause a scandal London would remember for years, decades perhaps.

One last breath. Everything was ready.

This was what she wanted, she reminded herself fiercely. A life she could enter with her head up and her own name inside her chest. Freedom.

And yet the treacherous truth pressed in all the same: if marriage had ever come to her looking like conversation, laughter, sharp green eyes, and a man who listened as though her mind mattered, she might have wanted that too. Not rescue. Not pity. But a husband she could have chosen.

Which was precisely why she could not afford to see Jason now. And why she was glad she'd asked him to stay away.

She glanced out the door again—and froze.

Her thoughts skidded to a stop.

Standing at the back of the church, partially in shadow but unmistakable all the same, was…

Jason.

Of all the people she had braced herself to see that morning, he was the one she had most wanted but most dreaded.

Her chest went painfully tight.

No.

She had asked him not to come. Asked him sincerely. Asked him after he'd kissed her—after she'd requested a favor of him.

Her heart fluttered traitorously. *Why are you here?*

Had he come to witness the scandal? To stop it? Or— more alarming still—to offer help she had no business wanting from him?

He wasn't smiling. He wasn't intervening. He simply stood there, watchful and intent, his arms folded as though holding himself in check.

As though every instinct in him urged movement and he was resisting it by force. The sight of that self-command unsettled her more than interference would have.

A nervous chill skated down her spine. He had better not say a word. Better not look at her again. Better not do *anything* that might draw attention or unravel what she had spent weeks planning.

"Ah, Pembroke's arrived," Henry said mildly. "I thought he told me he couldn't make it."

He pushed himself up and hobbled toward the aisle, presumably to greet his friend.

Georgie's fingers clenched in her bouquet. *Why would you accept, Jason?*

He had stayed away for a sennight, just as she'd asked. Why choose today of all days to reappear, unless he meant to matter?

She forced herself to look away. Whatever he was doing here—whatever it meant—she could not afford to think about it now.

She had bigger problems.

Much bigger.

If she let herself wonder whether he had come for her, she might lose the precious thread of her resolve—and that, this morning of all mornings, would be fatal.

One more breath.

Then the music began.

Mother stood, smoothing her gloves. "Well," she said coolly, "the next time I see you, you'll be Lady Henderville. Try not to embarrass yourself. Or us."

Georgie smiled faintly and said nothing.

Poppy shot her a panicked glance and fell into place behind her, bouquet in hand.

Georgie stepped into the nave, her gaze fixed somewhere beyond her father's shoulder.

Halfway out—exactly as planned—she faltered, pressing a hand to her middle.

Poppy darted forward. "Are you all right?" she whispered, loud enough for nearby guests to hear.

Georgie shook her head weakly. "I… I feel ill. I think I need a moment. Some air…"

Poppy straightened. "The bride needs a moment," she announced in far too conspicuous a voice.

Mother's head snapped toward them.

Georgie caught Bea's barely concealed smirk as she pivoted, pulling Poppy with her toward the side door, her heart pounding.

They reached the archway. Georgie turned, clutching her bouquet. "Thirty seconds," she murmured. "That's all I need."

Poppy nodded and turned back to Mother.

But Mama's sharp voice cut through the air. "Where do you think you're going?"

Georgie froze—

Poppy stepped into Mama's path. "She just needs—"

But Mother surged forward, pushing past the much smaller woman.

That was it.

Georgie didn't hesitate. She tore off her veil, flung her bouquet backward, gathered her skirts…and ran.

The sound of her mother's furious cry echoed behind her. "Stop her!"

But Georgie didn't look back.

Not at her family.

Not at the church.

And not—no matter how her heart thundered—at the man she had begged to stay away.

If he meant to follow, let him. If he meant to stop her, he would fail. And if he meant something else—something far more impossible—she must leave that hope behind with the veil and flowers.

Freedom first. Heartbreak after.

# CHAPTER TWENTY-THREE

Jason had told himself a hundred times on the way to the church this morning that he was *not* going to do anything.

He wasn't here to interfere.

Not to watch her, not to stop her, and certainly not to help if she planned to escape.

He was simply an invited guest. Never mind that he'd been specifically asked by the bride herself to stay away.

And yet, here he was, leaning against a pillar at the back of St. George's, watching the entire farce unfold with his arms lodged tight across his chest and his jaw clenched so hard it ached.

And—though he'd never admit it aloud—he was already restless.

Restless in the particular way a man became when he knew he ought to leave well enough alone and had already failed three times before breakfast.

He'd told himself—firmly, repeatedly, like a prayer—that he was attending this wedding out of courtesy.

To Chadwick.

To Society.

To common bloody decency.

Fine. He'd risen earlier than necessary. Dressed too quickly. Left the house too soon.

And, inexplicably, had stopped by the mews for a mount rather than his usual carriage.

The stable boy had looked at him strangely when he'd swung into the saddle in his formal morning coat and cravat, but Jason had ignored him.

When he arrived, he'd tied the horse to a post just outside the church and told himself it was for convenience.

Not because he expected anything. Not because he intended to involve himself or anything absurd like that. Absolutely not.

Though some misguided instinct in him had plainly preferred being prepared to being helpless.

He barely had time to greet Chadwick, when the murmur began to ripple through the congregation, the kind of uneasy, scandal-tinged whisper that prickled at the back of his neck like a warning.

Jason's eyes lifted to the aisle just in time to see Georgiana's white skirts disappearing through the side door.

Her mother's sharp cry—*"Stop her!"*—echoed in the vaulted ceiling.

For half a second, he stood frozen, watching the anarchy begin to unfold. Miss Poppy Montfort darted about, while Lady Beatrix Winslow sat in perfect, unruffled composure in the front, and the elderly groom fumbled with his cane while barking for order. Lady Chadwick was nearly apoplectic.

Jason watched all of this as if in a blur. And then—against all reason—he moved.

Not because she needed rescuing from her own plan. Not because he meant to drag her back. But because the sight of her vanishing had struck him with a force that felt suspiciously like losing her.

He shoved off the wall, shouldering past startled guests and emerging into the pale spring sunlight just as Georgiana's skirts flashed around the corner at the far end of the church.

He turned swiftly, racing back toward his mount. His horse snorted and danced as he swung into the saddle.

"I'm not doing this," he muttered aloud, his hands already gathering the reins and galloping around the side of the church. "I'm not—"

He was not chasing her to stop her escape. He was chasing her because he could not bear to let her disappear without knowing where she meant to land—or whether she truly meant to leave him behind.

But then he caught sight of her—a flash of white as she hurtled into a plain black coach waiting at the road—and that was it.

By the time more shouts came spilling from the church doors behind him, he was already turning the next corner at a full gallop, giving chase.

The London streets flew past in a blur of brick and cobblestone. His horse's hooves thundered over the stones, the wind stinging his face as he leaned low, his eyes fixed on the black coach ahead.

It barreled down Oxford Street, its driver urging the horses faster, weaving through morning traffic as startled pedestrians leaped out of the way.

Jason urged his own mount harder, the leather reins biting into his palms. Somewhere behind him, he could still hear faint cries—of outrage, of confusion—as wedding guests spilled into the street, presumably in varying states of horror and disarray.

He glanced back and caught only a glimpse of them—

Lady Chadwick gesticulating wildly, Miss Montfort pretending faintness, the groom tottering down the church steps like an indignant tortoise—before Jason left them behind entirely.

The black coach careened around another bend, the wheels skidding hard on the damp stones.

Jason followed without hesitation.

He didn't stop to question himself, didn't stop to think about how idiotic it was, how it would look, how it would end.

He simply followed.

Which was unlike him. Jason preferred strategy, foresight, a clean understanding of his own motives. This felt more primitive than that. More honest, perhaps, and therefore considerably more dangerous.

The horse's breath came hot and fast beneath him, its muscles bunching and stretching as it ate the ground between them.

Through Cheapside.

Across Ludgate Hill.

Past Holborn, the smell of coal smoke and bread mingling in the air as the coach hurtled on.

It was headed—quite obviously—toward the coaching station north of town.

Jason swore under his breath and leaned lower, urging his horse into a final burst of speed as they rounded the last corner.

And there, just ahead, was the station.

Dust and commotion and the sharp scent of horses hung thick in the air as passengers bustled about, porters shouting and heaving luggage onto waiting carriages.

The black coach clattered to a halt near the farthest post, and he saw Georgiana emerging in a swirl of white satin and determination.

She'd already discarded her veil, and her hair was coming loose from its pins, wild in the morning sun.

She did not look like a woman in need of saving. She looked like a woman in motion—one who had chosen her own course and meant to keep it. The realization should have slowed him. Instead, it only made him admire her more.

Jason didn't stop to think.

He swung halfway down from the saddle before his horse had fully stopped.

She saw him at the last moment, her eyes widening as he reached her, her lips parting to speak.

But he didn't give her the chance. One arm looped around her waist, he lifted her clean off her feet as she let out a startled gasp.

If she said his name in that tone and asked him what in God's name he thought he was doing, he rather feared he would have no answer fit for daylight.

He swung her up and into the saddle in front of him in one smooth motion, her skirts tangling with his boots as she clutched at the reins in surprise.

"Jason—!" she cried, breathless.

But he was back up into the saddle behind her, gathering her firmly against his chest with one arm while his other hand gripped the reins.

He could feel her heartbeat hammering through the thin fabric of her gown, her breath warm against his jaw as she twisted to glare at him.

"What do you think you're—"

He didn't say a word, just turned the horse and kicked it into motion, galloping away from the station as the driver of the black coach and a few bystanders began to shout after them.

They tore through the streets of London again, hooves

ringing over stone and dust kicking up behind them, Georgiana's skirts fluttering wildly in the wind.

Jason didn't look back.

He didn't dare.

He just held her steady in front of him, her body pressed against his, her scent—something faintly floral, maddeningly warm—filling his senses as they flew through the city streets.

And for the first time in days, perhaps in weeks, he stopped telling himself he wasn't involved.

Because, clearly, he was.

And there was no turning back now.

The truth was simpler and more damning than any excuse he had rehearsed. He had not come to the church out of courtesy. He had not mounted that horse for convenience. He had come because some stubborn, inescapable part of him meant to be where Georgiana Chadwick was…meant to keep her from marrying another man…meant to keep her from leaving his life for good…and today, at least, that part had won.

# CHAPTER TWENTY-FOUR

Georgie sat stiff-backed in a chair near the window of an unfamiliar upstairs room, her skirts still rumpled from the ride, her coiffure askew, and her demeanor filled with outrage.

She'd been too stunned to speak at first when Jason had all but carried her through the front door of his town house, barking something about privacy and propriety to his butler before hauling her up the stairs and shutting them both in this room.

But she'd found her tongue soon enough.

"What exactly," she began, arms tightly folded over her chest, slippered foot tapping on the floor, "is your plan here, my lord?"

He stood by the fireplace, hands clasped behind his back like some self-satisfied general who had just captured an enemy fort.

"My…plan?" he repeated slowly, as though the word itself were foreign.

"Yes," she said, rising to her feet and glaring at him. "Because it seems to me you've gone to considerable trouble to…to *abduct me,* so surely you must have some notion of what comes next."

The faint hitch before *abduct* caught his attention—so brief he might have imagined it. As though outrage was not the only thing she was struggling to name.

He turned to face her. "Abduct you? That's preposterous."

"Oh?" she shot back. "What would you call it then? You can't have been working for my brother or you would have returned me to the church."

"Of course I'm not working for your brother. I…" He faltered, running a hand roughly over his jaw. "I'm simply…"

Trying to keep you from vanishing before I understood what in God's name I was losing, he nearly said.

Instead, he only stared at her, because that truth was far too raw—and far too ridiculous—to say out loud.

She planted her hands on her hips. "You're simply *what* precisely?"

Her tone was sharp, but there was something else in her face now too—something wary and searching, as though she were braced for an answer she might not wholly despise.

He exhaled sharply. "I don't know yet."

Which was the most maddening part. He knew perfectly well what he did *not* want: Henderville, Chadwick, or any other grasping fool laying claim to her. It was the rest—the part that involved himself—that remained maddeningly unresolved.

She arched a brow. "Well. At least you admit it."

Jason didn't know exactly *how* he'd expected her to react. Anger seemed as good as any other sentiment at the moment. And she clearly *was* angry. Glaring at him from beneath drawn brows, her eyes narrowed and her mouth pinched.

He groaned and began pacing the room, his boots thudding softly against the rug. "I couldn't let you ruin yourself *and* run off to God-knows-where," he muttered.

It was a wholly inadequate explanation. And even as he said the words, he knew they were wrong. It was not the running that had unstrung him. It was the thought of her being gone—truly gone—and himself left standing uselessly behind.

"Bath," she supplied. "I was going to Bath. And the ruining is already over," she informed him pointedly, "so the running off part is hardly the scandal."

She said it crisply enough, yet her eyes lingered on him half a beat too long after the word *scandal*, as if waiting to see whether scandal was truly what troubled him most. As if she assumed he'd done this in some sort of foolhardy attempt to save her from ruinous gossip. Only they both knew it was *far* too late for that.

He stopped pacing long enough to say, "If you and I are found together—"

"What does *that* matter?" she asked, lifting her brows. "You've already made certain plenty of people saw you snatch me up at the coaching station, so it seems you've ruined me far more effectively than I ever managed to ruin myself. If you had some ill-conceived notion of saving my reputation, it's long since gone."

*Fuck.* She was right. All he'd done was pluck her from one scandal and place her solidly in another.

Her words had come out with deliberate coolness, but Jason had the distinct impression she was not merely accusing him. She was probing. Watching him far too closely for a woman who cared only for escape.

He froze at that, clearly struck. "There has to be a way out of this," he murmured, mostly to himself, pacing again.

Her eyes flashed fire. "There is," she said at once. But before she spoke further, there was the slightest pause—as though she had, for one reckless instant, considered some answer other than the obvious one.

His head snapped up to face her. "What?"

She slowly expelled her breath, and gave him a wary look that clearly indicated she believed she was speaking to someone who had almost certainly gone mad. "Take me back to the coaching station. My friend will be waiting in Bath. She'll be worried if I don't arrive."

She spoke briskly, almost too briskly, as if speed alone might spare her from hearing what he had not yet chosen to say.

But Jason was already shaking his head, muttering under his breath as he resumed pacing, scrubbing a hand through his hair until it stood on end.

"There's *got* to be another way," he said grimly.

At that, something flickered across her face and vanished. Not hope exactly—he would not flatter himself so far—but a sharp, unwilling alertness, as though the words had touched some hidden bruise.

He did not mean to hand her back. Never that. But sending her on alone no longer felt possible, and keeping her here without a name for what he meant to do felt worse.

She flopped back into the chair and glared at him. "Well. Do let me know when you've thought of it."

The irony was intact, but she did not look away afterward. She kept her eyes on him, waiting—as if despite herself, she wanted to know what sort of answer he might reach.

He continued to pace, still muttering to himself and wearing a path into the rug, when a knock came at the door.

Jason's head whipped toward the sound. His eyes narrowed. "Who could that be?"

A moment later, his butler appeared, looking harried. "My lord," he began, "it's—"

But the man didn't have the chance to finish before Georgie's parents pushed their way into the room. Her mother's skirts practically caught fire from the speed with which she entered, her father quickly following with a self-satisfied smirk.

"She's here!" Lady Chadwick cried, triumphant. "I *knew* it!"

Georgie sank deeper into the chair, groaning quietly.

Jason blinked at the sudden onslaught, his hands lifting instinctively as if he could physically hold back the madness barreling toward him. "Now wait just a—"

"You've thoroughly disgraced us!" Lady Chadwick continued, pointing a shaking finger at Georgie.

"It's not what it looks like—" Jason tried to say, but her father cut him off with a dismissive wave.

"We don't care what it looks like," Lord Chadwick insisted. "All we care about is returning Lord Henderville's bride to him. He's still at the church waiting, poor fellow."

Something cold and final moved through Jason at that. Not bride. Property. That was how they meant it. How they had always meant it.

"What?" Jason blurted, visibly flabbergasted.

"Let's go," Lady Chadwick demanded, her head jerking toward the door in a silent order.

At that moment, Henry made his entrance, hobbling awkwardly into the room on a cane of his own. His voice soon added to the cacophony.

But in the midst of all the yelling—Henry calling Jason names, Lady Chadwick calling Georgiana names, Lord Chadwick threatening to call out Jason—Georgiana must have seen her opportunity.

She slipped from the chair, moved toward the window, and, when no one was looking, shoved it open and swung one leg over the sill.

That, at least, got everyone's attention.

Jason whirled toward her just in time to see her white skirts billowing in the breeze.

"Georgiana!" he cried, real fear pounding through his chest.

"I will jump to my death," she announced coolly, "if any of you try to take me back to that church."

Her gaze cut first to her father, then her mother, then Henry. Only at the last did it find Jason—and linger there for the briefest instant, as though daring him to prove he was no better than the rest.

Jason believed her. Not because she was hysterical—she was the opposite of that—but because he had seen, again and again, the terrible calm that came over her when she had truly reached the end of what she could bear.

Her mother gasped. Her father sputtered. Her brother gawked.

And Jason just stood there, his face no doubt a mixture of horror and disbelief as he raked both hands through his hair. "Oh, hell," he muttered under his breath. "I've created a bloody mess."

A mess of his own making, yes—but one that had at least stripped away every polite fiction in the room. Georgiana was cornered. Her family meant to force her back to the church to marry Henderville. And Jason, having dragged her into this half-ruin, no longer had the luxury of pretending he was only passing through.

*That did it.*

"ENOUGH!" Jason roared suddenly, his voice cracking like a whip through the room.

Everyone fell silent at once.

Even Georgiana, poised precariously on the windowsill, froze and blinked at him.

Jason drew himself up to his full height, his jaw set. "*How much*," he demanded, his voice low and even, directed at Lord Chadwick, "was Henderville set to pay you?"

If they insisted on speaking the language of bargains, then let them hear, plainly, how monstrous they sounded.

Georgiana's father, who looked utterly confused now, opened his mouth—then closed it again.

Jason stepped closer, the muscle in his jaw ticking. He'd had quite enough of Georgiana's family's nonsense. "Well?"

Lord Chadwick swallowed. "Ten…thousand pounds," he admitted at last, tugging at his lapels and glancing away.

Georgiana made a small sound at the window—barely audible, but enough to slice through Jason. There it was at last, the neat price of her future, spoken into the open air as baldly as the price of horseflesh.

Jason did not think. If he had, perhaps he would have found some gentler phrasing, some nobler arrangement, some way of keeping her from Henderville without sounding as though he, too, meant to enter the auction.

But Georgiana was still perched on that damned windowsill, pale and proud and one breath from catastrophe, and Chadwick had just named his daughter's price aloud. Something savage in Jason refused to let the moment pass unanswered.

His nostrils flared. "I'll give you *twenty-five thousand*," he said, his voice cutting through the heavy air, "to marry her tonight."

The words landed with a brutality he felt at once. Too blunt. Too crude. Too perilously close to the very ugliness he had meant to destroy.

But he did not take them back. He'd meant every word he'd said.

The room went dead still.

Georgiana's eyes widened. Not merely in outrage. There was confusion there too—a stunned, searching disbelief, as though she could not decide whether he had just claimed her, insulted her, or done something far more perilous than either.

*Damn.* He had just done the one thing she would no doubt hate most—made marriage to her sound like a financial counteroffer. And yet beneath the shock on her face, he thought he saw something worse…hurt. As though some part of her had wanted very much to hear one answer from him and had received quite another.

Her mother's mouth fell open. Her father actually stammered. Henry sat down with an *oof* in a nearby chair.

And Jason just stood there, unflinching, watching them all with grim determination, daring anyone to argue.

He was no longer certain whether he had made things better or appallingly worse. He only knew he would not hand her back to Henderville. Not for twenty-five thousand pounds. Not for fifty. Not for *anything*.

# CHAPTER TWENTY-FIVE

Jason remained in the center of the room, his hands at his sides, the echo of his voice still vibrating in his chest.

*I'll give you twenty-five thousand to marry her tonight,* he'd said.

And the strangest thing was…

The moment he said it, he felt…calm. Relieved, even. As though something that had been gnawing at him for weeks had finally settled into place.

"Pardon?" Georgiana's voice snapped him out of his thoughts.

She was still perched in the window, her skirts ruffling faintly in the wind, her brown eyes wide with outrage…or was it disbelief? As though she had not yet decided whether he had done something monstrous, magnificent, or merely mad.

She shook her head violently. "No," she said firmly. But the refusal came a shade too quickly, with the sharpness of a woman batting away not only an offer, but the hope buried within it.

Her father squinted at him, incredulous. But finally found his voice. "Are you *quite serious?*"

Jason straightened. "I am *entirely* serious," he said evenly, his jaw still ticking.

Lady Chadwick let out a scandalized laugh. "Well, you're mad," she sniffed, already flouncing toward the door. "Completely mad. I'll be in the coach while you men work out the details. Come along, Georgiana."

"I'm not going anywhere with you," Georgiana bit out.

Jason's lips twitched faintly. "Georgiana stays with me," he commanded.

Her gaze flew to his at once, startled and searching, as though the words had landed with more force than either of them expected.

Henry, who had been glaring at Jason from his awkward seat near the door, finally spoke up. "I should call you out for ruining my sister," he growled.

Jason's head snapped toward him. "I did *not* ruin her," he said sharply. "I'm *attempting* to do the opposite, actually."

"Henry, you dimwit," Lord Chadwick said, rolling his eyes, "Pembroke's about to save her reputation and give us twenty-five thousand pounds to boot. A fortune! You shouldn't be calling him out. You should be shaking his hand."

Henry looked thoroughly confused by this information. He had never been the sharpest foil in the rack. His mouth opened, closed, then opened again before he simply stood and hobbled out after his mother, muttering under his breath.

Jason exhaled slowly, then turned back to Lord Chadwick. "One more condition," he said, his voice calm but firm.

The older man's brow rose.

"I need a few minutes alone with Georgiana before we

discuss any contract. I will not proceed without her full agreement."

Georgiana's expression changed almost imperceptibly at that—not softer, precisely, but less closed. As though she had expected to be spoken over yet again and did not quite know what to make of being consulted instead.

Lord Chadwick barked a dry laugh. "We don't *need* her agreement," he scoffed.

Jason's eyes hardened. "You do if you want my money," he said flatly.

That shut him up.

After a moment, Lord Chadwick sniffed and adjusted his waistcoat. "Very well. I'll wait for you downstairs in your study."

When the door closed behind him, the room fell quiet except for the faint rattle of the window where Georgiana still perched.

Jason dragged a hand through his hair and turned toward her slowly.

She didn't look at him. Her eyes were fixed on the street below, her fingers clutching the sill, her shoulders rigid.

She was obviously scared. And furious.

And he couldn't blame her.

But beneath both, he sensed another tension he could not yet name. Not simple fear. Not pulsing rage. Something more watchful than that, as if she were waiting to discover what he meant by all this before deciding how deeply to hate him.

He took a careful step closer. "Georgiana," he said softly.

She didn't move.

Another step. "I know you want to escape," he said, more gently this time. "I know you're angry with me. And you have every right to be. Of course. But please…come back inside. Sit down. Hear me out."

Her fingers tightened on the sill.

"I will not insist on *anything*," he continued. "You have all the choice here. If you say no, I'll take you to the coaching station myself if that's what you want. I promise you, I can get you there undetected, your family be damned."

He meant it. Even now, even after all this chaos, some stubborn part of him would rather lose her entirely than have her think he meant to trap her.

*That* got her attention. She glanced back at him, still suspicious but interested.

"I *promise*," he said again, hand on his heart.

Her lips pressed into a thin line, but after a moment, she swung her leg back over the sill and allowed him to help her to the floor.

She stalked to the chair she'd abandoned earlier and sat with her arms crossed, still glaring at him.

Jason lowered himself into the chair opposite her. "I won't pretend this is how I imagined any of this," he began with a quiet laugh.

Her eyes narrowed.

"But I would *never* force you to marry me," he said quickly. "I want you to understand that. I...want you to choose. You can continue with your plan and go to Bath, or—"

"Or what?" she asked coolly. Yet there was nothing casual in the question. Her gaze held his too steadily, her voice too controlled, as though what she truly asked was not *or what* but *what am I to you, exactly?*

He dipped his chin. "Or you can marry me."

Her brows shot straight up.

Jason huffed a laugh, rubbing the back of his neck. "We already know there's an attraction between us. At least, I think there is."

Even as he said it, the words sounded miserably inadequate. Attraction was too bloodless a word for Georgiana Chadwick. Too tidy. Too cowardly. And she was probably remembering, the same way he was, how vehemently he'd denied wanting to marry.

She blinked at him. Her shoulders loosened a bit. "Yes," she admitted. "I think so too." But her eyes did not soften. If anything, they sharpened—still watching him, still measuring, as though waiting to hear whether attraction was truly the best he could offer.

"I didn't plan this," he continued quietly. "At least...well, not before your family entered this room." He smiled faintly.

Which, again, was not the whole truth. He had not exactly named marriage, no. But he had thought of her too often, wanted her too sharply, and followed her too far for this to be called sudden in any honest sense. And it certainly wasn't the first time he'd *considered* it. But if he blurted that out now, it would sound completely fabricated. Far too convenient.

Georgiana took a deep breath. She stared at him then— really stared—until he finally realized what she must be waiting for.

"I can't promise I'll be a good husband," he said with another shaky laugh. "But I can promise I'll try my best. And —at the risk of sounding arrogant—I can't possibly be worse than Henderville."

Her mouth curved, yes, but there was still strain beneath it. As though she was grateful for the jest and wounded by it too, because she had not asked whether he would be preferable to Henderville. She had asked, in her own way, whether he wanted her enough to mean this.

She lifted her chin in that same proud way she always did when she was feeling less than confident. "I don't want you to marry me unwillingly." Her voice shook. "I don't want you to save me. And I certainly don't want the *ton* to think you married me to keep me from scandal."

There it was at last. Not merely pride, though she had that in abundance. Something rawer. She was not asking whether he could be kind. She was asking whether he could truly choose her.

He nodded slowly. "I *promise you* I'll make certain they hear I married you because I wanted to."

The answer was not elegant, but it was true. And from the way her breathing hitched—not with pleasure, but with startled, painful attention—he knew she felt the difference.

He pushed himself out of his chair and dropped to one knee and—because it felt right, because it felt necessary—reached for her hand.

Her breath hitched.

"Please," he said softly. "Georgiana…*marry me.*"

He was asking. *Truly* asking. Not because Henderville wanted her. Not because Chadwick would sell her. Not because scandal demanded repair. But because, somewhere between the first dance, the first argument, and the first kiss, the idea of letting her go had become intolerable.

# CHAPTER TWENTY-SIX

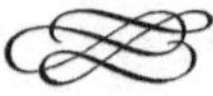

Jason didn't breathe as he watched her.

Georgiana's hand was still in his, her fingers slightly cool but steady enough that he thought—just perhaps—she wasn't going to run again.

Her gaze darted between his face and the door, then back to his face, as though weighing all her options one last time. Not merely whether to stay, he thought, but whether he himself was a risk worth taking.

The silence stretched out between them, broken only by the soft creak of settling floorboards.

And then...

"All right," she murmured at last, her voice so quiet he almost didn't catch it.

There was no romance in the sound of it. No excited flutter. Only decision. Which, somehow, made it mean more.

His chest loosened all at once, though he didn't dare let it show. "You're saying yes?" he asked carefully.

She let out a long breath and nodded, her jaw clenched with quiet resolve. "Yes," she said more firmly. "But we must marry tonight. I will *not* go back home with my family."

Even now, even in agreeing to him, she was choosing against them first. Jason understood that. And still, some selfish part of him wanted to believe she was choosing him too.

Jason closed his eyes for half a second, letting the tension drain from his shoulders before he rose to his feet and offered her his hand.

"Then let us not delay," he said. He wanted to add, "Before anyone comes to their senses," but thought better of it.

The words sounded too blunt for the moment, but if he let himself feel too much relief, too much gratitude, he feared it would show plainly on his face.

Her mouth quirked, though she didn't say anything. "Stay here," he said. "I'll send up a maid with some food and other necessities while I take care of your family."

A look of utter relief passed over her face, but Georgiana only nodded. Relief, yes—but not delight. He noticed the difference, and for some reason it mattered to him more than was probably wise.

DOWNSTAIRS, Lord Chadwick was already pacing in Jason's study, a sheaf of paper spread across the desk and a quill at the ready.

The negotiation was brief. Jason listed off a score of things he demanded in exchange for twenty-five thousand pounds to be paid upon mutual signature of the contract.

His demands included but were not limited to…Georgiana would not be leaving with her family, her family was not to contact her or visit her unless expressly invited by Georgiana herself, and her family was not to ever request or expect another farthing from either Jason or Georgiana.

They also agreed to a story to mitigate the gossip. One in

which Jason would take the blame. He would tell everyone he was madly in love with Georgiana and had decided he could not live without her. She had merely been going to use the convenience at the church before her wedding to Henderville, and Jason had abducted her.

Of course, he would have Henderville to contend with—and pay off as well, but that was Jason's problem, not Chadwick's.

There would still be a scandal, but it would die down eventually.

Georgiana's father, clearly eager to get his hands on the promised purse, eagerly scrawled his signature to the contract, and Jason followed suit.

"There," Chadwick said with a satisfied sniff. "Done. She's your problem now."

Problem. As though Georgiana were a debt to be transferred or a nuisance to be settled. Jason had to lock his teeth together to keep from putting his fist through the man's face, but he said nothing. He simply took the folded paper, slipped it into his coat, stood, and turned to fetch the money.

But in his heart, he couldn't help but think...*yes, she's mine now*. Not *mine* as Chadwick meant it. Not bought, not bartered, not possessed. *Mine* because she had said yes with her own mouth and placed her hand in his. And the thought filled him with something that felt suspiciously like...joy.

"You may wait in the foyer for your payment," Jason intoned. He had no respect for this man, a man who would sell his only daughter for the largest purse. Jason had no doubts that had he been an ogre who promised to beat Georgiana nightly, the outcome here would have been the same, given the amount of money involved.

"I will send a footman out with your money," he told Chadwick. "And let me be clear. After the ceremony, I never want to see you again."

Chadwick merely tilted his head, studying Jason as if he were a curiosity in the museum. "May I ask you a question?"

Jason inclined his head, more curious now than cautious.

"Why would you spend so much for Georgiana of all women?" Chadwick asked lightly. "She's hardly the prettiest of the lot and far from the most well-connected. If you were planning to steal a bride, the Winslow girl would have been a much better choice."

The question was so grotesque in its ignorance that Jason nearly laughed. As though a woman might be judged the way one judged a fencing bout: by position, advantage, and the likelihood of a cleaner finish.

For a heartbeat, Jason simply stared at him.

Not in anger. In disbelief.

*You don't know her at all,* he thought. Not the way she argued as if truth mattered, or kissed as if she had surprised herself by wanting. Not the fierce dignity with which she demanded to be chosen rather than rescued. Not her quick wit. Or the way her eyes lit when she spoke of history. Not the dry humor and the quiet courage it took to stand alone in rooms that had never made space for her. This man had lived under the same roof as Georgiana for years—and had somehow missed every remarkable thing about her.

Jason's mouth curved, slow and deliberate.

"That," he said evenly, "is where you and I differ."

Because to Chadwick, Georgiana was a disastrously undervalued asset. To Jason, her worth was incomparable.

Chadwick blinked.

"I do not value a woman for her connections," Jason continued calmly. "Nor for the advantage her name might lend to a drawing room." His gaze held steady. "I value intelligence. Resolve. A mind that refuses to bow simply because it is told to."

Something flickered across Chadwick's face... Confusion, perhaps. Or irritation.

Jason did not relent.

"Lady Georgiana," he added quietly, "is clever, funny, and possessed of more courage than anyone else in this house—including you…and me. And if you cannot see that, then you were never worthy of knowing her at all, let alone being her father."

And as he said it, Jason realized with a kind of startled clarity that he was not assembling compliments for effect. He was naming, one by one, the things he most admired in her.

Chadwick sniffed, unimpressed. "You're a romantic," he scoffed, turning away.

Jason couldn't help his answering smile. A romantic? Perhaps. Or perhaps he had merely met one woman worth the inconvenience of honesty.

Jason didn't stop Chadwick.

He watched him leave, utterly untroubled, knowing with a quiet certainty that whatever Georgiana became—whatever life she chose—it would be infinitely richer than anything her father had ever imagined for her.

# CHAPTER TWENTY-SEVEN

They arrived at the archbishop's residence well after midnight. It had taken the rest of the day to arrange everything. A special license was in order, after all. And then there was the matter of planting the desired story about the wedding in the *Times*.

The archbishop—a family friend who had known Jason since he was a boy—greeted them at the door in his dressing gown, his expression equal parts surprise and amusement.

"You have a talent for choosing your moments, Pembroke," he said mildly as he ushered them inside.

Jason managed the faintest of smiles. "I'll owe you for this," he murmured.

"You already do," the archbishop replied, though he was already shuffling toward the study to gather what he needed.

The ceremony was brief, quiet, almost surreal.

Jason stood at Georgiana's side as the words were spoken, watching the way her lashes lowered over her eyes, how her hands tightened and loosened in the folds of her gown.

She looked exhausted—bone-deep weary, her shoulders

sagging as though the weight of everything had finally settled on her at once.

Not unhappy, exactly. Not relieved either. More like a woman who had run so long on sheer will that now, at last, she could do nothing but feel the cost.

Her boorish family stood behind them, silent and brooding…her father with his arms crossed, her mother stiff with indignation, and Henry leaning heavily on his cane, looking bewildered and vaguely resentful.

When the archbishop declared them man and wife, Jason glanced down at Georgiana, half-expecting her to flinch or recoil.

But she didn't.

Which unsettled him more than either reaction might have. A flinch he could have understood. This quiet acceptance—this grave, deliberate stillness—felt far weightier. She simply looked up at him, her eyes dark and unreadable, and gave the faintest of nods.

As though to say: *Very well. I am here. I have chosen this. Do not make me regret it.*

Jason felt utter and complete relief. Followed almost instantly by something sharper. Responsibility, yes—but also a fierce, humbling awareness that this woman had just placed the rest of her life in his keeping, and he had better prove worthy of it.

IT WAS NEARLY three in the morning by the time they returned to his town house.

The streets of London were quiet now, the gas lamps casting long, soft shadows over the cobblestones as Jason helped his wife down from the carriage.

She swayed slightly when her feet touched the ground, and without thinking, he swept her into his arms.

"Jason—" she started.

"Don't argue," he said gently. "I'm putting you to bed. You're clearly exhausted."

For once, she *didn't* argue.

Not because the old spirit had gone out of her, he thought, but because she had simply reached the end of what one day could ask of any human.

Instead, her head dropped against his shoulder, her hair tickling his jaw as he carried her up the staircase.

The maids had already prepared a room—not his own but one of the guest chambers—and Jason pushed the door open with his shoulder, then strode over and set her carefully on the edge of the bed.

She blinked up at him, her lips parting as though she wanted to say something but couldn't quite find the words.

He crouched in front of her, his hands resting lightly on her knees.

"You're safe now," he said quietly.

The words felt inadequate the moment he spoke them. Safe was only the beginning of what he wanted to give her. Safe was the least of what she deserved.

Her lashes fluttered.

"I don't…" she began, but trailed off, her eyes falling shut.

He did not know what she had meant to say—*understand this, forgive you, trust you*—and the not knowing lodged beneath his ribs.

He didn't press her.

Instead, he bent over her with careful, deliberate hands, drawing off her clothing as gently as he could before pulling the new nightgown down over her head as she swayed sleepily beneath his touch. The soft linen slid over her skin, whisper-light and fresh, and he guided her arms through the sleeves with every care a gentleman owed his wife—and perhaps a little more than wisdom advised. He would not let himself think about the warm line of her shoulder beneath his knuckles, or the way her loosened hair spilled over the white fabric once the gown was settled properly into place. He only smoothed the folds gently, made certain she was covered, and told himself the strange tightening in his chest came from relief alone.

Once she was dressed, he rose, pulled the blankets up over her, and smoothed them into place.

Then—unable to help himself—he leaned down and pressed a kiss to her temple.

She murmured something unintelligible, already half-asleep.

Jason straightened slowly, letting his eyes linger on her one last time—the gentle rise and fall of her chest, the delicate curve of her cheek, the faint crease still etched between her brows even in sleep.

And as he stood there, he thought—not for the first time tonight—that it was, without question, the best twenty-five thousand pounds he'd ever spend. But the only bargain struck that day that truly mattered was the one Georgiana herself had made when she chose to stay.

# CHAPTER TWENTY-EIGHT

Georgie woke to the scent of beeswax and fresh lemon.

At first, she lay perfectly still, her eyes closed, waiting for the familiar chill of her small bedchamber at her father's house, the usual thin coverlet and threadbare curtains that didn't quite keep out the morning sun.

But there was no chill.

Instead, the sheets beneath her were soft—*luxuriously* soft—and warm, smelling faintly of soap and something far more expensive than anything she'd ever owned. Fresh lavender, perhaps?

Her lashes fluttered open, and the sight that met her eyes made her breath catch in her throat.

She was not at home.

She was in a bed—a massive bed—draped in pale blue damask with delicate gold embroidery. Above her, the ceiling was painted with cherubs and clouds, and on either side of the bed hung rich, thick draperies of a blue so deep it could only have come from the finest dye.

The room itself was enormous—easily three times the

size of her entire bedchamber at home—with tall windows framed by gleaming white molding and heavy brocade curtains.

An exquisite Aubusson rug stretched across the polished wood floor.

The walls were lined with paintings, landscapes, hunting scenes, and one that appeared to be some kind of Italian seaport bathed in sunset light.

On the mantel stood a row of sterling silver candlesticks, polished to a gleam, and the fireplace was flanked by two armchairs upholstered in rich velvet.

A small writing desk stood by the window, already set with quills and fine paper, and there was even—good heavens—a dressing screen embroidered with golden lilies.

She'd woken up inside a dream.

But then the memory came back. Of she and Jason riding in a coach, him half-carrying her into a grand residence, a man in robes greeting them, a ceremony, some words mumbled and then...a ride back in the coach and then... nothing.

She was married to Jason...which meant...she was at Jason's house. Oh, God, she might be in Jason's bed. But more unsettling than the bed itself was the thought of Jason choosing to put her here. Not in some cold guest room at the back of the house, but somewhere soft, beautiful, and unmistakably intimate.

The rest of yesterday's events came hurtling back into her mind. The church, the escape, Jason scooping her up like a wraith on a horse. Then the confrontation with her parents and...Jason asking her to marry him.

He'd sounded so earnest. Like he truly *did* want to marry her. Only...he hadn't said it. And she, coward that she apparently was, hadn't found the courage to ask him how or why he'd suddenly changed his mind about the institution of marriage.

A cold dread formed in the bottom of her stomach. What if he'd only done it out of guilt? What if he'd only done it in another attempt to 'save' her?

She didn't have long to contemplate either horror because the sound of the door opening drew her attention.

She sat up a little, clutching the coverlet to her chest as a young woman in a neat cap and apron stepped inside, curtsying immediately.

"Good morning, my lady," she said cheerfully. "I'm Hester. I'm to be your maid."

Georgie blinked at her. "M—my maid?"

Hester smiled. "Yes, my lady. His lordship gave me the instruction himself."

His lordship?

Another memory filtered through Georgie's mind. She'd fallen asleep inside the coach last night. At least…she'd thought she had.

She quickly pulled the coverlet from her chest and then looked down. Oh, dear. She was not wearing the last thing she'd been wearing when she remembered things. Instead, she had on a gossamer night rail that felt like pure silk. Clutching the coverlet to her chest again, she blurted out the question before she could stop herself. "Who undressed me last night?"

The question came out sharper than she intended, driven by equal parts embarrassment and the deeply disorienting need to know whether he had treated her with tenderness— or only detachment.

Hester, who was pulling out a pale morning gown, froze. Then she pinkened just a little.

"Lord Pembroke," she admitted. "He insisted on seeing to

it himself. I did go to the dressmaker's yesterday to purchase a few things for you."

Georgie's pulse gave an inconvenient throb. He had seen to her himself? Carefully enough, apparently, that she had woken comfortable and warm and dressed in finery. The question was why. Because he was kind? Because he felt responsible? Or because, in some perilous corner of his heart, he truly wanted her?

She glanced down. She was nude beneath the thin nightgown.

Completely nude.

He had seen all of her, then—or nearly all—and yet the memory that rose first was not shame, but the quiet way he had said, *You're safe now.*

Her face flamed as she scrambled to tug the blankets higher, even though it was already too late for modesty.

Hester, wisely, pretended not to notice and simply busied herself with laying out undergarments and stockings.

Georgie continued to look around. She truly had woken up inside a dream. Her fingers curled into the thick, soft sheets.

She'd *known* Jason was wealthy—he had to be to pay twenty-five thousand pounds for a wife.

But she hadn't truly comprehended until now just how wealthy he was. Yesterday, she hadn't been looking at the furnishings.

And today…she had a maid.

Georgie flushed faintly. "My maid at home was… dismissed long ago," she said slowly. "We couldn't afford…"

"Well, you don't need to worry about that here," Hester said briskly, already moving toward the wardrobe. "You're Lady Pembroke now."

*Lady Pembroke.*

The title landed heavily, yes—but not because she thought

herself unequal to it. Until her unthinkable betrothal to Henderville, she'd dreamed of being a married lady in a fine home. No, what unsettled her was not whether she could be Lady Pembroke, a countess, but what sort of *wife* Jason expected her to be.

"Are you ready to dress now, my lady?" Hester asked with a bright smile on her face. No one at her father's house ever wore a bright smile on their face. Not even poor Martin. There wasn't much to smile about at Chadwick House.

Nodding, Georgie returned the smile and slid out of bed. Then she padded over to the vanity and sat upon a tufted stool. She stared at her reflection in the gilded looking glass. Apparently, this is what a countess looked like.

She bit her lip and smiled to herself at the thought as Hester combed out her hair and dressed her with deft, practiced hands, all the while chattering about how much she loved working in this house, how kind his lordship was to the staff, how well everyone was treated, how beautifully kept everything was.

Georgie tried to nod and smile in the right places, but she was still overwhelmed by the sensation of being…cared for.

It was utterly foreign.

At home she'd been ignored at best, berated at worst. Here she was being treated like a princess.

It was…disorienting.

More disorienting still was the long-neglected part of her that responded to it at once, as though she had been starved for such gentleness so long she hardly knew what to do when it was offered.

"We must hurry," Hester told her. "His lordship said he'd be up to collect you at nine."

"Nine," Georgie echoed, a flicker of unease stirring in her chest. "Whatever for?"

Unease—and curiosity. She wanted, rather desperately, to

see Jason's face in daylight. Wanted to know whether yesterday's wild, impulsive tenderness would survive the morning…or whether he had already begun to regret it. Whether he meant to look at her as a burden hastily acquired, or as a wife he had truly chosen.

"I'm not entirely certain, my lady, but I think he wants to show you the house."

Show her the house? Or show her her place in it? Very well, then. Georgie drew herself up. Whatever waited for her —welcome or regret, hope or disappointment—she would meet it head-on.

# CHAPTER TWENTY-NINE

Hester fussed with the last of the buttons on the pale pink day gown and stepped back, clearly pleased with her work. Georgie, however, stared at herself in the looking glass as if a stranger had taken her place.

Lady Pembroke.

The woman in the mirror certainly looked the part. Her gown was simple but exquisitely cut, the silk flowing over her figure in a way no gown ever had before. Clearly the work of a highly skilled modiste. Her hair—tamed by Hester's quick, competent hands—was coiled into an elegant chignon with a few soft curls left to frame her face.

It was the sort of reflection one might expect of a woman born into comfort and admiration. But Georgie felt only like an interloper in a life so unlike her former one that she scarcely knew how to inhabit it.

"Is it to your liking, my lady?" Hester asked, a touch of uncertainty in her tone.

Georgie swallowed. "It's...lovely," she managed. "You've done wonders."

Hester's smile returned in full force. "His lordship said you were not to want for anything," she offered. "He gave very clear instructions."

Of course he did.

Because this was what Jason did, apparently. He bought women out of wretched situations and then gave them things. Soft sheets, silk gowns, cheerful maids, and entire rooms that looked like they belonged to someone else.

The question was whether he meant her to be a true wife —or merely provide comfort until they both learned how to live inside the consequences of yesterday.

Georgie smoothed the skirt with damp palms. "Did he say anything else?" she heard herself ask, hating how eager she sounded.

Hester tilted her head, considering. "Only that you were to be treated with the utmost respect," she replied. "And that if anyone upset you, he would consider it a personal insult."

Georgie's throat tightened unexpectedly.

*Oh...my.*

Before she could decide what to do with the uncomfortable warmth spreading in her chest, a firm knock sounded at the bedchamber door.

Hester bobbed a curtsy. "That'll be his lordship," she said, far too knowingly. "Shall I show him in, my lady?"

No, Georgie's heart shrieked. Absolutely not. She was not ready to face the man she'd married while half-conscious. The man who'd spent twenty-five thousand pounds on her. The man who—

"Yes," her traitorous mouth said. "Of course."

Because hiding from him now would answer nothing. And Georgie found she wanted answers far more than she wanted shelter.

The door opened a moment later, and there he was.

Jason filled the doorway in a way no mere mortal had any

right to. Dark coat, crisp cravat, sunlight from the corridor catching in his hair and turning it a warm, burnished brown. His gaze flicked over her, quick and assessing, before he inclined his head.

"Lady Pembroke," he said.

It was ridiculous how her stomach flipped at the way he said it. As if the title belonged to her as naturally as it did to him.

"Lord Pembroke," she returned, grateful her voice didn't wobble.

Hester vanished with a discreet dip, shutting the door behind her and leaving Georgie alone with one very large, very unsettling husband.

For a moment, neither of them spoke.

Then Jason cleared his throat, shifting his weight and staring toward the wall as if he suddenly found the wallpaper of exceptional interest. "I came to see how you were faring," he said. "Hester had orders to fetch me if you attempted to escape out the window."

Georgie couldn't help the smile that popped to her lips. "Did she?"

"One can never be too careful," he replied, with perfect seriousness. "You have something of a reputation."

She lifted her nose in the air. "I do not have a reputation," she insisted. "I have...one incident."

His mouth curved ever so slightly. "An incident involving a second-story window and a runaway bride," he said.

Despite herself, a smile tugged at her lips. "I suppose you think you're terribly amusing."

"On the contrary," he said solemnly. "I've never been particularly amusing. Ask anyone."

Her smile escaped then, bright and uncontrollable. The answering flicker in his eyes told her he'd seen it.

Jason shifted again, as if remembering why he'd come. "If

you're feeling up to it," he began, "I thought perhaps I might give you a tour of the house. It occurs to me that you have been unceremoniously deposited into it with very little context."

Her fingers tightened in her skirts. A tour. Of *her* house. Not a prison, then. Not a gilded arrangement to be endured in separate corners. A house to be walked through, inhabited, perhaps even shared. The distinction mattered more than she cared to admit.

"Yes," she said, a bit too quickly. "I should like that. Thank you."

He offered his arm.

For a heartbeat, she hesitated. It was a perfectly ordinary gesture between a husband and wife. Proper. Expected. And yet the simple act of placing her hand on his sleeve felt momentous, like stepping onto a ship whose destination she did not know.

As she slid her fingers into the crook of his arm, she couldn't help but wonder if he felt as unsettled as she did. Surely, she wasn't the only one navigating the strange new shape of them.

His muscles tensed briefly under her touch before relaxing again. If she hadn't been so attuned to him, she might have missed it.

"This way," he said quietly.

They walked down the stairs together and into the first corridor. Jason paused in each room they passed, offering brief, wry commentary—the small morning room no one used, the formal drawing room his mother had preferred, the music room with its polished pianoforte.

"Do you play?" he asked as she ran her fingers lightly along the instrument's edge.

Georgie shook her head. "We didn't keep a pianoforte,"

she said simply. "They're expensive. And loud. Neither of which my parents care for."

His jaw worked, just once. "You're welcome to this one," he said. "Or another upstairs, if you prefer. I'm told some modish households have two."

"I wouldn't know what to do with one, let alone two," she said, attempting a jest. "I suppose I could stack them and escape from the second-story windows more efficiently."

He huffed a laugh, but his eyes were soft when he looked at her. "You shouldn't have to *know* what to do with them," he said quietly. "You should simply be allowed to…want things. Or not."

The words did more than soothe her. They sharpened her. If he truly meant that, then perhaps she *could* want more…a husband who had married her with open eyes, not merely honorable instincts.

She looked away under the pretense of examining the delicate inlay. Wanting things. It had never seemed like an option. Her life had been a series of obligations—be pleasant, be quiet, be grateful, be sold.

And now here Jason was, telling her she was allowed to want.

"Careful, my lord," she said lightly, though her voice wasn't quite steady. "If I grow accustomed to wanting, I may become greedy."

Something flickered in his expression, sincerity, unguarded and startling. "I don't believe that for a moment," he said.

The conviction in his tone hit her squarely. She smoothed her gown down her middle to hide the sudden tightness in her chest. "You do think well of me," she murmured. "Far more than I'm accustomed to."

He shook his head, not in dismissal but disbelief. "Anyone who ever met you should think well of you, Georgiana."

The quiet certainty of it—spoken like fact rather than flattery—caught her so off guard she forgot to breathe. Her throat tightened. She looked away for a moment, blinking against the sudden sting in her eyes.

When she lifted her gaze again, something inside her had shifted—something fragile and far too bold. The question escaped before she could stop it, barely above a whisper. "What do you see," she asked, "when you look at me?"

It was not vanity that prompted the question, nor insecurity. It was hunger—clean and sharp. If they were to share a name, a house, a bed perhaps, she meant to know whether he saw merely the woman he had rescued or the wife he had actually chosen.

His throat worked. He considered her briefly before biting his lip. "I see a woman who climbed out a window because no one listened when she said no," he said slowly. "I see a woman who refused to be auctioned off, even when it meant an uncertain future. I see a woman who laughs in the face of pain and won't be controlled. In short, I see someone extraordinary."

They were standing closer than she'd realized. The air between them felt suddenly thick, charged with something that had nothing to do with house tours or pianofortes.

His gaze dropped briefly to her mouth before snapping back to her eyes.

Georgie's heart pounded.

He wasn't going to kiss her. They were in his music room, for heaven's sake, with servants somewhere nearby and the door half-open. Even though they were husband and wife, he was far too honorable, far too controlled—

His hand lifted, fingers brushing a wisp of hair at her temple.

"A curl," he said, his voice a little rough. "Hester left a mutinous one."

"It's recalcitrant," she whispered.

"So I see."

His fingers lingered a fraction too long, the barest graze of knuckles against the delicate skin at her temple sending a shiver down her spine.

Somewhere in the corridor, a door banged.

Jason stepped back as though burned, dropping his hand to his side. His expression closed, polite and distant once more.

"Come," he said, clearing his throat. "I've yet to show you the library. It would be irresponsible of me not to introduce Lady Pembroke to the only truly respectable room in the house."

"Only one?" she managed, forcing her lips into a wobbly smile as she took his arm again.

"Oh, yes," he said gravely as they stepped into the hall. "You should see the card room. Positively debauched. Books are its only redeeming feature."

His tone was teasing, but as they walked on, Georgie felt the echo of his touch at her forehead and the weight of his words settled, warm and terrifying, in her chest.

*Anyone who ever met you should have thought well of you.*

Her family. That's who he meant.

She was not yet fool enough to mistake admiration for love, or kindness for certainty. But as they stepped into the library together, Georgie knew one thing with painful clarity: she wanted this marriage to become something real, and she wanted Jason to want that too.

# CHAPTER THIRTY

The library was magnificent. The card room not nearly as debauched as she'd been promised. But the dining room was somehow even grander than her bedchamber.

The walls were painted a warm ivory with gilded molding, and tall windows lined one side of the room, spilling sunlight over the gleaming table.

A glittering chandelier sparkled above her head, and the mahogany sideboard was stacked with shining silver platters and fine china.

Fresh flowers—white roses and lilacs—stood in a tall vase at the center of the table, and everything spoke of quiet, understated wealth.

After their tour, Jason had deposited her back at her bedchamber and asked her to meet him here for breakfast at half past.

And there he stood, at the entrance to the room, still looking unfairly composed and devastating in his dark coat and perfectly tied cravat.

"Good morning, Lady Pembroke," he said politely,

inclining his head. The hint of a smile played around his firmly molded lips.

Ooh. The title again (and the way he said it) sent a strange little twist through her stomach. That was the third time she'd been called Lady Pembroke today. She had best begin to get used to it.

"Good morning," she murmured, taking the chair opposite *her husband* as he pulled it out for her.

He took his own seat as a footman poured her tea and set a selection of eggs, toast, fruit, and pastries in front of her.

She glanced intermittently at Jason as the quiet clink of silverware filled the silence between them.

She nibbled at her toast, painfully aware of how elegant and handsome he looked across the table—and how awkward she felt in her own skin. And for the first time, she began to think about—*truly think about*—everything that had taken place yesterday.

How, precisely, had she ended up here, nibbling on this toast?

Because she had chosen, however hastily, however wearily, and she would not insult herself now by pretending otherwise. The better question was what, exactly, she had chosen.

First, there was the undeniable fact that Jason was handsome. He always had been. Is *that* why she'd said yes to him yesterday? Her attraction to him? It had been nearly irresistible after all. Him yelling "enough" to quiet her family, him offering an ungodly sum of money to get her father to agree, him making all of them leave and demanding that she be the one to decide. While all the while, he'd looked unbearably gorgeous and the memory of his kisses had played through her mind as if they were on a roundtable.

Then there was the simple case he'd made... *"I can't possibly be worse than Henderville,"* he'd said. Beyond an understatement, of course, but perfectly true. Yesterday, it had made quite a lot of sense to her frightened, tired, frantic mind.

But there was more, wasn't there? Additional reasons. Reasons about being a countess instead of being a lady's companion. Reasons involving remembering their tour of the museum, their private waltz, and their unforgettable kisses. Other reasons she couldn't think of at the moment. But valid ones, just the same. She bent her head and concentrated on pretending to eat her food.

She had not said yes merely to a handsome face or a dramatic rescue. She had said yes because Jason listened, because he had put the choice into her hands when no one else would, and because some optimistic part of her had wanted to believe a life with him might be more than tolerable. It might even, in time, be good.

Hope. She had said yes because of hope.

After a while, Jason cleared his throat, setting down his fork. "I thought," he began carefully, "that you might like to redecorate one of the wings of the house."

Her head came up, startled. "I beg your pardon?"

"This place has more rooms than I know what to do with," he continued evenly. "You may choose whichever wing you like and make it entirely your own. New wallpaper, furnishings—anything."

Georgie went still. It was not an unkind offer. Quite the opposite. But it sounded perilously like distance wrapped in generosity.

She forced a polite smile. "How…generous of you," she murmured.

He tilted his head slightly, looking a bit puzzled by her tone, but said nothing. Instead, he returned to his meal.

Georgie set her teacup down with great care.

So that was the shape of it, then. Not rejection. Not indifference. Something more complicated—and, in its own way, more inscrutable. Jason meant to be generous. To be considerate. To make room for her, quite literally, in his house.

But was he making room for her in his life?

That was the question that tightened suddenly in her chest. Not whether he thought well of her—she knew he did. Not whether he desired her—she knew that too. But whether, having married her in haste, he meant this to become a real marriage or merely a very comfortable kindness.

Georgie had not fled one bargain only to drift blindly into another, softer one.

Very well. If he was offering space, she would take it—but on her own terms. Not as a woman put gently aside, but as one giving herself time to understand the man she had married before yielding anything more.

"I'd like my own room," she said, her voice firmer than she expected.

Not forever, perhaps. Not if this marriage proved capable of becoming something warmer, truer, and chosen by both of them. But for now, yes. She wanted a room of her own and the dignity of not pretending certainty she did not yet feel.

Jason's brow furrowed faintly. "Of course," he said after a moment.

For just an instant—the briefest flicker—she thought she saw something in his eyes. Not relief. Not polite agreement. Something sharper. Something that looked very much like he had hoped she would ask for something else.

And then it was gone, hidden behind his usual unflappable composure.

He rose, folding his napkin with quiet precision. "I'll see to it immediately."

Of course he would. Jason was very good at doing. Solving. Providing. The trouble was that Georgie no longer wanted only solutions from him. She wanted truth.

She watched him go, leaving her alone at the table, staring down at the delicate roses in the vase. Her heart beating double-time in her chest.

She refused to believe that she'd made a mistake in marrying him. But she had stepped into something far more complicated than rescue, or a simple flight from a ballroom, and now she would have to discover whether Jason Pemberton meant to be merely a generous husband...or truly hers.

# CHAPTER THIRTY-ONE

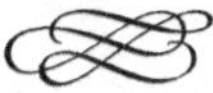

The faint rasp of steel on steel filled the air, sharp and rhythmic.

Jason lunged, the point of his foil striking the burlap sack dead center.

*Thrust, recover. Thrust, parry, recover. En garde. Riposte. Again.*

The fencing room was quiet, save for the scrape of his boots on the polished floor and the faint creak of the leather grip in his hand.

Sunlight filtered through high, narrow windows, catching motes of dust that swirled lazily in the air. The room smelled faintly of wax and wood.

Against the far wall hung an assortment of blades—foils, sabers, epees—gleaming in their racks. Two burlaps sacks made to resemble opponents stood in one corner, padded and scarred from years of practice, and the floor was lined with marks to measure proper distance for lunges and retreats.

He adjusted his grip and lunged again, driving the point

of the foil into the straw-stuffed sack hanging from the ceiling.

*Point. Recover. Riposte.*

He should have felt better. Fencing always calmed him. It was clean, precise. A contest of skill and focus.

But this morning, every move felt heavy. Every thrust felt off.

He dropped the foil to his side, raking a hand through his hair and glaring at the poor sack as though it were to blame.

Georgiana.

He couldn't stop thinking about her.

She'd been so...*cool* at breakfast. She'd barely smiled. Polite, yes...but distant. And that request for her own room...

What had *that* been about?

She wasn't frightened of him. He knew that. She wasn't disgusted either. Far from it. It was something more measured than that, and far harder to fight. She had looked like a woman drawing a line and waiting to see whether he would honor it.

Fair enough. She had married him in confusion and woken to a life neither of them had properly named. If she was keeping her distance until she understood what sort of husband he meant to be, he could hardly blame her.

He closed his eyes, groaning softly.

He'd thought—foolishly, it seemed now—that suggesting she redecorate one of the wings would make her happy.

His mother adored decorating. She'd spent years fussing over wallpapers and draperies, thrilled to make the house her own.

Wouldn't Georgiana want the same?

He shook his head. Georgiana was not his mother, and this was not some cheerful bride's first triumph over curtains. She had not asked for wallpaper. She had asked, in her own way, what sort of husband he meant to be.

He set his feet again and lunged hard, the foil biting deep into the straw.

Or had she simply understood something he had been too clumsy to name—that offering her a suite of rooms was not the same as offering her a place in his life?

He pictured her at the breakfast table, her lashes lowered, her hands delicate and still against the porcelain. Her eyes had met his only once, and even then they'd been unreadable. Not empty. Not cold. Merely watchful, as though she were weighing him still—his words, his silences, the shape of the marriage he had thrust upon them both.

Did she think him merely generous? Merely honorable? The thought sat worse in him than outright resentment might have.

He pulled back and struck again, harder this time, the foil tearing a small hole in the burlap.

She would be a fool not to mistrust the shape of it. She had been cornered, and he had intervened with all the subtlety of a cavalry charge. He had given her a choice, but only after narrowing the field with his own hands.

And now, having married her after the debacle that was yesterday, he was behaving like a man who could solve discomfort with rooms and furnishings and good intentions. No wonder she had looked at him so carefully across the breakfast table.

He dropped the foil entirely, bracing his hands on his knees as his breath came heavier.

He didn't want her to feel cornered. He didn't want her to feel obligated. The realization hit him like a blade to his chest. *He wanted her to want him.*

Not because he required admiration to soothe his vanity, but because anything less would begin to look too much like the kind of marriage he had spent half his life despising: duty without joy, proximity without choice. And he couldn't bear to share that sort of life with Georgiana.

Not merely because she was beautiful, though she was. Not merely because he desired her, though God knew he did. He wanted her laughter at his table, her opinions in his rooms, her hand in his sleeve because she chose to place it there. He wanted her as a wife in every way that mattered, and the knowledge of it left him peculiarly winded.

And that was precisely what made the whole business so damned complicated. His father had once wanted his mother too—ardently, sincerely, enough to marry her with every confidence in the world. Look how that had ended. Years of discord. Resentment. A household thick with strain. Jason had spent most of his life promising himself he would never build such a marriage for anyone, least of all a woman as brave and courageous as Georgiana.

But he'd already made mistakes, hadn't he? He had given her every reason to believe that duty stood at the center of their marriage. He had spoken of attraction like a fool, marriage like a practical necessity, and safety as though it were enough. All true, perhaps. But not the whole truth. Not even close.

But what in God's name was he supposed to do about it? March into her room and announce, after one frantic day and a wedding conducted at dawn, that he wanted more than duty from her? That he had begun to want her in earnest, inconveniently, perhaps irrevocably? He would sound like a lunatic. Worse—he would sound like a man trying to dress up obligation in prettier clothes.

No. Georgiana deserved better than some breathless declaration made in the smoking wreckage of scandal. She deserved time. Clarity. A courtship of sorts, however backward the order of things had become. She deserved tender care, not some hasty claim laid over scandal.

He straightened slowly, wiping a sheen of sweat from his forehead.

If she didn't want him in her bed…well then, so be it. The bed was the least of it. Tempting, yes. Difficult to stop thinking about, certainly. But what he wanted now was more difficult and far more complicated than physical ease. He wanted her trust before her surrender, her willingness before her warmth.

He walked to the wall and carefully replaced the foil in its rack.

The fencing room felt colder now, the silence heavier.

He had wanted to save her from Henderville. True. But somewhere between the first argument, the first dance, and the first kiss, that had ceased to be the whole of it. He did not merely want her safe. He wanted her near. Wanted her laughing in his house, choosing him in the daylight, coming to him because she wished to and not because circumstance had cornered her there.

And that meant the next move could not be his alone. Georgiana had been given too little choice for too long. He would not be another man deciding her life for her, however noble his intentions. From this moment on, he would give her all the time and space she required to come to terms with their marriage.

Moving forward, it would be her choice. Always.

# CHAPTER THIRTY-TWO

Georgie stood in the center of the formal Pembroke drawing room, twisting her hands together and trying quite hard to look composed.

The room was perfectly elegant, with tall windows draped in pale green silk, a gleaming rosewood escritoire tucked into the corner, delicate French chairs upholstered in cream damask, and a chandelier dripping with crystal.

The air smelled faintly of fresh flowers, and the silver tea service gleamed on the low table in front of the settee.

She'd seen grand houses before. She was a member of the *ton*, after all, but *this* was another thing entirely. Why, this was as grand as Bea's father's house.

But despite her gilded surroundings, all Georgie could think about was whether she'd made a mistake asking for her own room this morning at breakfast. Not because she regretted drawing the boundary. She did not. But because she still could not tell whether Jason had understood it as caution, rejection, or a simple request for time.

It had seemed the obvious thing to do after he'd offered her a whole wing to make her own. Space. Privacy. Comfort.

All generous things. But generous was not the same as intimate, and that was the trouble. She still did not know whether he meant to fold her fully into his life or simply make her comfortable at its edges.

But Georgie refused to invent humiliations before they arrived. She did not know yet what sort of husband Jason intended to be. She only knew she would rather discover the truth clearly than drift into false ease.

The question now was not whether she could undo yesterday. She could not. The question was what she meant to do with today. She'd worry about her room and the wing she lived in later. At the moment, she was waiting for someone. Two someones, actually. If she could not yet make sense of her husband, she could at least begin by gathering her allies.

She smoothed her skirts and checked the tea tray one last time, as though it might somehow help her feel more settled. She chastised herself for being silly. She had spoken the vows and signed the register. If she was Lady Pembroke, then she had better begin acting like it.

She'd already written her friend, Martha, a letter and had it dispatched to Bath posthaste. No doubt it had been an inadequate missive. And certainly one that would confuse her poor friend with its contents. But Georgie had shared the relevant facts, namely that she'd married Jason instead of escaping Lord Henderville and would write to explain more at her earliest opportunity.

It would just have to be enough…for now. Oh dear, what Martha would think when she read it. Indeed, what the entire *ton* was thinking right now. She couldn't even guess. Instead, she resumed her hand twisting.

She hadn't waited five minutes longer before the door opened, and a well-dressed footman announced, "Lady Beatrix Winslow and Miss Poppy Montfort."

Georgie briefly closed her eyes. Oh, thank heavens both of them had made it. She expelled her breath with relief as her two friends swept into the room.

Bea looked as composed and regal as ever in a bright green walking dress, while Poppy practically bounced with excitement, her coppery-red hair a fiery halo under her yellow bonnet.

"My dears," Georgie said warmly, rushing forward to greet them.

They embraced her in turn before settling themselves on the settee, their eyes already darting around the room with unconcealed curiosity.

As usual, Poppy was the first to speak.

"Well," she breathed, "I must say...*this* is very fine. I could scarcely believe it when I got your note this morning."

Bea arched a brow. "Indeed," she said coolly. "When you wrote to request we visit you at *Pembroke House*, I was quite certain you'd made a mistake. Or perhaps you'd fallen out of the coach and experienced an injury to your head during your flight."

Georgie flushed faintly as she poured tea. "Yes, well. I nearly thought so myself."

Once the tea was served, Bea fixed her with a penetrating gaze. "Well? Out with it. How did this happen? The last we saw of you, you were rushing from the church in your wedding gown. And now here you sit—*married*. To an entirely different man."

Poppy leaned forward eagerly. "Yes," she said, picking up her cup. "Do tell."

Georgie spent the next half hour recounting the details of what had happened since she'd last seen her friends. She told it as evenly as she could, though saying it aloud made the shape of it stranger: flight, pursuit, bargaining, vows. A life overturned in less than a day. And still, beneath all the madness, the same question remained. What had Jason actually meant when he chose her?

"Well," Bea began, "so much for the first volley of the Wallflowers' Revolt."

"Yes, but you have to admit, Georgie," Poppy added, "it's rather romantic, the way Lord Pembroke swept you up on the horse like that. It's practically a fairy tale."

Bea snorted. "Nonsense. Pembroke shouldn't have put his nose where it didn't belong. No one asked him to interfere."

Georgie did not answer at once. Bea was not wrong. And yet neither was that the whole of it any longer. She opened her mouth to reply but was interrupted by the faint sound of a throat clearing behind her.

Her stomach dropped as she turned to see Jason standing just inside the doorway, his green eyes inscrutable.

Oh, no.

How much had he heard?

He inclined his head to the ladies with impeccable courtesy. "My apologies," he said smoothly. "I don't mean to interrupt."

Poppy's cheeks pinkened, while Bea met his gaze without flinching.

Jason's mouth quirked faintly, though it was impossible to tell if it was amusement or something else. "I simply wished to let Lady Pembroke know," he continued, his eyes flicking to Georgie, "that I took the liberty of arranging for Madame Duval to come by within the hour to see to her new wardrobe."

There it was again, Jason doing things for her with effortless decisiveness, as though provision came naturally to him. The difficulty was that Georgie no longer wanted only provision. She wanted to know what place she occupied in his heart, not merely in his household accounts.

Georgie froze. "Oh, that won't be necessary—" she began,

already shaking her head. Madame Duval was the most expensive, most sought-after modiste in town.

But Bea cut her off briskly. "Lady Pembroke shall be ready at the allotted time," she declared.

Jason's brows rose faintly, and one corner of his mouth curved just slightly before he bowed again. "Very good," he murmured. "I'll leave you ladies to your visit."

As soon as the door closed behind him, Poppy let out a low whistle. "Is he real?" she demanded.

Bea huffed softly. "I suppose he *is*, though I still maintain he oughtn't have meddled. And you deserve a new wardrobe, Georgie. It's no more than his duty to provide it."

Duty. There was that wretched word again. Useful, respectable, impossible to build a marriage upon by itself.

Poppy nudged Georgie with her elbow. "All I'm saying is —revolt or not, if my husband looked like that and hired Madame Duval to dress me, I wouldn't argue."

Georgie flushed hotly and stared into her tea, feeling more overwhelmed than ever...and more aware of Jason than she cared to admit.

But she could not agree with Poppy either. This was neither fairy tale nor nightmare—at least not yet. It was something far more precarious: the beginning of a marriage she very much wanted to understand before she dared to trust it.

# CHAPTER THIRTY-THREE

Georgie stared at herself in the long gilt-edged mirror the footmen had delivered to the salon shortly after Bea and Poppy left. She barely recognized the woman reflected back.

Madame Duval, a whirlwind of French-accented flattery and swishing silk skirts, fussed with the final fastening on the bodice and stepped back with a satisfied nod.

"There," she announced triumphantly. "You see? *Magnifique.* A true lady of zee *ton.* You are a countess now, no?"

Georgie blinked at the vision before her, the shimmering gold gown, cut to perfection, the delicate lace at her bodice, the way the fabric caught the light and made her eyes look… almost luminous.

She swallowed hard.

It was…beautiful.

Far more beautiful than anything she'd ever worn in her life, and that was awkward enough without the inconvenient twist of pleasure it gave her. Jason had thought of this. Anticipated it, even. Which was kind. Generous. Thoughtful.

But kindness still was not clarity. A husband might provide gowns out of duty just as easily as out of devotion. Georgie ran her fingertips over the fine silk and admitted, with some irritation, that she didn't want only his provision. She wanted to know what, exactly, she was to him.

"Now," Madame Duval continued briskly, "zee evening gowns will arrive later zis week, and zee walking dresses zee week after. I've left you a few specials pieces to wear until then. But you must tell me if you have preferences. Embroidery? Beading? Colors? You have an excellent figure. We must show it off. You'll come to zee shop soon, *oui*? And see everything."

Georgie flushed at that and murmured something noncommittal, but Madame Duval seemed to take it as agreement and launched into a torrent of instructions to her assistants.

Once the bustle of measuring, pinning, and adjusting finally subsided, Georgie found herself once again alone in the drawing room, the soft sheen of the new gown still clinging to her skin.

She sat down on the edge of the settee, her fingers smoothing over the fabric almost absently.

Once more, she had the thought that it *had* been kind of Jason to arrange this.

It was terribly *unkind* of her to believe he had only done it out of obligation. After all, she'd already been dreading facing the *ton* again with nothing but her tired, outdated gowns…and the little matter of her *scandal*.

And Jason had thought of it without her even asking.

Her throat tightened at the thought.

He was not the arrogant, interfering brute Bea claimed him to be. Nor was he simple to account for. Jason did not behave like a man indifferent to his wife. She needed to come out and ask him. She knew she did. But that thought frightened her more than leaving it to unfold. Because what if he said he *had* only married her to 'save' her. What if he didn't want a real wife…or a real marriage?

A faint rustle drew her gaze toward the door. The footman entered, carrying a silver tray. "Forgive me, my lady," he said, bowing. "The afternoon's paper—as requested."

She startled slightly, then nodded, her fingers curling against her lap. She had asked for it to be brought to her the moment it arrived—could hardly help herself. She needed to know what had been said. What London was already whispering about her wedding.

The footman set the folded newspaper on the table and withdrew.

The moment he'd shut the door behind him, she nearly launched herself at the paper, her pulse quickening. There had to be *something* in it—some speculation, some cruel amusement. The rumors would be rampant by now. And curiously, there had been nothing in the morning's paper.

She quickly scanned the headlines, the usual prattle about Parliament, the latest military news, an announcement of the Duchess of Dunworthy's ball.

But then her gaze froze on a smaller column halfway down the Society page.

*An Unexpected Union: Lord Pembroke's Hasty Nuptials.*

Her stomach dropped. There it was.

She scanned the text, her cheeks growing hotter with every line.

*Last evening, in a quiet and private ceremony, Lord Pembroke —long regarded as one of London's most eligible bachelors—wed Lady Georgiana Chadwick in what can only be described as a sudden and unexpected match. Particularly because the bride had been set to marry Lord Henderville that same morning. This author has it on good authority that Lord Pembroke is said to have acted with admirable haste to rescue the lady from further scandal after she attempted to run off from her own wedding. Lord Pembroke is known to be a close friend of Lady Georgiana's brother and one wonders if the marriage was completed in haste in order to save the young woman from her own recklessness. No doubt whispers shall continue to abound as to the true circumstances of this precipitous marriage...*

The blood drained from Georgiana's face.

*Rescue her from further scandal? Save the young woman from her own recklessness?*

Her fingers tightened on the page. So that was the version of the story already racing through town…Jason the dutiful gentleman, Georgiana the heedless girl he had scooped up before she could ruin herself entirely.

It was the worst possible interpretation of what had happened. Jason had been painted as a martyr doing a favor for a friend, while Georgiana was made to look like a fool who would marry any man who'd have her.

And what possible "good authority" could have provided such rubbish to the newspaper? Surely, her family wouldn't have provided such damning material? They didn't wish to look foolish either. It had to have been Lord Henderville. Or someone near enough to him to know exactly where the knife would slide in. It was not the scandal itself that stung most. It was the shape of it. The story stripped her of every ounce of will and made Jason's choice look like charity.

She quickly re-read the article and winced. Ugh. It sounded worse the second time. The whole thing made her out to be some silly waif plucked from ruin, grateful to be saved by her magnanimous new husband, who was simply doing her family a favor.

Which didn't help her own uncertainty one whit.

Georgie dropped the paper back onto the table, the words blurring before her eyes.

So this was how Society would prefer to see her? Not as a

woman who had refused one fate and chosen another, however hastily. Not as a countess newly installed in Pembroke House. But as a foolish young woman passed from one man's hands to another's.

She lifted her chin sharply, her chest tight.

Well. So be it. If they thought she would hide in shame from them, they would be in for a surprise.

She blew out her breath and straightened her shoulders. She would not be pitied. Not by Society. Not by Jason.

And most certainly not by herself.

Let them whisper. Let them decide Lord Pembroke had rescued her if that made the tale tidier. Georgie knew better. She had made a choice in that upstairs room, and if the marriage that followed was to mean anything, it would begin tonight…with her.

She would not hide. She would not let the *ton* mistake silence for meek gratitude. If Jason meant this marriage to be real, he would find her ready to meet him in it. And if he did not, then she would still be Lady Pembroke with her head held high.

# CHAPTER THIRTY-FOUR

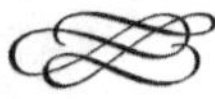

The study was quiet, save for the faint tick of the clock on the mantel and the low crackle of the fire in the grate.

Jason sat behind his oak desk, leaning back in the leather chair that had molded to him over years of late nights, the weight of the room pressing in around him.

It was a comforting space. Dark wood paneling, books lining every wall, the rich scent of old leather and beeswax mingling with the faint smokiness from the hearth. The warmth should have been reassuring. Once, it had been.

Tonight, it felt like a cage.

His glass of brandy sat on the blotter before him, untouched. He'd poured it when he'd come in, thinking it might dull the restless energy coursing through him, but instead it sat there, catching the firelight like amber, mocking him.

He stared at it a moment longer before dragging his hand down his face, exhaling hard through his nose.

Lady Beatrix's voice still rang in his ears, sharper than the foil he'd driven into the straw dummy earlier.

*Pembroke shouldn't have put his nose where it didn't belong. No one asked him to interfere.*

It hadn't even been said to him. That was the worst of it. She hadn't known he was standing in the doorway. That made it all the more cutting.

No one *had* asked him to interfere. That much was true. But the uglier truth was that he had interfered because he couldn't bear not to—and had never once stopped to ask whether desire and righteousness were becoming too entangled to separate cleanly.

And now Georgiana was his wife. Not unwilling, exactly. But wary. Careful. As well she should be.

He rubbed his temple and leaned forward, elbows braced on the desk, feeling the familiar ache beginning at the base of his skull.

He'd spent the entire night imagining what their marriage might become if given half a chance. He may not have been searching for a wife, but that didn't mean he didn't want one—or children, for that matter. It was simply that his past had left him too wary to even try. But with Georgiana…it was different. It seemed as if they might actually stand a chance. She made him feel as if he might have the courage for it after all.

His past had also taught him something else…that wanting to protect someone could become its own kind of ruin.

He pushed the glass of brandy aside and reached for the small velvet case in the top drawer. His fingers hovered over it for a moment before he finally opened it.

Inside, nestled against the dark velvet lining, was the miniature of Evelyn.

His breath hitched despite himself, the familiar pang of grief and guilt slicing through him.

His sister's young face gazed back at him from the

painted ivory—her dark hair curled loosely at her nape, her cheeks flushed with life, her green eyes bright with laughter. Even though she'd been barely seven when the artist had captured her likeness, the sight of her never failed to twist something inside him.

He remembered the day as though it had been yesterday.

He'd been meant to watch her—just for a few hours, while their parents visited with neighbors. He'd promised them he would look after her.

He'd promised.

And yet…

He closed the case with a quiet snap and pressed the heels of his palms to his eyes.

He had been trying to save her ever since.

Every reckless duel, every ill-advised wager he'd interrupted, every woman he'd tried to protect from some fortune hunter's designs—all of it, in some irrational corner of his mind, had been for Evelyn.

And now he'd gone and done it again.

Only this time it was worse, because Georgiana was no abstraction. No convenient object for atonement. She was sharp, living, entirely real—and he had married her before fully disentangling what he felt for her from the old compulsion to prevent disaster.

He thought of Georgiana, the way her eyes had narrowed at him this morning when he'd dared suggest she take over a wing of the house, the stiffness in her spine as she'd asked for her own room.

She was wary of him…of his motives…and she had every right to be.

He shoved the velvet case back in the drawer and stared unseeingly at the far wall, trying to quiet the churn in his chest.

He reached for the brandy out of habit and caught sight

of the newspaper lying half-buried under a sheaf of letters on the edge of his desk.

He pulled it closer and flattened it with his palm, his eyes automatically scanning the headlines.

At first he thought nothing of it, the usual prattle about politics and duels and the Duke of Denly's latest folly.

But then his gaze fell to it. The largest column in the Society section. Of course it was about them.

*An Unexpected Union: Lord Pembroke's Hasty Nuptials.*

He stilled.

The words swam into focus. He read them quickly, his gaze sliding over them as if he could erase them as they went.

The brandy glass tilted in his hand, and he set it down with a dull clink before he crushed the newspaper in his fist.

*To rescue the lady from further scandal! To save the young woman from her own recklessness!*

It was not merely false. It was insulting. To Georgiana most of all. The article stripped her of her will, her courage, her choice—and cast him, yet again, as the very sort of grand male savior he was beginning to loathe in himself.

Who in God's name had authorized *this* version of events? He'd gone himself to the publisher yesterday afternoon— slipped the man an obscene sum—to guarantee the paper reported a version of events more favorable to her...that he had pursued her because he could not bear to lose her to Henderville. Overblown, perhaps. Embarrassingly romantic, certainly. But infinitely preferable to *this*.

His gaze snagged then on one of the folded notes half-hidden beneath the rest of the correspondence. He recognized the hand at once and felt his jaw tighten before he had even broken the familiar seal.

*Jason—*

*I have seen the papers. You have acted in haste, exactly as I always feared you would, and you will regret it. One day, when this ill-considered marriage has made you miserable, do not say I did not try to warn you.*

He did not read it twice.

With a sound of disgust low in his throat, he crumpled his mother's note in his fist and tossed it into the fire. It caught at once, the edges blackening, the script curling in on itself before vanishing into ash.

To hell with her. If he had any say in the matter, Georgiana would never be subjected to his mother's company.

And now, he realized, he had failed in two directions at once. He had not warned Georgiana of his attempt, and the paper had made her sound like some fragile little creature in need of saving.

It was the precise opposite of what she'd wanted… What she'd specifically asked of him, even. *"I don't want you to save me. And I certainly don't want the* ton *to think you married me to save me."* That was literally all she'd asked of him when she'd agreed to marry him. After standing in that window with fire in her eyes, threatening to jump rather than let them drag her back to Henderville.

He'd promised her, damn him. And this—this was precisely the sort of failure she had every right to remember.

If he meant to win her trust, he would have to do better than rescue, better than provision, better even than apology.

He would have to show her, patiently and in full daylight, that he saw the woman she actually was—and meant to be a husband equal to her.

Georgie stood outside the closed door to Jason's study, her knuckles hovering just above the polished wood.

On second thought, she didn't bother with the polite knock. Instead, she pushed the door open.

He was there, sitting behind the massive desk, as she suspected he would be, jacket removed, sleeves rolled, a single candle and the hearth casting long shadows around him. He looked up, startled, and his eyes sharpened the instant they saw her.

"Have you seen it?" she asked, her voice even but low.

His gaze didn't waver. But anger was etched on his features. Anger and…regret? "Yes," he said simply.

She nodded once, stepped farther inside, and folded her arms over her chest. "Good. Then we both know."

Not merely what the paper had printed, but what it meant if left unanswered. People would believe the story because it was easy. Georgie had no intention of making ease of it for them.

The silence between them was thick, the sound of the fire popping in the grate far too loud in her ears.

"Georgiana, I—"

"No." Her hand shot up. "No apologies just now. No pity either. I only came to tell you I'll be ready to leave for the Hartleys' ball at nine."

His brow furrowed. "You wish to go out tonight? After that?" He gestured vaguely to the newspaper crumpled on the corner of his desk. As though the thought of exposing her to such company pained him—which, for some reason, made it harder rather than easier to hold her ground.

She lifted her chin, summoning every ounce of the composure she'd never learned from her mother. "The only thing worse than gossip," she said coolly, "is hiding from it. I am not some fragile creature to be hidden away until the whispers die. And I will not begin my life as Lady Pembroke by letting Society decide I have something to be ashamed of."

A faint smile curved his mouth, not mocking but something almost…proud. "You're right," he murmured, inclining his head. The look unsettled her more than argument would have. It was one thing to be opposed. Quite another to be seen—and approved of—by the man whose opinion had begun to matter far too much.

She swallowed hard, turned on her heel, and left before he could see how badly her hands were shaking.

ONE HOUR LATER, Jason stood beside his new wife as they entered the Hartleys' ballroom, and for the first time all evening, he could breathe. Not because the worst was over. Quite the opposite. But because Georgiana had chosen to face the scrutiny head on, and seeing her do so made him understand afresh that whatever else she was, she was never someone to be quietly managed. Or underestimated.

Georgiana was radiant.

Not in some overdone way, but quiet and devastating, her dark hair gleaming under the chandeliers, her head held high as if the venomous whispers in the corners didn't touch her at all.

Which, of course, they did. But she didn't let it show. And damn if he wasn't proud of her. Proud—and something deeper than pride. The kind of admiration that made a man ache to deserve the woman walking beside him.

Her gown—new and worthy of a countess—was a masterpiece of deep sapphire silk that hugged her slender waist before spilling into a sweep of skirts edged in delicate silver embroidery. The off-the-shoulder neckline framed her collarbones with understated allure, while a scattering of seed pearls at the bodice caught the light like a constellation. A matching ribbon encircled her throat, and her gloved hands rested with perfect poise at her sides. Madame Duval had outdone herself. He would be sure to pay her handsomely.

Georgiana paused at the top of the marble stairs, long enough to scan the room. Then she descended with measured grace, her skirts gliding over the steps like water.

They entered the crush, and though Jason could sense the gazes following them, the speculative murmurs, the lifted fans, the envious smirks, Georgiana kept her chin aloft, her mouth soft but resolute.

He wanted to reach out and take her hand. Just to steady her. But he didn't.

Instead, he walked by her side as they moved through the crowd. That was the trick of allowing her the choice. Not offering comfort she had not asked for. Not assuming. But staying near enough to be chosen, if she wished it, and no nearer.

Lady Beatrix and Miss Montfort materialized near the refreshment table in a flurry of silk and fan-fluttering.

"Look at you, Georgie," Miss Montfort gasped, clapping her hands together. "You're perfect."

Georgie? Was that what her friends called her? Jason smiled. It suited her.

Lady Beatrix gave Jason a pointed glare before turning to Georgiana.

"Good evening, Lady Pembroke," she said smoothly. "Your husband does know he's the most fortunate man alive, does he not?"

He was just about to say, "Of course he does," when Georgiana gave a small laugh and murmured something he couldn't hear before turning to him and excusing herself politely.

He let her go. He had no intention of doing anything other than whatever she wished tonight. She disappeared into the throng with her friends at either elbow, their heads bent together conspiratorially.

If she wanted distance, he would give it. If she wanted his arm later, he would be there. For perhaps the first time in his life, restraint felt less like self-denial than courtship. A courtship that was entirely hers to define. She already had too many choices taken away from her in life.

Jason let out a slow breath and angled toward the card room, where a knot of his acquaintances had already gathered. Best to get it over with—the inevitable barrage of questions and overly familiar remarks.

It didn't take long before Lord Weedham approached him. The man was tall and thin, with an expression just insolent enough to set Jason's teeth on edge.

"Pembroke," Weedham drawled, swirling his brandy.

"You've gone and astonished us all, you know. Marrying that Chadwick chit."

Jason's shoulders stiffened, his blood turning to ice.

"She's quite pretty," the man continued, as though that explained anything. "But...with no dowry? And all that scandal? God knows you could have done a sight better. Suppose you always have been one to martyr yourself for friendship. I say, Chadwick owes you one this time, old chap."

There it was again—the same filthy story in a different mouth. Georgiana diminished, Jason ennobled, as though the marriage made sense only if she were a burden and he a saint.

Jason set his glass down very, very carefully. Then he turned to Weedham fully, his voice calm but cutting. "The papers," he began, "are wrong. I married Georgiana because I wanted to. And if anyone here thinks I would marry for any other reason, they have sorely misjudged my character. Is that clear?"

The words came out harsher than he intended, but no less true for that. For once, bluntness served him better than caution.

Weedham swallowed and nodded. "Yes," he said in a reedy voice.

"Good. Now, if I ever hear another word—from you or anyone else—disparaging *my wife*, I will see you at dawn on the field, pistols in hand. Do you understand me?"

Weedham blinked, paling slightly. "Pembroke— I—"

Jason's mouth curved into a humorless smile. "I assure you," he continued, his tone smooth as silk, "that's not a threat. It's a promise." He glanced around at the other men, who all had the sense to look away.

Weedham muttered something unintelligible and backed away, disappearing from the room.

Jason turned on his heel to leave.

And stopped short.

Georgiana stood not ten paces away, just outside the door. Not hidden, exactly. Not eavesdropping. Simply there —as though fate, having found him clumsy in private, had decided he might speak truly only by accident in public.

Her lips were parted, her eyes shining not with anger but with something he couldn't quite name...soft, wet, and unguarded.

She'd heard. Every word.

And she was looking at him now not with simple gratitude or startled awe, but with a new, searching steadiness— as though some piece of him had just shifted into view, and she meant to consider it quite carefully.

# CHAPTER THIRTY-SIX

The ballroom had become too warm.

Heat prickled at the nape of Georgie's neck and the candlelight in the chandeliers blurred ever so slightly as she stood frozen outside the door to the card room, her breath trapped somewhere between her chest and her throat.

Jason's words echoed in her ears.

*If I ever hear another word—from you or anyone else— disparaging my wife, I will see you at dawn on the field, pistols in hand. Do you understand me?*

The way he'd said *my wife,* with such unflinching certainty, as though there were no shame in it, no pity, had twisted something inside her.

A few minutes ago, Bea had wisely suggested that to further mitigate gossip Georgie should dance with her new husband to present a united front.

Georgie had immediately gone looking for Jason. And she'd found him…in the card room. She'd been about to turn and go back to her friends, reluctant to bother him in a room full of his peers.

And that's when she'd heard what he'd said. The words, spoken so evenly, yet with such fierce sincerity, had stolen the breath from her lungs.

Their eyes met, and in that moment, it had been too much. All the emotions from the last two days surged through her at once. She'd quickly turned and hurried away.

Now, she found herself weaving through the crowd, drawn like a moth to the open balcony doors where the cool night air beckoned.

Of course she should have known he'd follow her. Just as he had those nights at the parties she'd escaped. She was leaning on the stone balustrade, her shoulders rigid, one hand gripping the edge of the railing, when she heard him approach.

He came to stand beside her and she turned her head to look at him, sucking in two lungfuls of air.

She watched him for a few moments. The moonlight painted him in silver, catching the sharp line of his jaw, the faint furrow between his brows, the steady rise and fall of his chest.

He looked…*tired.*

Not just in body, but in soul.

Something tugged in her chest.

"It's quite cold," she said quietly, wrapping her arms about her shoulders.

He whipped off his coat and covered her with it. It smelled like him. Warm and masculine, with a hint of soap and something quietly intoxicating beneath it.

"I thought you'd gone off with your friends," he said, his voice low.

"I did," she said simply. "But then I overheard you."

His head bowed, just enough for his eyes to meet hers.

They were darker than usual in the moonlight, the green

muted, but they still held that quiet intensity that made her stomach flutter.

"You weren't meant to hear that," he said at last.

"I gathered. I can only imagine what that man said first."

They stood in silence for a moment, the sound of laughter and music drifting faintly through the doors behind them, mingling with the rustle of the breeze.

Jason shook his head. "It doesn't matter."

Georgie stepped toward him, resting her hands lightly on his abdomen. She felt his muscles jump. "You defended me," she said softly.

His gaze burned into her. "Of course I did," he murmured. "You're my wife."

She sucked in her breath. The words shouldn't have meant so much. But they did.

"You didn't have to," she said after a beat, dropping her gaze to his broad chest.

"I didn't have to marry you either," he said evenly.

A startled gasp flew from her lips and her eyes darted back to his. "*What did you say?*"

His gaze was already on her, steady and unflinching. "You heard me," he murmured.

Instead, she asked the question she'd been fearing the answer to ever since they'd wed. "Why did you?"

He blinked at that, then straightened slightly, his fingers covering hers.

For a long moment, she thought he wouldn't answer. But then he said quietly, "At first, I told myself it was because I couldn't stand to watch you be dragged back into that church. Not to him."

"At first?" she echoed, hope and apprehension equally etched in her features.

"Then I realized I couldn't stand to think of you in Bath. Or wherever you were planning to go afterward."

She expelled her breath. "You still haven't answered the question."

That faint crease deepened between his brows. "You didn't deserve a life in exile, Georgie. And you certainly didn't deserve being married to Henderville. Someone should have stopped it long ago."

The rawness in his voice startled her as much as the words. But she pulled her hands away from his and took a step back. "You wanted to be the hero? Is that it?" For the first time, she wondered if there was something he wasn't saying, something deeper, older, behind that compulsion to protect her.

One corner of his mouth curved faintly. "No," he said. "Not at all. I married you because I wanted you. In every way."

# CHAPTER THIRTY-SEVEN

The air outside felt too warm now, or perhaps it was simply that Georgie's blood was still humming from what Jason had said.

She followed him back through the doorway, the familiar strains of a waltz rising up to greet them, and for the first time all evening, she was acutely aware of how close he walked at her side.

She could still hear his words echoing in her mind. *I married you because I wanted you. In. Every. Way.* Not because the words solved everything. They did not. But because they shifted something essential. The marriage no longer felt like a kindness she must endure. It felt, suddenly and unmistakably, like a thing they might have both chosen.

And that mattered. It mattered *so* much.

Then there was the fact that he'd called her Georgie. It felt perfect the moment the name left his lips.

As they moved through the crowd, she kept her chin high. The hum of gossip still surrounded them like gnats, fans fluttering, voices dropping to conspiratorial whispers, heads turning wherever they passed.

And yet now, instead of feeling suffocated by it, she found herself standing just a little taller.

Because at her side was the man who'd told another gentleman tonight—in no uncertain terms—that anyone who spoke ill of her would answer to pistols at dawn.

He may not have fallen to his knees and declared his love for her. She hadn't expected that. But it meant something that he'd stood up for her. More than something, if she was honest. It was the first time since the wedding that she had seen him act not out of haste or rescue, but from open allegiance.

They paused near the edge of the dance floor, and she reached into her reticule for her fan, to give her hands something to do.

The waltz swelled to its peak before the musicians let the final notes drift into silence, and a smattering of applause followed.

Then another waltz began.

Jason glanced at her then, his expression unreadable.

"Will you dance with me, Lady Pembroke?" he asked, his voice low enough to keep the question just between them.

She hesitated for the barest moment, then slipped her glove-clad hand into his. "In public this time?" she murmured.

The corners of his mouth curved, not quite a smile, but something close. "I wouldn't have it any other way."

He led her onto the floor, his hand warm and firm at the small of her back as they joined the other couples already moving to the graceful rhythm.

It wasn't the first time they'd waltzed, of course, and this time, much like the first time, she was aware of every single point of contact, the press of his palm, the faint brush of his coat against her skirts, the steady weight of his gaze.

Around them, she could feel the stares, hear the whispers.

But tonight, she found herself almost daring them to look. If they were going to gossip, let them. She refused to cower in a corner while they did it. Let them see her dance with her husband. Let them make of that what they pleased. Georgie was through with being narrated by everyone else.

Jason's eyes found hers as he guided her through a particularly tight turn, and for a moment she forgot what she'd been thinking entirely.

The music, the murmur of voices, the whispers, they all fell away until it was just the two of them, moving in perfect time. Not easy, exactly. Not settled. But possible. And for now, possibility felt like more than enough to unsettle her.

When the final notes faded and the couples began to clap once more, Georgie caught sight of Poppy and Bea near the edge of the floor, their eyes shining with something between delight and mischief.

After the music stopped, they both waved her over with such unladylike enthusiasm she couldn't help but laugh under her breath.

"I believe my friends are conspiring," she murmured as she curtseyed to Jason.

His mouth curved faintly again. "I have no doubt," he replied, bowing.

She stepped away to join them—only to find they were not alone.

Lady Clare Trentham stood with them as if she'd always belonged at their little post on the sidelines, impossibly composed amid the crush of bodies. She was all pale-gold elegance and cool grace, her blond hair arranged with such effortless perfection it seemed almost an affront. Her dark brown eyes—startling against her fair lashes—tracked Georgie's approach with an aloof serenity that would have been intimidating on anyone else.

Yet there was a spark there too. A quiet, knowing amusement, as if Lady Trentham had also seen every whisper and survived them all.

Georgie gathered herself and dipped into a proper curtsy. "Lady Trentham," she said, keeping her voice steady. "I wished to thank you. For...your help. With my... At the church." She tugged nervously at her gloves. "You did not have to intervene on my behalf."

Lady Trentham's mouth tipped into the faintest curve—more suggestion than smile. "Of course I did," she said, as calmly as if she were commenting on the weather. "Ladies touched by scandal must make a habit of protecting one another. Society is never eager to extend us its mercy."

Something in Georgie's chest loosened, like a knot pulled through. "That is...extraordinarily kind of you."

"Nonsense." Lady Trentham's gaze flicked briefly—very briefly—toward the dance floor where her husband, Ashford Drake, was speaking with another gentleman, his profile handsome enough to make more than one debutante forget her own name. Then her attention returned to Georgie, and the aloofness softened into something warm and formidable. "If you ever find you require an ally again, Lady Pembroke, you need only send for me."

Georgie felt that invitation more keenly than she would have expected. Not because she wanted rescuing again, but because it reminded her that stepping into scandal did not mean stepping out of the world. One could survive it. Even wield it.

And then—utterly to Georgie's shock—Lady Trentham gave her a quick, conspiratorial wink.

Before Georgie could decide whether she'd imagined it, Lady Trentham drifted away, pale skirts gliding through the crowd as if it parted for her by instinct. She moved toward her husband with the serene certainty of a woman who knew precisely where she belonged—beside him, yes, but also entirely on her own terms.

Poppy let out a delighted little sigh. "Well," she whispered, eyes bright, "I think you've just been adopted."

Bea's expression was dry, but her eyes were dancing. "By someone *quite* magnificent," she murmured.

Georgie's laugh came softly. And as she glanced back once—just once—she found Jason watching her again, his expression softer than she'd ever seen it.

For the first time since her wedding, Georgie let her thoughts stray to a place she had been carefully avoiding. Jason had said he wanted her in every way. And that could only mean one thing when night fell.

# CHAPTER THIRTY-EIGHT

The carriage ride home was quiet, but there was no mistaking what filled it—tension, restraint, and enough unresolved desire to make the very air feel hot.

Jason sat opposite Georgie, his long legs stretched toward hers, his gloved hands resting on his knees. He didn't speak, and neither did she, but she felt his gaze now and then—quick, scorching glances that landed on her like fingertips brushing bare skin.

Every time the carriage hit a small rut, their knees drifted closer, the breath between them growing tighter, warmer. Her pulse still thudded from the ball, from the waltz, from the way he'd looked at her while everyone whispered behind their fans. From the way his hand had rested at the small of her back—steady, certain, claiming.

She told herself it had just been a dance.

But her body knew better.

More disconcertingly, so did the rest of her. Tonight had altered something between them. Not solved it. Not settled it. But altered it all the same.

When they arrived at Pembroke House, Jason helped her down with quiet, impeccable manners. His hand lingered at her waist a fraction too long—just enough to make her breath catch, just enough to remind her of the feel of his palm through silk.

Inside, the butler took her shawl and gloves. She murmured something about retiring, but her feet didn't move toward the stairs. That, at least, was no accident. Georgie knew perfectly well where the staircase was. Knew perfectly well what retreat would look like. And still she did not choose it.

Instead, she drifted to the foot of the grand staircase, fingers grazing the polished banister as she watched Jason shrug out of his evening coat. He handed it to a footman, his eyes already lifting to hers.

Their gazes locked across the marble floor.

Neither moved.

Neither breathed.

Something hot and hungry unfurled in her chest.

She turned toward the drawing room instead of the stairs. She didn't look back. She didn't have to.

He followed.

Of course he did. And she desperately wanted him to.

The room was dim, lit only by the fire and a single lamp on the sideboard. Shadows moved along the walls, soft and suggestive.

She stopped in the center of the rug, her back to him, her pulse a fast, trembling thing.

He shut the door and came up behind her, close enough that the heat of his body brushed her spine. The air thickened.

"Georgie," he murmured, voice low and roughened with something that made her knees weaken.

She turned.

Whatever restraint had held them both in check all evening snapped like a thread pulled too taut. Not because either of them had misunderstood the other, but because, by now, understanding had become its own kind of strain.

His mouth was on hers before she could draw a full breath—hungry, reverent, consuming. His hands framed her face as though he were afraid she might vanish if he didn't hold on. She clung to his waistcoat, fingers digging into the fabric as he kissed her like a man who had been waiting far too long. And she kissed him back with equal intention. No confusion. No fear. Only the sharp, thrilling knowledge that this was the man she had married and that, tonight, she wanted him.

He walked her backward toward the settee with slow, deliberate steps, kissing her between each one. When she sank into the cushions, he followed her down, his weight settling over her in a way that made her entire body light up.

His hands slid over her hips, her ribs, the curve of her breasts.

She arched into him helplessly.

Her breath broke when his thumb brushed her nipple through her gown—too soft, then firmer, until she gasped into his mouth. He swallowed the sound greedily, deepening the kiss until she felt drunk on him.

He pushed her skirts up—slow, devastating—his knuckles grazing her skin as he did. Her legs parted without thought, her body answering him before her mind could catch up.

And then her mind did catch up—and instead of recoiling, it urged her closer. That was what startled her most. Not that she wanted him, but how little she wished to pretend otherwise any longer.

His fingers slid higher, then paused—just to make her ache for it—before continuing with deliberate intent.

The first touch stole her breath. The second stole her

composure. And then he began a slow, relentless rhythm that had her clutching at his sleeve.

He kissed the corner of her mouth, her jaw, the frantic beat at her throat, as if he could soothe her while he ruined her.

"Jason…" she breathed.

"I've got you," he whispered.

And he did. He absolutely did.

Not as rescuer now. Not as the man who had bargained and intervened and chosen for both of them. But as the husband he was. And at last, they met in the dark as equal participants in their desire.

His hand moved, one finger sliding into her with patient precision, the kind that promised he wasn't guessing—he was deliberate.

He drew it out, coaxing, easing her higher, then higher again, until she was trembling with it, breath stuttering, hips pleading in small helpless motions.

She tried to speak his name again and only managed a shaky exhale.

He smiled against her skin like he felt every shiver as a victory.

By the time she unraveled beneath his hand, she was shaking, crying out softly into his shoulder as her release tore through her. He held her through it, kissing her, murmuring her name like a promise.

When she finally blinked up at him, dazed and unsteady, she felt his unmistakable hardness against her hip.

He was shaking too.

Straining.

One look at him—his mussed hair, his ragged breath, the raw need in his eyes—and something wild rose in her. She wanted him to lose control. Here. Now. With her.

But he drew back with a ragged exhale, slipping his hand from beneath her skirts.

The sudden distance felt like a punch. She nearly sobbed. Not because she thought he did not want her—God, that much was plain—but because wanting, apparently, was still not enough to bridge the careful distance he had set between them.

He pressed a hand over his mouth, as if steadying himself, before speaking.

"The last thing I want to do is pressure you, Georgie," he said, his voice rough. "I have patience. And I intend to give you all the time you need."

Which might have sounded noble if she had not been shaking from wanting exactly what he had just denied them both.

He stood. And with one lingering look—full of longing, frustration, and something terribly close to reverence—he turned on his heel...and walked out.

Georgie was left flushed, trembling, aching...and desperately wanting more.

She stared at the doorway after him, breath still uneven, and understood with a clarity that frustrated her: this was to be the new battle between them. Not whether desire existed. That had been settled. But whether either of them would be brave enough to stop protecting the other from what they both plainly wanted.

# CHAPTER THIRTY-NINE

Jason lay flat on his back in the massive bed, one arm flung over his eyes, the sheets tangled around his legs like unwanted restraints.

Sleep was an impossibility. Every time he closed his eyes, Georgie appeared behind them. Not merely as she had looked on the settee, though God knew that would have been enough, but as she had looked all evening: proud, watchful, fierce, and increasingly impossible to think of as anything but his wife in the fullest sense of the word.

The way she'd looked sprawled on the settee beneath him —her lips parted, her hair tumbling in soft disobedient curls, her gown rucked indecently high on her thighs…it drove him mad. Her cheeks had been flushed with heat and astonishment, her chest rising and falling in those quick, breathless little pants that had nearly destroyed every ounce of control he possessed.

He could still hear her whimpers. Those soft, desperate sounds she hadn't meant to make, the ones she tried—beautifully, unsuccessfully—to swallow.

That sound… God help him, that sound was etched into

him now, carved beneath the ribs where a man kept his most vulnerable places.

And the look on her face when pleasure overtook her—eyes wide, lashes trembling, lips parted in a silent cry…

He groaned, dragging his hand down his face, as though he could wipe the memory away. Impossible. She was in every part of him now.

He wanted to give her that feeling every night.

Wanted to erase every harsh word ever thrown at her.

Wanted to replace every wound with something soft, something tender.

He wanted her to know she was wanted.

Cherished.

His.

Not his in the ugly, grasping way men like Chadwick or Henderville might mean it. Not owned, not cornered, not kept. His because he wanted, with a force that startled him still, to build a life in which she might one day choose to belong beside him.

He should have said more tonight—told her he was falling in love with her, that every hour spent in her company only pulled him deeper under. But he'd held back. Too soon, too sudden, and the last thing he intended to do was frighten her into retreating. Not when he'd only just coaxed her out from behind the walls she'd built.

Besides, what sensible woman would trust a declaration made in the wake of scandal, half-dressed on a settee, from the same fool who had married her in a storm of impulse and good intentions? Georgie deserved more than truth blurted out at the height of desire. She deserved the kind of attention that could bear daylight.

He exhaled a shaky breath into the dim quiet of the room.

He'd meant what he told her—God, how he'd meant it. The last thing he wanted was to pressure her. He wasn't a man without honor. Yes, desire thrummed through him like blood itself, but he wasn't ruled by it. Not when it came to her.

Especially not with her. Too much had already been decided at speed, by force of circumstance and his own over-reaching hand. If this marriage was to become real, then the next steps had to be taken freely—or not at all.

There were things still between them. Unspoken, fragile things that mattered far more than the ache tightening every muscle in his body. He wouldn't take her to his bed until she wanted him in every way—not just in a moment of passion on a drawing room settee.

Because he wanted more now than surrender. He wanted trust. He wanted her certainty. He wanted the look in her eyes when she came to him to say not merely *yes* but *you. Here. Now.*

Which meant—for the sake of his sanity—he might well be damned.

He rolled onto his side, glaring hopelessly at the soft flicker of moonlight on the far wall. Every part of him felt strung tight, hot and restless.

He tried—honestly tried—to think of anything else.

But all he saw was her.

Her in blue silk under the Hartleys' chandeliers. Her in the carriage, silent and burning. Her turning not toward the stairs but toward the drawing room, making a choice he had felt all the way down to his bones.

The curve of her perfect breast under his hand. The taste of it beneath his tongue. The softness of her sweet thighs parting for him. The slick, desperate heat of her as she ground helplessly against his fingers.

A harsh, fractured sound escaped him. He shoved the sheet down, as if air alone could cool him.

It couldn't.

His hand slid lower before he could summon a reason to stop himself. Her face was all he saw. Her soft cry. Her trembling limbs. Her whispered, broken "Jason…"

He gripped himself, his breath shuddering as his hips arched into his own palm. It was her he felt, her he chased, her he wanted with a ferocity that bordered on insanity.

Which was inconvenient enough. More alarming was that the wanting no longer ended at her body. It reached further now—to breakfast tables, drawing rooms, dance floors, quiet laughter, shared glances, and the impossible hope of being welcome in all of it.

He stroked himself—once, twice—slow enough to torture, fast enough to betray him. Her name crowded his tongue, the image of her mouth on his, her body yielding, the memory of her sounds in his ear.

His climax tore through him with a guttural curse, his body tightening and then falling apart, leaving him shuddering and breathless in the thick quiet of the room.

The only sounds were his uneven breaths and the steady tick of the clock on the mantel—counting down the unendurable hours until morning, when he would have to look her in the eyes and pretend he hadn't spent the night wanting her more than he'd ever wanted anything in his life.

Morning would be worse, not better. Because daylight always asked more honest things of a man. In darkness, he could admit he wanted her. In daylight, he would have to decide what, exactly, he meant to do about it.

# CHAPTER FORTY

*A sennight later*

The bell above the door of Madame Duval's shop tinkled merrily as Georgie stepped inside, the soft scent of starch and expensive fabric immediately enveloping her.

Madame Duval's was more than a dressmaker's. It was an experience. The polished wood floors gleamed, and sunlight streamed through tall windows and glinted off the delicate buttons and ribbons that lined the walls in neat boxes. Bolts of silk and satin spilled across display tables in jewel tones and soft pastels, while dress forms stood like silent sentinels, draped in the latest Parisian fashions.

Bea trailed just behind her, immaculate in a light-green pelisse trimmed in sable, her blond head held high, looking as though she owned the place.

Georgie herself wore a dove-gray walking dress with a soft rose sash that Madame had insisted flattered her coloring perfectly. Still, she was aware of the watchfulness new clothing invited. Only because it was such a difference from how her life had been for so long.

She hadn't breathed a word to Bea or Poppy about that night in the drawing room with Jason. Nor had she confessed that their marriage remained unconsummated. It was far too personal…and, if she were honest, far too humiliating.

Not humiliating because she doubted he desired her. Humiliating because she did not know why he still held back, and she disliked not understanding the terms of her own marriage.

Since the wedding, she and Jason had settled into a comfortable routine. Comfortable enough to fool anyone watching. Perhaps even themselves, on weaker days. But Georgie had begun to understand that comfort was not the same as certainty. They had found a rhythm, yes. What they had not yet found was an answer.

They shared breakfast each morning before going their separate ways—she with the decorators, poring over endless swatches and sketches for Pembroke House, and he in his study, at his club, or—she'd learned—in the fencing room for hours at a time.

They dined together, trading laughter and easy conversation, then attended whatever *fête* was currently dazzling the *ton*. They danced, took refreshments side by side, and, to all appearances, presented the picture of a hasty marriage that had already blossomed into a warm companionship—friendlier, in fact, than many of Society's most celebrated unions.

And Hester had been right. Jason was kind and generous with all of his servants. He tossed a coin to the butler's young son whenever he saw him, ruffling his hair and asking how his schoolwork was coming along. The butler had informed her that Jason himself paid for Timothy's tutor.

She'd also overheard the housemaid recounting to

another that when her mother had taken ill, Jason had sent the woman home for a fortnight with full pay—and had quietly arranged for a physician to visit her in the country.

Only yesterday, when a footman had wrenched his ankle carrying crates down to the cellar, Jason had ordered him to sit, sent for the apothecary, and paid the bill himself—remarking that no errand was worth a man's health.

Then there was the way he treated her. With kindness, gentleness, and an endless well of patience. He made her laugh until her cheeks ached and made her press her thighs together with a wanting so sharp it stole her breath. He was clever, kind, and utterly devastating in the way he could disarm her with a single look—leaving her both safe in his presence and perilously close to forgetting why she'd ever intended to keep her heart to herself.

But for all his charm and attentiveness, Jason had not once crossed the threshold of her bedchamber. Georgie was beginning to wonder if she'd imagined that night in the drawing room—when his touch had very nearly set her aflame.

She was also beginning to wonder, with no little frequency, exactly what she could do to entice her husband to her bed.

Which was not, she had decided, a meek or shameful thing to want. If this marriage was to become real, then wanting him—fully, honestly, joyfully—seemed a perfectly sensible place to begin.

As Georgie and Bea made their way farther into the shop, Madame Duval bustled toward them in a cloud of flowery perfume, clapping her hands in delight.

Draped over her arms was a gown so exquisite it could have stepped straight from a Parisian sketchbook. "Try zis one first, Lady Pembroke," she implored.

Sweeping Georgie toward a curtained alcove, she pulled

back the heavy purple velvet with a flourish and ushered her inside.

Twenty minutes later, Georgie emerged, the gown flowing around her like poured silk. Madame Duval trailed in her wake, beaming.

"Ah! *Ma chère!* You are a vision!" she cried, taking Georgie by the shoulders and spinning her toward a long gilt mirror.

Georgie barely recognized herself. The new gown she wore, a creamy pale gold muslin with delicate ivory embroidery and tiny seed pearls scattered over the bodice, *was* exquisite.

"Perfection," Bea said, with a warm smile and an approving nod.

"You will have zee *ton* on zeir knees," Madame Duval declared.

Georgie laughed, but some small part of her stood a little straighter all the same. If Society insisted on looking, then let it have something worth staring at.

"Preferably not literally," Bea drawled, casually examining a length of silk.

Georgie gave a faint laugh while Madame fussed over her hem, nodding when the woman declared she must fetch a final accessory from the back.

As Madame disappeared behind the velvet curtain, the shop door chimed again.

This time the effect was…different.

Every seamstress in the room froze. Shopgirls scattered to line up by the door like soldiers awaiting a queen.

The air shifted perceptibly as the newcomer entered—a tall woman in a perfectly tailored emerald velvet pelisse, the collar lined in white fox, her gloved hands resting lightly on an ebony cane that was surely more ornament than necessity.

Her hair was a rich chestnut threaded liberally with

silver, swept back under a feathered hat, and her eyes—sharp and nearly as green as her coat—seemed to take in everything at once.

She carried herself with such imperious elegance that Georgie instinctively straightened.

"Dowager Countess," one of the shopgirls murmured, hastily curtsying as if bracing for judgment.

*Dowager Countess?* Who was this woman?

The answer arrived in her bones before it reached her mind. Something about the woman's carriage, her confidence, the emerald eyes—too close a match to Jason's to be coincidence.

The girls rushed to take her gloves and offer her tea, but she waved them off with a faint smile that didn't reach her eyes. Instead, she walked slowly toward the mirror where Georgie stood, her cane clicking softly on the floor.

"You," she said, her voice smooth as satin, "are the new Lady Pembroke, are you not?"

Georgie blinked, startled into speechlessness for a beat before she nodded. "Yes. I am," she replied carefully, feeling Bea come to stand close beside her.

A faint, knowing smile curved the older woman's mouth.

"I thought that was you," she murmured, eyes sweeping up and down Georgie's figure with an appraisal that made her cheeks heat.

Bea's hand slid through hers, her grip firm, her chin lifting.

"I do so enjoy seeing how quickly the gossip pages work," the dowager continued idly, as though she were remarking on the weather. "Why, it was only last week they described you as 'a penniless wallflower from a tarnished family,' and yet here you stand bedecked in finery. Miraculous, really."

Bea stiffened at her side.

Georgie met the dowager's appraisal with calm composure, refusing to give her the satisfaction of a smile.

The woman took another slow step closer, her eyes narrowing slightly. "I thought I ought to come and see for myself," she said softly, leaning in just enough that Georgie could smell her perfume—something spicy and expensive, like cloves and roses.

Her voice dropped to a conspiratorial whisper. "My son always did like to take in strays."

The insult landed cleanly, but it was not the cruelty of the word itself that struck deepest. It was the ugly suggestion beneath it—that Jason's tenderness had never been particular to her at all.

The dowager straightened, her eyes glittering, then tilted her head and leaned in again, her tone almost pitying now.

"It's not about you, you know," she said, her words deliberate and quiet. "It's about her. Evelyn. He never got over not being able to save his sister. Now he saves any poor creature he can find to make up for it."

Georgie narrowed her eyes. She did not believe it wholly. That was what made the blow so treacherous. If the dowager had spoken an obvious falsehood, she could have dismissed it at once. But there was just enough shape to it, just enough hidden knowledge that aligned to her deepest fears, to slip under her guard and lodge there.

The woman allowed her gaze to sweep down Georgie's new gown with a faint, almost imperceptible sneer. "Clearly."

And just like that, she turned on her heel, cane tapping smartly against the floor as the shopgirls all scrambled to escort her out.

The bell above the door chimed one final time as the dowager swept out into the street.

The silence that followed was deafening.

Bea squeezed her hand. "Georgie?" she asked gently.

Georgie heard her, dimly, from very far away. But she couldn't answer—not yet.

Because the dowager had not given her a neat lie to reject. She had handed her a cruel possibility instead, one tangled enough with truth to hurt. Jason *had* tried to save her. The older woman's words had torn open a wound that had just barely begun to heal.

Georgie stood very still, forcing breath back into her lungs. This, then, was the question she could no longer avoid. Not whether Jason desired her. Not whether he was kind. But whether, beneath all his patience and care and good intentions, there was something more particular. Something chosen. Something that belonged to her and not to his grief.

And she would have an answer. Not from gossip. Not from dowagers. From Jason himself.

# CHAPTER FORTY-ONE

Jason bit into his lamb with undue precision, though he scarcely tasted it.

Across the table, Georgie sat perfectly still, her hands folded primly in her lap, her eyes on her plate, though she had barely touched a bite.

For once, he found himself at a loss for words. An irritating sensation, particularly because words had lately become the very thing he seemed most to lack when she needed them.

For nights now, they had fallen into an easy rhythm.

Dinner, sometimes followed by a quiet game of chess or cards. Other times, simply sitting in companionable silence, both of them reading by the fire, the air between them warmer than it had any right to be.

By the third evening, he realized he'd begun to *look forward* to it.

He'd found himself watching her mouth curve faintly when she took his rook. Noticing the way her lashes caught the candlelight when she looked down at her book. The quiet sound of her laugh when he muttered something sardonic about Parliament.

He'd begun to crave it. Not merely the peace of her company, though that would have been novelty enough. He sought the sense—delicate and growing stronger by the day—that they might be edging toward a marriage chosen in truth rather than forged in haste.

He hadn't tried to touch her again—not even a kiss. He was waiting for a sign. From her. And not just a flutter of lashes paired with a coy smile, though she'd given him both on several occasions. He wanted something unmistakable before he risked taking her to his bed. The waiting was agony, but he knew it mattered. How he navigated these first weeks could shape the course of their entire marriage.

He had done enough choosing for both of them already. If this next step came, it must come with her full heart in it—not merely passion.

She had been warming to him—of that he felt increasingly certain. Not all at once, and never carelessly, but in glances, in laughter, in the way she no longer seemed braced for disappointment at every turn. And then tonight happened.

Tonight, she was a stranger again. Her replies to his questions had been short and polite. Her eyes didn't quite meet his.

She sat straighter in her chair than usual, her posture so rigid it made his own back ache just watching her.

Something was wrong. And he couldn't for the life of him figure out what.

Had he offended her somehow? Or had something finally made plain to her a question he had been avoiding too long himself?

He pushed another bite of lamb around his plate, glancing

up at her once more. "You don't care for the meal?" he asked finally, trying to keep his tone light. *Fool. As if lamb were the problem.*

She started slightly, as though she'd forgotten he was there. "It's fine," she said softly, her gaze still fixed somewhere over his shoulder. Which it plainly was not. Georgiana lied badly when hurt; she went very still and very polite, as though emotion itself were something best denied entry.

He set his fork down and studied her in silence.

Her face was calm, expressionless, but there was unmistakable tension in her shoulders, and her jaw was just a shade too tight.

Something had changed. He knew it in his gut.

GEORGIE KEPT her eyes on her plate, though she'd already given up any pretense of eating.

Jason sat opposite her, his posture perfect as always, his expression unreadable in the soft glow of the candles. He cut into his lamb methodically, chewing in silence.

It was intolerable.

The words she'd been swallowing all evening pressed harder against the back of her throat until she thought she might choke on them.

She wanted to ask him about his mother. About what she'd said this morning in the shop, her sharp voice and sharper smile still etched in Georgie's mind. The woman had struck too near a fear Georgie had been trying to reason away.

*It's not about you, you know. It's about his sister. He never got over not being able to save her. Now he saves any poor creature he can find to make up for it.*

She could not get his mother's words out of her mind.

Her stomach turned as she replayed them. She hadn't even known he *had* a sister.

And a horrible thought had occurred to her. If he *had* married her out of obligation, or worse, pity, Georgie never would have known it if she hadn't met his mother.

Georgie laid her fork down carefully, smoothing her napkin in her lap just to have something to do with her hands. This was untenable. She had to give him a chance…to tell him herself. She owed him that much.

She drew in a quiet breath and ventured, "I…I don't know much about…your family."

Jason's knife paused just briefly before continuing its steady work. When he looked up, his expression was as inscrutable as ever. "There's not much to tell," he said evenly, his voice low.

Which was answer enough to indicate there was, in fact, a great deal.

Her pulse ticked higher. "Are you…" She hesitated, choosing her words carefully. "Do you have any siblings?"

This time he did stop. His fingers tightened subtly on the hilt of his knife, and she thought she saw the muscle in his jaw flex. His throat worked as he swallowed, and for the first time since she'd met him, his composure faltered.

"Yes," he said at last, the word quiet but heavy.

"I have…" He exhaled, and she saw it—the flicker of pain behind his eyes, the way his gaze drifted somewhere far beyond the walls of the room. "…*had* a sister."

Georgie's heart thudded dully against her ribs. She swallowed, choosing quite deliberately not to say more.

The silence stretched, heavy and thick, as he stared at some invisible point on the tablecloth.

"She…" He stopped, his jaw tightening as he searched for the words.

"Her name was Evelyn," he said finally, his voice softer

now, and Georgie could hear it—the grief buried deep, the kind that never really left a person.

Georgie's breath caught. It was not confirmation exactly —nothing so neat—but the first hard edge of the truth she had been circling.

Her chest felt tight, her throat dry, but she couldn't look away from him, from the faint shadow of anguish on his face, the way his gaze stayed fixed on some distant memory.

"What happened to her?" she finally ventured.

"I'd rather not discuss it," he said, his voice firm and resolute.

Georgie nodded at once. She did not press. She had never heard that edge in his voice before, and it was plain the subject cost him something.

The silence that followed was not heavy so much as unsettled—like a question left deliberately unanswered. Jason returned his attention to his plate, his movements precise once more, as though nothing had been disturbed. But something had been.

More than one thing, perhaps. His composure. Her certainty. The pleasant little routine they had been constructing between them as though routine alone might spare them harder conversations.

Georgie folded her hands in her lap again, her thoughts turning inward despite herself. She had not meant to stir old grief. And yet his mother's words no longer felt like a passing cruelty. They had lodged themselves in the silence between them, where too many other things already lived.

She studied his face across the table—the restraint, the careful distance, the old pain he had permitted her to glimpse only for a moment—and felt the question sharpen. Whether the first impulse that had bound him to her had begun with *Georgie* herself, or with some older wound he had never managed to lay down.

That distinction, she realized, was not small at all. It might be the very thing upon which the rest of their marriage turned.

# CHAPTER FORTY-TWO

Jason stood by the tall window in his study, one hand braced against the sill, the other a loose fist at his side.

Outside, the square was quiet. A lone carriage rattled by, wheels crunching over the cobblestones, the sound faint and distant through the heavy pane.

He'd been standing here for the better part of an hour, telling himself he wasn't *waiting*. Waiting, and hating himself a little for it. A husband ought not feel so helpless in his own house merely because his wife had gone out with her friends and taken her silence with her.

But he was.

He hadn't seen Georgie since she'd left the dinner table last night, rising so abruptly after his confession about Evelyn he'd barely had time to stand before she was gone.

She hadn't spoken another word.

Not a single one.

Not in anger. Or accusation. Somehow that would have been easier. Silence required a man to think, and thinking was precisely what Jason had spent too long postponing.

This morning, she hadn't come down to breakfast.

Instead she'd sent a note with the footman—two crisp lines in her even hand.

*I've gone shopping with Lady Beatrix and Miss Montfort on Bond Street. Please do not wait on me for dinner.*

Bond Street made sense. And he certainly didn't begrudge her time with her friends. But dinner was fast approaching, and it seemed an awfully long while to linger over shopping.

He'd told himself not to think about it. Not to read too much into her sudden silence, or the fact that she'd sent her regrets this morning rather than simply face him.

And yet…he couldn't stop thinking about it. Because Georgie was not petty, nor theatrical. If she withdrew, she did so for a reason. Which meant whatever had passed over dinner last night had struck deeper than he wanted to admit.

He should have told her more last night…should have answered her question. Explained what happened to Evelyn. Instead, he'd been cold, sharp. He'd only managed to widen the space between them.

Not because she had demanded what was not hers to know, but because he had panicked at the thought of laying bare the oldest wound he possessed. And in panicking, he had done what he always did best—retreated behind control and called it necessity.

His mouth tightened at the thought.

The truth was, he'd never meant to tell her about Evelyn, not like that, perhaps not at all. But she'd asked about his family, and in that quiet moment over dinner, when her gaze had been so intent and her voice so tentative, the words had simply…slipped out.

But the moment she'd asked what happened, it was as if

all the pain had rushed back to haunt him. He didn't like to think about it, let alone talk about it.

Which, under ordinary circumstances, might have been excuse enough. But Georgie was no longer outside the matter. She was his wife. And if his old grief was shaping the life they were trying to build, then perhaps silence had become its own form of cowardice.

He cursed softly under his breath.

He'd practically snapped at her. It wasn't the kind of thing one could take back.

And the look on Georgie's pretty face before she left—stricken, shuttered, and…almost wounded—had not left his mind since.

Had she thought it was a rebuke? That he didn't want her to know anything about his family? Or worse, had she mistaken his refusal for confirmation that she didn't mean anything to him? The thought sat badly enough in his gut to make him pace again.

He scrubbed a hand over his face and sighed.

She did mean something to him. Of course she did. Which was precisely why he hadn't introduced her to his mother.

Not because he was ashamed of Georgie—how could he be?—but because he had no intention of subjecting her to his mother's poison.

The dowager may have been his only living relative, but she was a snake, and he knew better than anyone how sharp her tongue could be.

Georgie already had enough wretched relations to contend with. She didn't need his added to the list.

Still, the silence between them gnawed at him now.

He glanced at the clock—well past five.

The deepening light of early evening stretched thin over the square. And still no sign of her.

A small muscle worked in his jaw as he moved away from the window.

Bond Street wasn't so very far, and shopping with two chaperones—well, of sorts—should have been entirely safe.

But something twisted in his chest regardless.

Not because he doubted her good sense. God knew she had more of that than most of the men he knew. But because absence sat differently now that he had something real to lose.

A faint, restless prickle at the base of his spine told him something was wrong.

He couldn't have said how he knew…only that he did.

And as the clock chimed another lonely quarter hour, he found himself reaching for his coat. Not because she required rescuing. He would do well to remember that. But because this time, if he went after her, he meant to bring something different than intervention. He meant to bring honesty.

# CHAPTER FORTY-THREE

The Duke of Winston's coach wheels clattered over the cobblestones as Georgie leaned back against the velvet squabs, her gloved hands folded in her lap.

The sun had long since begun its descent, painting the sky in hues of pale gold and violet.

She was late.

Unquestionably late.

But she couldn't bring herself to feel truly guilty about it.

For the first time in…years, if she was honest…she'd had a truly fun day with her friends.

A proper day.

A day that had not been about duty or expectation or obligation, or planning a revolt, but laughter, shopping, and gossip, with two loyal friends who didn't seem to care a whit about the story in the papers.

The world had not ended because she had become Lady Pembroke. Scandal had not swallowed her whole. Life, stubbornly enough, had gone on.

Bea sat opposite her, as poised and sharp as ever in her

green pelisse, idly tapping her gloved fingers against her knee while she gazed out the window.

Poppy, seated beside Georgie, was already fussing with her reticule, a frown on her pretty, freckled face.

"Can you believe," Bea was saying, her tone dry as parchment, "that Nicholas Archer had the audacity to send me flowers?"

"Flowers?" Poppy exclaimed. "Why, that sounds lovely?"

"Flowers are lovely unless they come from him. He's simply mocking me," Bea insisted. "They weren't even roses. They were peonies, of all ridiculous things."

"Why are peonies ridiculous?" Poppy wanted to know.

Georgie stifled a laugh. "I thought you and Nicholas Archer merely disagreed on politics, not flowers," she teased. The ease of it startled her a little—this laughter, this banter, this sense that her life had not become some solemn thing beyond ordinary pleasures.

Bea's lips thinned. "We disagree on *everything*," she said flatly. "Including the weather, should the topic arise."

Poppy leaned forward, huffing. "Well, I'd gladly trade you Nicholas Archer and his peonies if it meant my mother would stop telling everyone she intends to waltz at Almack's in a sheer Turkish robe this Season. *A sheer Turkish robe*," she repeated, throwing her hands up in quiet despair.

Georgie laughed outright at that, the sound bubbling up before she could stop it. "That *does* sound rather…scandalous," she admitted.

Poppy groaned and dropped her head into her hands. "She claims it will 'rekindle her spirit.' I claim it will cause a megrim in the patronesses," she muttered into her gloves.

Bea merely arched an eyebrow. "I expect it will do both."

Georgie pressed her fingers to her lips to stifle another laugh but found herself sobering as the conversation shifted.

At some point, somewhere between Bond Street and tea at

Gunter's, she'd repeated to Poppy what the dowager had said in Madame Duval's shop, that Jason only married her to atone for his sister, that he "collected strays" to salve his conscience.

Even saying it aloud made it sound uglier. Smaller. And there was something distinctly unpleasant in giving voice to another woman's cruelty.

Bea's mouth had gone thin and sharp, her eyes flashing. "I told you the dowager was awful," she'd said crisply.

"Did you tell him?" Poppy had asked softly. "About running into her at the modiste?"

Georgie shook her head.

Bea frowned at once. "Why not?"

Georgie glanced down at her gloves. "I wasn't entirely certain how to bring it up. How exactly does one say, *By the by, your mother stopped me at Madame Duval's and informed me you married me out of guilt?*"

Poppy had winced. "That does sound dreadful."

Bea shrugged. "But it's true. It's precisely what happened."

Georgie had gone on to recount what Jason himself had said last night at dinner—about Evelyn, and how he'd refused to share more.

That part had come out in a whisper, her gloved hands knotted in her lap, her gaze fixed on the table so she wouldn't have to see their faces.

For a moment, neither of them spoke. Then Poppy had reached over and squeezed her shoulder.

"Did it occur to you," she'd asked gently, "to…ask him *why* he doesn't want to talk about it?"

Georgie blinked at her, taken aback. "Ask him?" she repeated blankly.

"Yes," Bea said, leaning back in her chair, her voice cool but firm. "You know…words. Directed at his face. In the form of a question."

Georgie had nearly laughed, then nearly winced. The notion of pressing him sat strangely with her. She was too accustomed to yielding when a subject was closed—too practiced in stepping back before she gave offense. She looked at her friends, feeling faintly foolish. "He said he did not wish to discuss it," she said at last.

Bea had snorted at that, and Poppy rolled her eyes.

"Georgie," Bea said with a faint smile, "you married him. You may ask him whatever you wish."

Poppy nodded.

Those words had lodged in Georgie's chest and echoed. Could she truly ask him, and have him answer honestly? The very idea felt foreign. She'd been raised in a household where lies and deceit were the currency of daily life, where questions weren't asked with any expectation of a forthright reply. And one certainly didn't press further after being curtly told a subject was off-limits. Was Jason the sort of man who welcomed such openness? She did not know. But ignorance itself was beginning to feel less tolerable than the risk of asking.

But now, as Bea's father's coach came to a halt outside Pembroke House, Georgie found herself considering it. Not because Bea had mocked her into courage, though that had helped, but because she was suddenly tired of building a marriage on guesses.

The footman opened the door, and she lifted her skirts, stepped down, and bid her friends goodnight.

The air was cooler this late in the day. It bit pleasantly at her cheeks as she glanced up at the grand facade of the house, warm light glowing from behind the tall windows. Her house now. Her husband somewhere within it. The thought no longer felt unreal. Only unfinished.

She adjusted her gloves and climbed the steps. At the

door, she hesitated only a moment before drawing in a steady breath.

Very well. Let the answer hurt if it must. Better that than silence. Better that than fear doing all the speaking for her.

Whatever lay ahead, she would meet it honestly. And this time, she would ask until she understood.

# CHAPTER FORTY-FOUR

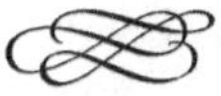

Jason ripped open the door to the town house so quickly it slammed against the inside wall.

To his infinite surprise, Georgie was standing on the threshold, her eyes wide and startled, one gloved hand lifted toward the knob as if she'd been about to enter.

Jason's own breath caught. "There you are," he said, the words coming out lower and rougher than he'd intended.

Georgie's lips parted, and she blinked up at him. "I'm sorry I'm late," she said quickly, stepping into the foyer, her skirts brushing past his boots as she moved to stand just past him.

He closed the door behind her, still watching her, still feeling that restless tightness in his chest that had been there all afternoon.

He turned to the footman waiting nearby. "Send the coach back to the stables," he ordered.

The footman bowed and hurried off, leaving them alone together.

Jason's eyes stayed on her. "I was about to come looking

for you," he admitted, his voice quieter now, but no less intense.

She glanced up at him then, and there was something in her gaze, nervous, yes, but also…hopeful?

"I'm sorry to have worried you," she murmured. Then, hesitating, she drew in a breath and added softly, "But I… want to talk to you too. Will you…come to my bedchamber?"

Her words stopped him cold. He stared at her, blinking. "Your bedchamber?"

Her cheeks flushed a lovely shade of pink, but she held his gaze and gave a small, decisive nod.

Jason's heart thudded once, hard.

Well.

That was…unexpected.

But he managed to find his voice and incline his head.

"Of course."

~

BY THE TIME she heard the quiet knock on her bedchamber door, Georgie's hands were already trembling.

She stood by the fire in the soft, pale-lavender gown she'd chosen with deliberate care—one of Madame Duval's creations. It was nothing indecent, but softer and lighter than usual, with a neckline just a touch lower and sheer lace sleeves that left her shoulders feeling bare…and a little thrilling.

The candlelight caught the faint shimmer of the silk, and she pressed her hands to her middle, trying to calm her breathing.

She might be married, but she'd never invited a man into her private chambers before. The very idea left her oddly breathless.

But she'd spent the last hour turning her friends' advice over and over in her mind. *Try it. Ask him. Tell him.*

If there was any chance—any at all—of something real with Jason, it had to begin with honesty. Tonight, she was determined to be brave enough for it. Not because honesty guaranteed safety. It did not. But because she could no longer bear the half-life of guesses.

A decisive knock sounded at the door.

She swallowed hard and called, "Come in."

The door opened and he was there. For just a beat, he didn't move.

His eyes swept over her, and his throat worked as he swallowed, his gaze darkening slightly as it returned to her face.

That single look—the way he seemed momentarily undone—sent a strange thrill through her middle.

She took a step toward him and nodded faintly to the bed.

"Will you...sit with me?" she asked softly.

His breath quickened just enough to betray him, but he nodded and crossed the room to stand near the edge of the bed.

After she lowered herself to the mattress, he sat beside her, leaving just enough space between them that she could feel his warmth without quite touching him.

For a moment, neither of them spoke.

Then she drew in a breath and said quietly, "I...want to tell you about something...something that happened at Madame Duval's."

His head turned sharply at that, his green eyes narrowing. "What happened?"

She met his gaze and did not look away as she told him everything. How the dowager had approached her, the sharp little smile, the word *stray*, and the way she'd claimed it was never about Georgie at all—but about Evelyn.

She said it all in a quiet, measured voice, but when she finished, her nails dug into her palms, her hands motionless in her lap.

His jaw tightened visibly. "Damn it," he murmured, his voice low, rough.

Georgie nodded faintly.

"I should have warned you about my mother," he said bitterly. "But I didn't think she'd stalk you down like that. Make no mistake," he added, his eyes hard now, "that was no coincidence she found you at Madame Duval's. She meant to find you and say exactly what she said."

Georgie inclined her head, though she'd already suspected as much. Still, it helped—more than she wanted to admit—to hear him confirm it. Because it meant he was not trying to make her doubt her own instincts. He was simply acknowledging the truth of it.

He exhaled then, his shoulders slumping slightly as he turned to take her hands in his. "I'm sorry, Georgie," he murmured, his thumbs brushing lightly over her knuckles. The apology hit her harder than the confession might have. Not because it solved anything, but because it was offered without defense, without explanation, without asking her to excuse what had hurt.

Her breath hitched. And it occurred to her in that moment that no one, not her parents, not her brother, no one, had ever apologized to her before. Everything had always been her fault.

"I'm sorry for all of it," he continued, his voice thick with something she couldn't quite name. "I'm sorry I interfered with your plans at that first ball. I'm sorry I abducted you on your wedding day. And I'm very sorry I coerced you into marrying me. But the truth is…"

He stopped and shook his head faintly, searching her face as though trying to find the right words.

"Somewhere along the way," he went on hoarsely, "I fell in love with you. And I couldn't stand the thought of you marrying Henderville. Only…I knew if I told you I thought I was in love with you, you'd think I'd gone mad and…"

His words faltered, but his gaze didn't waver.

"What I'm trying to say," he said finally, his voice roughening, "is that somewhere in the middle of all my interference and all your resistance, I came to see you too clearly to let you go."

She stared at him, her vision blurring as tears welled in her eyes.

"Evelyn," he said, his voice shaking, "was my sister. My younger sister. I was watching her one day while my parents were away and—" His voice hitched. "It seemed as if I just turned my back for a moment and…she was gone." He closed his eyes. Georgie could tell it was costing him a bit of his soul to relive it. "She was an adventurous girl. She loved the outdoors. I should have known… By the time I searched the entire house for her, it was too late. She wasn't there. In the end, I found her in the creek. She'd been asking just the day before to go swimming." He expelled his breath. "She drowned."

The word seemed to empty the room of air. Georgie felt, all at once, the shape of the wound he had been carrying— not as excuse, but as fact. Old grief. Old guilt. And beneath both, still, the man who had chosen to tell her because she had finally asked.

She flung her arms around his shoulders and hugged him. "Oh, Jason. I'm so sorry." She pulled back a little, searching his face, sensing there was more he wanted to say.

"Yes, perhaps it's true I started out wanting to save you,"

he admitted, his lips curving into the faintest, rueful smile. "But that's not how I feel now. Not at all."

His eyes lifted to hers.

"I know," she said, swallowing. "At least…I know it isn't all of it. And I know you know by now that I never wanted to be pitied. Never wanted to be swept up because I was too weak to save myself." Her mouth trembled, but she held his gaze. "If you had only wanted to rescue me, I think I would have hated you for it."

Something flickered across his face—pain, recognition, perhaps even relief.

"God, Georgie," he said roughly, "I know that now. You would have fought your way free with or without me. You nearly did." His thumb brushed her cheek. "It was never your helplessness that held me. It was your courage. Your temper. Your sharp tongue. The way you kept standing there and meeting me blow for blow when any sensible person would have run in the other direction."

He let out a breath that sounded almost like a laugh. "Perhaps I first told myself I was protecting you because that was easier to admit than the truth. The truth was that somewhere along the way, I stopped thinking about saving you and started thinking only about having you. Loving you. Earning the right to keep you."

She swallowed again.

"Hell, maybe there will always be a part of me that wants to save you. Because I love you. And the truth is—if you think you could ever love me back—I'll wait forever."

Not to be forgiven for it, she realized. Not to turn his flaw into a romance. But to set the whole truth before her and let her choose what to do with it.

The moments that followed were filled with the sound of Georgie's heartbeat pounding in her ears. She didn't even realize she was crying until his thumb reached up to catch a tear slipping down her cheek.

She gave a watery laugh, shaking her head softly.

"Oh, Jason," she whispered, voice trembling. Because that was the final, impossible thing, wasn't it? Not that he had once wanted to save her. But that somewhere along the way she had ceased to care which feeling came first and begun caring only that what they had now was real.

But she couldn't say more...because before she could form another word, his hand cupped her cheek and he leaned in, and she found herself kissing him like she'd been waiting her whole life to do just that.

This time she did not kiss him out of panic, longing, or the ache of uncertainty. She kissed him because she had her answer—or enough of one to choose the next step willingly.

# CHAPTER FORTY-FIVE

There was no space left for thought. Only the feel of him—his hands at her face, his body close, his kiss slow and deliberate, as though he meant her to understand exactly what he was doing. Not haste. Not comfort. Not apology. Choice.

He pulled her tight against him, her cheeks cradled in his hands, her breath mingling with his as he kissed her slow and deep, as though he were pouring every unspoken word, every held-back feeling, directly into her mouth.

Her fingers curled into the lapels of his coat, desperate and trembling, pulling him closer, closer, as though she could climb into the very circle of his warmth and stay there for the rest of her life. And this time she did not check herself for wanting that. She had done enough doubting for one marriage.

"Jason," she whispered against his lips, her tears slipping down her cheeks even as she smiled through them, her body shaking with emotion she'd spent years believing she wasn't allowed to feel.

He pulled back just enough to look at her—only just. His

green eyes were dark, tender, searching her face as though he were memorizing every tear, every breath, every flutter of her lashes.

Before she could lose her nerve, she blurted it out—between kisses and tears, her heart pounding so hard it almost hurt.

"I think…" Her voice caught. "I fell in love with you the morning you swooped me up on your horse like a knight in shining armor."

His mouth stilled against hers for a fraction of a second, the hesitation unmistakable, and the awareness of it gave her a courage she hadn't known she still possessed. She wanted him to know she was here by choice, not gratitude.

"And I definitely fell in love with you," she continued softly, "the night I heard you defend me at the ball. When you stood there and told that awful Lord—"

"Weedham," he finished hoarsely, brushing the back of his fingers along her jaw with a reverence that made her knees weaken. He shuddered, as though the very idea of touching her gently was almost too much for him to bear.

"Yes," she breathed. "That night."

Something broke in Jason's expression then—something vulnerable and unbearably sweet—and he kissed her again with a desperate tenderness that left her swaying toward him. She clutched at his coat as his mouth moved over hers, deeper, hotter, a soft whimper escaping her when his hands slid into her hair.

The kiss deepened quickly, their lips parting on soft gasps, their breaths tangling as his coat slid off his shoulders under her eager hands. She tugged at him, wordlessly asking—needing—more.

He answered by trailing hot, open-mouthed kisses along her jaw, down the elegant line of her neck, to the hollow of her throat. Each press of his lips drew a shocked, helpless sound from her, small bursts of pleasure that made her cling tighter.

When his hands found the fastenings of her gown, he hesitated, pulling back just enough to search her face. His chest rose and fell in quick, unsteady breaths.

"Georgie," he murmured, his voice low and rough. "Do you want this as much as I do?"

She nodded fiercely, her breath shuddering. "Yes," she whispered, her voice trembling with want. "Possibly more."

He swallowed at that—hard—his eyes darkening with a hunger that made her whole body flush. Slowly, deliberately, he unbuttoned the back of her gown and slid it from her shoulders. It pooled at her waist, baring her skin to the warm glow of the candles.

Her chemise followed, the thin linen slipping down her arms like water. She stood to shed the last layers, breath catching as the cool air kissed her skin. Her shift clung to her curves, slipping off one shoulder, almost transparent in the firelight.

His gaze swept over her, reverent and starving all at once, and the way he looked at her—like she was miracle and temptation and salvation—made a delicious shiver run through her. Not saved, she thought wildly. Seen. There was a difference, and it was obvious he knew it.

When he stood to undress, she reached for his buttons, fumbling in her eagerness until he caught her hands and pressed them gently to his chest.

"Let me," he murmured, kissing her fingers in a way that sent a slow warmth pooling low in her belly.

She sank back into the mattress, her chest rising and falling as he undressed with deliberate calm—waistcoat discarded, cravat loosened and set aside, shirt drawn over his head to reveal broad shoulders and a chest made for her hands. Candlelight traced the planes of him, lean muscle, strength held in check, the quiet confidence of a man entirely aware of his effect.

She drank him in shamelessly, her pulse skidding as he stepped out of his breeches and stood before her at last, gloriously undone, nothing hurried, nothing hidden.

Only then did he come to her. The patience of it nearly undid her more than haste could have. He was not taking. He was giving her every chance to stop—and every reason not to.

He sank to his knees and kissed her again, slower this time, deeper, his hands sliding over her bare thighs, up to her hips, higher still, until a soft, broken whimper escaped her.

When he lifted her and laid her back against the cool sheets, she arched instinctively into his touch, her legs parting to welcome him as he settled between them, his breath warm against her throat.

The air between them thickened—hot, charged, trembling—with the rustle of linen and the sound of their uneven breaths. He kissed down her body, tasting her collarbone, the swell of her breasts, the soft curve of her waist. Each kiss was patient, adoring, devastating.

When his mouth moved lower, she felt the shift of his intent before she fully understood it, and the realization sent a shiver through her so sharp it stole her breath.

"Jason—" she began, but the rest dissolved into a gasp as he pressed a kiss to the inside of her thigh, then another, slow and deliberate, his hands spreading her gently as though this, too, were something to be reverenced rather than taken.

He looked up once, his gaze dark and searching, and whatever he saw in her face must have answered him, because his mouth curved with the faintest trace of satisfaction before he bent to her in earnest.

Georgie's head fell back against the sheets. Pleasure hit

her all at once—hotter and more intimate than she had imagined possible, so exquisite it bordered on unbearable. His mouth was patient and merciless by turns, coaxing, tasting, learning her as though he meant to memorize every tremor he drew from her. She clutched at the linen beneath her, then at his shoulders when that was no longer enough, her breath breaking into helpless little cries she could not have silenced if she tried.

"Oh—" she gasped, hips lifting instinctively, and he answered with a low sound against her that nearly undid her on the spot.

He did not hurry. That was what destroyed her. The patience of him. The care. The unmistakable sense that he was not merely driving her toward pleasure, but taking fierce delight in giving it. Every sweep of his tongue, every lingering kiss, every restrained shift of his mouth told her the same impossible thing: he wanted this for her.

The pressure inside her built swift and bright, until she was trembling beneath him, her thighs shaking around his shoulders, one hand tangled in his hair. "Jason, I—"

He glanced up again, eyes molten, and the sight of him there—undone by her, intent on her, wholly without shame in his wanting—sent her over the edge. Her cry broke free as pleasure tore through her, sharp and shimmering, leaving her breathless and shuddering in its wake.

He rose over her slowly then, pressing a final kiss to the inside of her thigh before returning to her mouth, letting her taste herself on him. The intimacy of it made her whole body flush anew.

His forehead rested briefly against hers, both of them breathing hard. Then, with his whole body still taut from restraint, he whispered, "Tell me you're certain."

He was still asking, still making room for her answer,

even now. Something in her softened and steadied all at once.

"Yes," she breathed, lifting her hips toward him. "Jason… please—"

Her plea undid him.

His jaw tightened, his eyes molten as he positioned himself over her, bracing his hands on either side of her head. She felt the broad, hot press of him, and her breath faltered.

Trust, she thought. He'd asked her once if she trusted him. And now she realized…she trusted him more than anyone. Not blindly. Not foolishly. But with the full, trembling knowledge of what it meant to place herself in another person's hands and not regret it.

When he pushed into her—slow, steady, careful—there was a brief sting, a pinch of pressure…then something overwhelming, consuming, breathtaking.

She gasped his name, nails digging into his back as he groaned low, his lips brushing her temple. They stayed there for a moment, tangled, shaking, basking in the sharp, exquisite shock of becoming one.

Then he began to move.

The pleasure rose swift and relentless, stealing her breath, pulling helpless sounds from her throat. There was nothing dutiful in it, nothing tentative or half-claimed. Only the overwhelming certainty that this—this joining, this surrender, this joy—had been worth waiting for. She arched into him, meeting each thrust with trembling need. Her legs wrapped around his hips, urging him deeper.

"Georgie…" he gasped against her mouth.

When she shattered beneath him again, crying out softly as her body tightened around him, he swallowed her cry with a kiss and followed her over the edge—groaning her name into her neck as he came undone.

They collapsed together, panting, trembling, wrapped in tangled sheets and each other. His weight was a warm, heavy comfort, his arms holding her as if he'd never let go.

She pressed her lips to his shoulder, still breathless, her heart overflowing. "My husband," she whispered.

He smiled against her hair, his hand sweeping over her back in a slow, lingering stroke. "My wife."

The words no longer sounded like titles borrowed in haste. They sounded earned. And for the first time since all of this began, the three things no longer felt separate. She was safe. She was wanted. And, in his arms, she was finally home.

# CHAPTER FORTY-SIX

Jason woke to sunlight streaming through the curtains and the faintest weight of her hair across his bare chest.

*No one had knocked.*

That alone told him a great deal. Pembroke House ran on quiet efficiency, and by this hour his valet or the housekeeper would ordinarily have made some discreet inquiry. Instead, the morning had been allowed to unfold undisturbed—no tray, no footstep, no polite clearing of the throat beyond the door. Someone, somewhere belowstairs, had drawn a conclusion and passed the word along.

Jason made a mental note to reward that restraint later.

For a moment, he simply lay still, drinking in the sight of her nestled against him, her breath soft and even, her arm draped across his middle as though it belonged there.

His wife.

Georgiana. Georgie.

And then she stirred, one long leg sliding over his, her lashes fluttering as her eyes blinked open and focused on him.

She smiled sleepily, and it damn near undid him. "Good morning," she murmured, her voice still thick and husky with sleep.

He grinned lazily. "Good morning," he echoed, brushing a stray curl from her cheek.

For a few quiet moments they lay like that, neither in any particular hurry to move, the warmth of her body seeping into his as she rested her chin on his chest.

Then she let out a small sigh, her lips curving wickedly. "Honestly, if I'd known it was that enjoyable," she said slyly, "I would have demanded you take me to bed on our wedding night."

Jason let out a startled laugh, rolling slightly to pin her beneath him, his eyes dancing.

"Would you?" he teased, his thumb tracing the curve of her jaw.

"Absolutely," she said, feigning solemnity, though her eyes sparkled.

"You were nearly asleep on our wedding night," he pointed out.

She sniffed and arched a brow. "I assure you, I would have woken up for *that*."

He chuckled low in his throat, leaning down to kiss her soundly before settling back beside her, their fingers intertwining.

It was perfect. Or as near to perfect as real life ever came —untidy, tender, and astonishingly unforced.

She tilted her head and asked softly, "Do you regret that your friendship with my brother seems to be...ruined because of our marriage?"

Jason's grin faded, replaced by something steadier, more certain.

"No," he said firmly. Then he glanced down at her, ensuring his gaze was resolute. "In fact," he added wryly, "I owe you another apology. If I'd known what a horse's ass your brother was, I would have swept you up and carted you off a long time ago."

She gasped lightly at that, her eyes wide as his thumb stroked gently over her knuckles.

"You're my priority now, Georgie," he murmured. "You. Not him. Not anyone else. Including my odious mother." He pressed her fingers to his lips, letting the words hang there between them before adding softly, "Now and forever."

The words landed with a satisfying steadiness between them. Not the fever of scandal this time, nor the rush of rescue. A choice, calmly made and plainly spoken.

"Jason?" she asked, meeting his gaze.

"Yes."

"I was thinking...how old were you when Evelyn...?"

He expelled a breath. It always hurt to talk about Evelyn, but he was committed to answering any question his wife had from now on. "I was nine. She was seven."

Georgie gasped. "Oh, my goodness. So young? How could you have possibly been responsible for your sister at such a young age?"

"I was older than she," he insisted.

Georgie nodded, thinking for a few moments before she said, "Timothy is nine years old. Did you know that?"

Jason frowned. "The butler's son? He's...nine?"

"Yes, nearly ten."

"But he seems so..."

"So childlike? That's because he is."

The thought did not set him free all at once. Nothing so miraculous. But it shifted something ancient and rigid inside him, enough for the first crack of light to enter. Jason shook his head slowly, as if trying to clear a fog. "All these years, I blamed myself."

He went quiet then, her words sinking into him with an inexorable weight.

When he spoke again, his voice was low. "I suppose I never stopped to think how truly young I was."

Georgie squeezed his hand. "And your parents allowed you to blame yourself, didn't they? Instead of blaming themselves, or the servants, or any other *adult* who might have been charged with watching *both* of you that day."

Jason swallowed. "I never thought of it that way."

Which was perhaps the true cruelty of it. Now that he thought on it…he had spent half a lifetime judging the child he had been by standards no child could ever have met.

Georgie moved her hand to his cheek. "You're a good man, Jason. You care more about others than yourself. You cared more about me, a near stranger, than my own family did."

She was not absolving him of every mistake, and somehow that made the tenderness of it truer. She was simply naming what she had seen all along and asking him, at last, to see it too. He closed his eyes and leaned into her hand. "I love you," he whispered.

"I love you too." It wasn't a confession torn out by crisis this time, but as something quieter and steadier—made stronger, not weaker, by having survived the truth.

Her answering smile was radiant, and she surged up to kiss him again, but this time it deepened quickly, heat sparking between them until she was pressed beneath him once more and he was groaning her name into her skin.

By the time they collapsed again, sated and tangled in each other's arms, she was grinning against his chest. It no longer felt like desire fighting uncertainty. It felt like the two of them, at last, on the same side of their own marriage.

"You're going to ruin me for polite company," she

murmured, her fingers drawing idle patterns along his shoulder.

"Good," he replied, nipping lightly at her ear. "Let them wonder why you're always smiling."

Eventually, she rose and slipped into a robe, her cheeks still faintly flushed as she began fussing with her hair in the mirror.

"Poppy's expecting me," she said at last, catching his eye in the glass. "She wants my advice about—oh, something or other. Draperies, I think? Or possibly a love letter she claims she found hidden in one of Lady Viva's gloves."

Jason chuckled at that and rose to dress himself, as he crossed to her side.

"Well," he said, leaning in to press a kiss just below her ear, "you're clearly indispensable."

She smiled at his reflection.

He caught her chin lightly, turning her to face him, and kissed her once more before adding, "I'll be in my study. Come and find me when you get home."

His mouth curved into a slow, wicked smile as he added, "We can…continue our discussion from this morning."

Her breath hitched faintly, but she arched a brow with a small, conspiratorial smile.

"I will," she promised, her eyes glinting.

He watched her sweep toward the door, teasing and flushed and entirely his equal, and felt something settle quietly into place inside him.

For years he had looked at marriage and seen only the wreckage his parents had made of it—coldness, bitterness, two selfish people grinding each other down. He had mistaken their failure for a prophecy.

But Georgie was not his mother. And he was not his father.

What lived between them felt nothing like that old,

joyless war. It felt like laughter over breakfast, honesty in bed, kind words spoken, and hands reaching for one another without fear. It felt like something living. Something chosen. Something they would build themselves.

And as the door closed softly behind her, Jason realized that for the first time in years, he was not merely hoping his marriage might be a happy one.

He fully intended it to be.

# CHAPTER FORTY-SEVEN

The moment Georgie stepped through the Montforts' front door, she knew she'd made a tactical error in wearing such a light color. Ivory silk had no business in a house where muddy paws, spilled wine, and flying hat boxes were clearly part of the daily rhythm.

Disorder reigned.

An excitable spaniel puppy shot between her ankles, barking as though defending a fortress. A footman staggered by balancing a teetering tower of parcels. And from somewhere in the back came the distinct, off-key strains of a harpsichord being played at more of a gallop than a stroll.

Georgie paused, taking it in, and felt a sharp, unexpected pang of sympathy. So this was what Poppy had been carrying —day after day—smiling through it as if it were all perfectly normal. Dealing with Lady Viva wasn't merely exhausting. It was a full-time campaign. And Georgie, who had spent so long surviving other people's madness, found she was rather good at stepping into the fray when someone she loved required reinforcement.

"Oh, you came!" Poppy appeared at the top of the stairs, her red hair mussed, her bright-blue gown charmingly wrinkled, and her expression a mix of harried and hopeful.

Georgie smiled faintly despite herself. "I said I would."

When Poppy reached the bottom, she blew a strand of hair out of her eyes and gestured wildly. "Mama is holding a luncheon. For herself. On a Thursday. And the guest list is more than questionable."

Indeed, Georgie could hear a raucous chorus of laughter from the back of the house, punctuated by the sound of shattering porcelain.

Georgie winced. "What can I do?"

Poppy clutched her arm like a drowning woman seizing a plank of wood. "Help me decide if it's more urgent to remove the punch bowl before she bathes in it, or to hide the harpist before she decides to sit on his lap. Either way, I *cannot* do both at once."

Georgie chuckled softly and spent the next hour alternately soothing servants, retying sashes on drunken guests, and somehow convincing Lady Viva not to perform an interpretive dance on the dining table.

By the time she managed to extract herself, she was smiling, genuinely smiling, as she squeezed Poppy's hand and promised to come again soon. It pleased her more than she expected, being useful in this way—not as pawn or ornament, but as herself.

"Bring your handsome husband next time!" Poppy called after her as she descended the front steps.

As she stepped back into the street, Georgie sent up a silent prayer—not for Lady Viva's good behavior (that was clearly beyond the reach of heaven), but for dear Poppy's sanity.

The moment Georgie settled back into the carriage, her smile faded.

Because she wasn't alone.

A figure sat in the far corner of the seat, shrouded in the shadows despite the sunlight.

"Good afternoon…Lady Pembroke," came the low, rasping voice.

Her head jerked up, her blood turning cold.

Lord Henderville.

The marquess himself.

Sitting in her carriage…waiting. How had he sneaked in without the coachman seeing him?

For one sickening instant she was back in the church vestibule, back in every moment she had ever been cornered by men who believed they had the right to do so. Then fury surged up beneath the fear and steadied her.

Her mouth went dry as she stared at him, his thin lips curling into something that was neither a smile nor a snarl, but something in between.

"What are you doing here?" she managed, her voice sharp.

When she started to rise, to fling open the door and flee, he lifted a gloved hand, palm out.

"I suggest you sit down, my lady," he said silkily. "You're going to want to hear this."

Despite her misgivings, she lowered herself onto the seat once more, her back ramrod straight, her hands clasped with a stiffness that betrayed her unease. She did it not because he commanded it, but because if Henderville meant to threaten her or her husband, she intended to hear every word and remember it.

He leaned forward then, his faded eyes glinting.

"I won't waste your time," he said, his tone low and full of quiet menace. "You're enjoying your little fairy tale, I see. The pretty new wife. The lovely new wardrobe. The doting husband."

Georgie did not rise to the bait. Let him sneer. He knew

nothing of what lay between her and Jason—not the truth of it, and certainly not their very *real* feelings for each other. What could Henderville possibly know of love?

Her heart thudded painfully, but she lifted her chin regardless. "Your business with me is over," she said icily. "You'll kindly remove yourself from my carriage."

But he only chuckled. "On the contrary, my business has only just begun."

He reached into his coat pocket and withdrew a folded piece of paper, which he tossed onto her lap.

She didn't dare touch it.

"I know things about your husband," Henderville said softly. "Things that would ruin him. Destroy him, if they came to light. Political...financial...and otherwise."

The words struck hard, not because she believed Henderville honorable enough to tell the truth, but because she knew already that Jason had secrets and old grief enough for a vulture like this man to peck at.

Her stomach turned to ice. "You're lying," she breathed.

"Am I?" He leaned forward until she could smell the faint scent of cloves and old brandy on his rancid breath.

"Do you think Pembroke is so very spotless? Untouchable? Do you think he has nothing to lose?"

Her fingers curled into fists.

"If you wish to keep your husband's name from the scandal sheets—and from Parliament's inquiry board—you'll arrange a meeting between us. One where he will...reconsider what he owes me. What you *both* owe me."

There it was at last. Not grief. Not wounded pride. Extortion dressed up as entitlement. And some cold, lucid part of Georgie was almost grateful for the clarity of it. Her mouth opened and closed. "You..." she began, but no more words came.

He smiled thinly, clearly savoring her shock. "I rather

think he'd prefer you deliver my message," he said softly. "Do let him know I'll be in touch."

Then he reached out and drew a gnarled finger down her cheek. She pulled away sharply, and he chuckled. With a grunt of effort, he reached for the handle, pushed open the carriage door, and climbed down slowly, his movements deliberate and unhurried, like a man with all the time in the world.

Henderville stepped out with chilling calm, straightening his coat and hat and balancing on his cane, before slowly disappearing into the street, leaving behind only the faint smell of his cologne and the heavy weight of fear in her chest.

Georgie sat frozen for a long moment, the paper still untouched in her lap. Her heart thudded wildly as she stared at the door, her mind reeling, her breath shallow.

When she finally gathered herself enough to lift the note, her hands trembled. She still didn't unfold it.

She couldn't. Not there. Not while that awful man's smell still lingered in the carriage and her pulse still beat like alarm in her throat. She wanted clear eyes for whatever he had written, not the fog of panic.

Instead, she clenched her jaw and forced her spine straight. Henderville had made the mistake of thinking he could use Jason against her—or her against Jason.

No. Impossible.

She would not carry secrets for other men. She would not decide alone what belonged to her marriage. Whatever this was, Jason would hear it from her—and together they would decide what came next.

# CHAPTER FORTY-EIGHT

She didn't wait for the footman to open the front door.

She shoved it open herself, sweeping into the marble-floored foyer with her skirts still swirling around her ankles, her heart hammering wildly in her chest.

The butler appeared from the hallway, blinking at her with faint surprise.

"Lady Pembroke—"

"Is he in the study?" she cut in, already striding forward.

"Yes, my lady—"

"Thank you," she called over her shoulder, not slowing her pace.

Her gloves were already half off by the time she reached the study door. She didn't bother knocking.

She flung the door open to find Jason seated at his desk, jacket off, shirtsleeves rolled to his forearms, quill poised over a stack of papers.

He looked up immediately, brows knitting as he took in her no doubt flushed cheeks and bright eyes.

"Georgie?" he asked, rising. "What's wrong?"

She crossed the room in a few quick steps and dropped the still-folded paper squarely in front of him.

He glanced at it, then back at her, his green eyes darkening. "What is this?"

"It's from Lord Henderville," she said breathlessly. And even as she said it, some tight, fearful part of her eased. She had not kept this from him. Had not tried to carry it alone. Whatever came next, they were already on firmer ground than they might once have been.

Jason's jaw tightened, and he picked up the paper, opening it carefully.

Georgie crossed her arms, tapping her foot on the floor as Jason scanned the note in silence.

When he reached the end, he let out a faint huff of something that sounded suspiciously like a laugh, though there was no humor in it.

She frowned. "You're laughing?" she asked, more than a little confused. Not because the threat was amusing, she realized a beat later, but because Jason had met it with recognition instead of alarm, which was oddly reassuring.

Jason shook his head, setting the paper down with deliberate calm. "It's exactly what I thought it would be," he said simply.

She blinked at him, caught off guard. "What is it?"

"I heard," he admitted, finally meeting her gaze, "Henderville's been sniffing around my affairs the last fortnight. I should have met with him before now. I knew he would not let you go easily. I certainly wouldn't if I were in his position. That much is my fault," he added, more grimly than before. "I knew he'd try something. I should have warned you he might come slithering after us."

His mouth tightened. "I sent him a bank draft last week. A generous one. Enough to pay your father's original gambling debt in full, with a bit extra besides to soothe Henderville's wounded pride. I thought it would be enough to make the old goat release his claim and limp away with what remained of his dignity."

Georgie just stared at him. "You paid my father's debt?" she asked at last, her voice quieter now.

Jason gave a short, humorless laugh. "I paid *Henderville*," he corrected. "Your father's debts seem to multiply like rabbits. I only dealt with the one that had attached itself to you."

Something in her chest twisted hard at that. Not because of the money itself—though the sum must have been enormous—but because he said it so plainly, as if freeing her from an old man's grasp were the most natural thing in the world. As if of course he would do it. As if of course *she* was worth it.

"Jason…" she said, and then stopped, because for one bewildering moment she did not know what to do with the ache rising in her throat. No one had ever spent money to protect her before. Men had only ever spent, bargained, and borrowed *against* her.

Almost without thinking, she crossed the space between them and laid her hand lightly over his where it rested on the desk. The contact was small, barely more than a brush, but his fingers stilled beneath hers at once.

His expression changed—just a little. Softened.

"Clearly," he said more quietly, turning his hand beneath hers until his thumb brushed her knuckles, "I should not have assumed he would give you up that easily."

Georgie eyed her husband carefully. "He implied the document contained a threat."

Jason's mouth curved faintly, though his eyes stayed serious. "It does…of a sort." He sighed. "There are…things about my past," he said carefully, "that aren't exactly scandalous, but also not something I'd want splashed across the gossip sheets."

He said it carefully, but not evasively, and Georgie felt another small shift inside herself. This, too, was new between them—truth offered before she had to drag it out by degrees.

Georgie nodded slowly. She knew Jason would have an explanation. "Like what?"

Jason straightened slightly, looking almost sheepish now.

"Several years ago," he began, "I invested—rather foolishly —in a shipping venture that turned out to be a front for smuggling French silks and brandy. The venture collapsed, of course. I withdrew as soon as I discovered the truth, but…"

He gestured vaguely to the paper. "…not before my name appeared on certain documents."

She stared at him for a long moment, then narrowed her eyes. "That's it?" she asked. Relief came first. Then indignation on his behalf. Henderville had barged into her carriage, touched her, threatened her husband, and all for this? A foolish investment and old paperwork? She was almost insulted by the thinness of it.

He arched a brow. "Well, I suppose some would find it damning."

She snorted. "Please. My father is the most shameless spendthrift in town. I think I can handle a husband who accidentally invested in contraband. If Henderville hoped to frighten me into trembling silence, he has chosen the wrong woman," she added. "I was raised by professionals."

That startled a laugh out of Jason, and the corner of his mouth twitched upward.

She, however, wasn't done yet. "And if Henderville wants to toss gossip about," she said, straightening her spine, "I… no, *we*, happen to have an ace up our sleeves."

The correction pleased her more than it ought. *We.* The word settled between them with a surprising rightness, as though their marriage had just taken on another layer of substance.

Jason's eyes glinted with interest at that. "Really? And what is this miraculous ace?"

"Not what," she corrected with a wide grin. "*Who.*"

Jason crossed his arms over his chest, leaning back in his chair with a faint smirk. "Oh?"

Georgie smiled sweetly, though her pulse was still racing. "Her name," she said, savoring the words, "is Lady Beatrix Winslow."

For the first time since Henderville stepped into her carriage, something like triumph flickered through her. Let old men scheme and threaten all they pleased. She had Jason now. She had Bea. She had allies. She was no one's isolated prey.

# CHAPTER FORTY-NINE

Bea sat in Georgie's drawing room like a queen—perfectly poised, one gloved hand resting delicately on the arm of her chair, her expression composed yet crackling with barely restrained amusement.

Across from her, Georgie and Jason exchanged a glance before Bea finally spoke, her voice low and measured. "Of course," she began with that arid calm of hers, "we never had this conversation. And I was never here."

Georgie's brows lifted slightly, but Bea only arched one of her own, her sea-green eyes glinting with quiet mischief.

"Because," Bea continued, her tone light but her words carrying unmistakable weight, "if my father ever discovers how his secrets get out, I will lose my greatest strength."

The warning was real enough beneath the wit, and Georgie felt a flicker of gratitude. Bea was not merely gossiping for sport. She was placing something valuable into their hands because Georgie had asked.

Jason, leaning casually against the mantel with his arms folded, inclined his head solemnly. "Understood," he murmured.

Georgie nodded just as gravely. "Of course," she agreed.

Bea allowed herself a faint, knowing smile before smoothing her skirts and crossing one elegant ankle over the other.

"Excellent," she said approvingly. Then she leaned forward, lowering her voice. "Now. You said you only needed one?"

Georgie straightened in her chair, her hands folded in her lap but her eyes sharp. "That's right," she said quietly. "One good strike. Something solid enough to keep Henderville out of our lives for good."

It was not vengeance for its own sake. She wanted an ending. Clean, final, and strong enough that no man would ever again mistake her marriage for leverage.

Bea tilted her head, considering them both for a long moment before she sat back, her fingers toying idly with the edge of her reticule. "Well then," she said at last, her voice dropping even lower. "Listen to this."

She glanced toward the door once to ensure it was closed, then beckoned them both closer.

Jason pushed away from the mantel, crossing the room in a few strides, while Georgie leaned forward, her pulse quickening as the three of them huddled close.

Bea lowered her lashes, her mouth curving into something sly and wicked. "There's a particular house on Half Moon Street," she murmured, her words barely more than a breath. "Very discreet. Very…specialized clientele. Henderville has been a patron there for years. And he prefers his *companions* younger. *Much* younger."

The room seemed to go colder around the words. Georgie felt disgust rise swift and clean through her, washing away any lingering temptation to think of Henderville as merely ridiculous or vain. He was dangerous.

Bea continued. "There are at least three young women

who've left his employ with a generous purse, but not all of them kept quiet. And at least one is back in London now… with a rather damning diary she's been attempting to sell."

Jason let out a low whistle under his breath, his jaw tightening as he straightened slightly. "That'll do," he said grimly.

His words did not hold a note of triumph. Instead, they were laced with the hard satisfaction of a man who had finally been handed the means to shut a monster's mouth for good.

Georgie's hand curled into a fist, but she forced a calm smile to her lips as she met Bea's gaze. "That," she murmured, "will do very nicely indeed."

Because if Henderville wished to trade in ruin, then, for once, the ruin would not flow only in one direction.

Bea leaned back, smoothing her skirts as though she'd just recommended a new milliner. "Good," she said lightly. "And remember, this conversation never happened."

Georgie allowed herself a faint, wicked smile as she exchanged a glance with Jason, then nodded at Bea. "What conversation?"

Jason's answering look was brief but unmistakable. Not surprise. Not correction. Respect. And Georgie found she liked that almost as much as the plan itself.

And as they bent their heads together again, whispering through the next steps, Georgie felt something settle more firmly into place. Not merely the plan, though that was important. Something else.

This was what it meant, perhaps, to start acting together. Henderville had mistaken her for the frightened young lady he once cornered. He had mistaken Jason for a man who could be manipulated through secrecy.

He was wrong on both counts.

# CHAPTER FIFTY

The ballroom glittered around her, all candlelight and crystal, champagne and whispers, but Georgie hardly saw any of it.

Her gown shimmered like moonlight, her gloves were perfectly white, her hair pinned just so…and yet her pulse thrummed in her throat like a war drum.

Because he was here.

Lord Henderville.

Standing at the far end of the ballroom, his beady eyes sweeping the crowd, his mouth curled into its usual smirk.

A month ago, the sight of him might have sent her searching for an exit. Tonight, it only sharpened her purpose. Let him smirk. He was not hunting her now. He was walking into ground she had chosen.

Her stomach turned as she watched him accept a glass of wine from a passing footman, his bony fingers clutching the glass like talons.

Georgie sipped her own champagne, then began slowly weaving her way toward him, her skirts whispering over the polished floor.

When she passed behind him, she didn't stop, only murmured quietly as she moved past, "The blue salon. A quarter hour."

She did not look back because she did not need to. For once, she was not fleeing a man's plans. She was setting her own in motion.

~

THE BLUE SALON was quiet when she slipped in, the din of the ball muffled by the heavy oak door.

Jason was already there, leaning against the mantel, his emerald coat catching the light of the fire. His jaw was tight, his eyes bright with anger.

She drew in a breath, her pulse calming slightly at the sight of him. Not because Jason would take the matter out of her hands, but because she no longer had to hold it alone.

When the door creaked open, Lord Henderville shuffled in, his cane tapping against the floor.

At first he froze, his gaze bouncing from Georgie to Jason, confusion flickering in his watery eyes. Then he straightened, his lips curling into something smug.

"Well," he drawled, "I see. Very clever. I assume we're here to…negotiate the terms then? Finally decided to be reasonable, have you, Pembroke?"

Jason's jaw ticked visibly, but he didn't move from the mantel. "And what," he asked coldly, "do you believe are the terms?"

Henderville gave a little shrug, his face oily with satisfaction. "I thought we'd start with a sum of…oh, an additional ten thousand pounds, and of course"—his eyes swept to Georgie, making her skin crawl—"one night. With her. Just to even the score."

Georgie did not flinch. Let him say the vile thing aloud.

Let him hear, in the silence that followed, exactly what sort of man he was.

Jason straightened slowly, his expression almost calm… Almost.

But Georgie, standing slightly behind him, saw his hands flexing at his sides, the muscle in his jaw jump.

"You," Jason said at last, his voice quiet but sharp enough to cut glass, "may go *straight to hell.*"

Henderville blinked. "I—what?"

Jason's lips thinned into something that wasn't remotely a smile. "I wouldn't negotiate with you if you were the last man on earth. And if you so much as *touch* my wife's hand, I will put you in the ground myself."

For the first time, Henderville's smirk faltered. He straightened, his bony fingers tightening on his cane. "You obviously don't understand," he stammered. "Didn't she tell you? The French shipping—"

"I received your letter," Jason cut in, his voice low and full of steel. "And I tossed it in the rubbish heap where it belongs."

Henderville's jaw worked soundlessly, his brow furrowing.

Jason stepped closer, his tall frame eclipsing the older man as he loomed over him. "Now," he said quietly, "allow me to give you a few facts that *I've* become aware of."

Georgie stayed where she was, neither shrinking back nor looking away. Henderville would leave this room knowing he had not intimidated either of them.

Henderville's eyes darted between them, a flicker of fear starting to creep in at the edges.

Jason's smile was cold and humorless. "Half Moon Street," he began softly. "A discreet house. Specialized clientele. You've been visiting there for years, haven't you?"

Henderville's face drained of color.

Jason pressed on. "Three young women paid off. One of them back in London now. With an extremely damning diary."

The marquess took a staggering half-step back, clutching his chest, his breath rasping audibly. "Who...who told you that?" he wheezed, his voice cracking. "How do you know any of that?"

Jason straightened to his full height, his gaze sharp enough to flay skin. "I don't just know it," he said quietly. "I have proof. In the form of the diary itself. And make no mistake, every word of it can be corroborated."

Henderville's fear was immediate and ugly. He let out a strangled noise, his face gray now, his hands trembling. Georgie felt something cold inside her settle. Good. Let him understand, at last, what it was to be the one without power.

"Now," Jason continued, his voice still calm but underpinned with lethal intent, "I'm perfectly willing to forget I know anything about this. Though rest assured, I'll keep the diary in a *very* safe place...in case you ever get the ludicrous notion that somehow the information will die with me."

He took one final step forward, his eyes narrowing to slits. "In exchange, *you* will never darken my doorstep or contact my wife, or our children, in any way, ever again. Do you hear me?"

Henderville's lips worked silently for a moment before he croaked out, "Yes. Yes. I hear you. Of course. You...you have my word."

Jason's smile was a blade. "Good."

Henderville glanced between them one last time, his eyes full of hate and humiliation, before he slunk toward the door.

"One more thing..." Jason tossed after him.

The older man paused, his craggy hand on the door handle.

"If I learn that you have so much as laid a finger upon a

*child* again, I will ensure you are forever relieved of the particular appendage that drives you to do so."

He smiled then—cold, precise. "Permanently."

There was an audible gulp from Henderville before he quickly exited the room.

When the door closed behind him, the room was silent for a long beat. Jason let out a slow breath and glanced back at Georgie.

She met his gaze squarely, her chest still heaving slightly from the rush, and allowed herself a small, satisfied smile. "Well," she murmured, "that went well."

Jason's lips quirked faintly, though his eyes were still dark with the echoes of what had just passed. "Yes," he said softly. "I quite agree."

Georgie's smile widened. She stepped toward him. "But did you say something about Henderville staying away from...*our children?*" The words had startled her, not because they felt presumptuous, but because they landed with such sudden, startling rightness.

"Yes," Jason replied with a wicked grin as he reached for her hand. She felt her pulse begin to steady again, her fingers threading through his with quiet certainty. "Children I hope to create with all due haste."

There was wickedness in the words, yes, but something steadier beneath it too—a future calmly assumed, built between them on purpose.

Georgie leaned up on her tiptoes and kissed him, smiling against his mouth. "By all means, my lord," she murmured. "I do believe we have a future to begin."

# EPILOGUE

***One month later, The Earl and Countess of Pembroke's Town
House***

Georgie was seated at the head of her dining table, flanked by Poppy and Bea on her left, and Jason at her right. Laughter rang off the gilded walls.

The long table gleamed with polished silver and crystal, the scent of roasted duck mingling with wax candles and the faintest whisper of roses from the arrangements spaced perfectly down the center.

Georgie took it all in, the soft murmur of conversation, the warmth of Jason's thigh brushing hers under the table, and marveled at how much her life had changed in only a handful of weeks.

Not by accident, either. That was the part she felt most keenly now. For all the turmoil, all the scandal, all the uncertainty, she had chosen her way into this life—and then chosen, day by day, to build it.

Lord Henderville, she was pleased to say, had not only

retreated from Society entirely but had even named his nephew his heir at last, quietly slinking away to the country like the defeated old crow he was.

It was a deeply satisfying end to a man who had spent far too long mistaking power for inevitability. Georgie had once been expected to submit to him. Now she scarcely thought of him at all unless the memory rose only to amuse her.

And Jason… Well, Jason had, at some point in the past four weeks, apparently paid a visit to his mother with much the same energy he'd brought to his showdown with Henderville. Georgie hadn't been privy to what exactly he'd said to the dowager countess, but he had returned that evening looking quietly satisfied, and his mother had not so much as *glanced* in Georgie's direction since.

Georgie had not asked for details. She had only noticed, with a private pulse of satisfaction, that Jason no longer tried to shield her with silence. He simply stood where he meant to stand and expected the world to adjust itself accordingly.

At the moment, all four of them—Georgie, Jason, Bea, and Poppy— were leaning comfortably in their chairs after the third course, sipping wine and laughing over Poppy's latest tale of her mother's antics.

"—and then," Poppy was saying, nearly breathless with indignation, "she declared she was forming her own opera company and began auditioning footmen in the drawing room. Two of them actually sang arias to her!"

Bea snorted elegantly into her wine, while Jason shook his head with a bemused smile.

"She has quite the…creative spirit," Jason murmured dryly.

"She's a menace," Poppy retorted, though her lips twitched with reluctant affection.

Georgie chuckled softly, resting her hand lightly on Jason's arm. He turned his wrist beneath her fingers just enough to catch her hand and hold it there for a beat, an absent, intimate gesture that still sent a small thrill through her. Marriage, she had discovered, was made as much of such quiet moments as of declarations.

"Oh!" Georgie said suddenly, remembering. "Bea, did you see the paper this morning? That *scathing* cartoon of Lord Nicholas Archer? I nearly dropped my teacup at the sight. The man looked like a puffed-up rooster wearing nothing but Parliamentary robes and a grin."

At that, Bea's eyes sparkled with unmistakable amusement…and something else, something sly and secretive.

"See it?" she repeated archly, setting down her glass with delicate precision. "I created it."

The room fell into stunned silence for a heartbeat. Georgie's jaw actually dropped. "You…*what?*"

Then, quite without warning, Georgie began to laugh. Of course it was Bea. Of course the most imperturbable woman in the room had been quietly setting fires under Parliament all along.

Bea smirked, a wicked gleam in her eye. "I drew it," she said simply, leaning back in her chair. "And delivered it to the paper under a pseudonym. And before you ask…yes. You're all sworn to secrecy."

Poppy gasped softly and clapped a hand over her mouth, while Jason merely arched a brow in faint disbelief.

"You're the artist?" Poppy finally managed, blinking at her friend as though she'd never seen her before.

Bea gave her a wicked grin. "I am."

Georgie just shook her head. Honestly, it made almost perfect sense. Bea had always possessed that sharp, watchful quality of a woman collecting ammunition.

Poppy leaned forward, her cheeks flushed with excitement. "Ooh, do you plan to make any more cartoons, Bea?"

she asked breathlessly. "Your father would be so angry if he found out."

Bea's gaze sharpened, and for the first time that evening, Georgie saw something almost fierce glitter behind her friend's usual cool composure. "Oh, indeed I do," she replied smoothly, her lips curving into a smile that promised trouble. "It's hardly my fault that my father and his cronies are on the wrong side of politics."

And then, "I'm so glad your revolt worked out in the end, Georgie," Bea added, her voice low but full of quiet fire, "because I do believe it's time for mine. I'm using my satirical sketches to influence the vote on the reform bill set to take place this summer."

Georgie felt that land more deeply than anyone else at the table perhaps could. Her own revolt had not ended at the altar. It had only changed shape. And now, looking at Bea, she saw the next battle forming just as clearly.

Bea's sea-foam eyes glinted as she raised her glass in a silent toast, and her smile turned downright daring. "And," she finished softly, "mine is going to be an all-out war."

Poppy gasped in delighted horror. Jason huffed a laugh into his wine. And Georgie, lifting her own glass to meet Bea's, felt not alarm but recognition. Yes, she thought. That was *exactly* how a revolt ought to begin.

Want one more hot scene with Jason and Georgie making very improper use of a bedroom at Pembroke Court? CLICK HERE to read the bonus epilogue and join my newsletter
or type
https://dl.bookfunnel.com/3q1s7zcrcx
into your browser.

Thank you for reading *The Wallflower's Great Escape*. If you enjoyed it, I would truly appreciate your recommendations and reviews.
Want more? Find out what happens when Bea finally clashes with Lord Nicholas Archer. CLICK HERE TO READ *The Wallflower's Secret War* now.

The Unlikely Lady (Book 3)

The Irresistible Rogue (Book 4)

The Unforgettable Hero (Book 4.5)

The Untamed Earl (Book 5)

The Legendary Lord (Book 6)

Never Trust a Pirate (Book 7)

The Right Kind of Rogue (Book 8)

A Duke Like No Other (Book 9)

Kiss Me At Christmas (Book 10)

Mr. Hunt, I Presume (Book 10.5)

No Other Duke But You (Book 11)

**Secret Brides**

Secrets of a Wedding Night (Book 1)

A Secret Proposal (Book 1.5)

Secrets of a Runaway Bride (Book 2)

A Secret Affair (Book 2.5)

Secrets of a Scandalous Marriage (Book 3)

It Happened Under the Mistletoe (Book 3.5)

Thank you for reading *The Wallflower's Great Escape*. I hope you enjoyed Georgie and Jason's story.

I'd love to keep in touch.

- Visit my website for information about upcoming books, excerpts, and to sign up for my email newsletter: www.ValerieBowmanBooks.com or at www.ValerieBowmanBooks.com/subscribe.
- Join me on Instagram: http://Instagram.com/ValerieGBowman
- Join me on Facebook: http://Facebook.com/ValerieBowmanAuthor
- Reviews help other readers find books. I appreciate all reviews. Thank you so much for considering it!

Want to read the other Wallflowers' Revolt books?

- The Wallflower's Secret War
- The Wallflower Takes All

# ABOUT THE AUTHOR

Valerie Bowman grew up in Illinois with six sisters (she's number seven) and a huge supply of historical romance novels.

After a cold and snowy stint earning a degree in English with a minor in history at Smith College, she moved to Florida the first chance she got.

Valerie now lives in Jacksonville with her family including her two rascally dogs. When she's not writing, she keeps busy reading, traveling, or vacillating between watching crazy reality TV and PBS.

Valerie loves to hear from readers. Find her on the web at www.ValerieBowmanBooks.com.

facebook.com/ValerieBowmanAuthor

instagram.com/valeriegbowman

goodreads.com/Valerie_Bowman

bookbub.com/authors/valerie-bowman

amazon.com/author/valeriebowman